Falconland

—ɯ—

The Story of Frederick II:
A Novel of Medieval Historical Fiction

Reggie Connell

ISBN: 0692340157
ISBN 13: 9780692340158
Library of Congress Control Number: 2014921341
Reggie Connell, Altamonte Springs, FL

Published and printed in the
United States of America

Dedication

To Christina; the love of my life.

Prologue

Rome 1245 AD

"Rome is surrounded, Your Grace," Ezzalino said. "The siege engines are in place, and we have secured all the gates entering and exiting the city."

"It's not Rome I have under siege," Frederick snarled. "It's the Vatican."

"I understand, Your Grace, but the siege has to surround Rome in order to control the Vatican."

Frederick snapped the reins and let his anxious horse turn in a circle before answering Ezzalino.

"Did you know the Vatican is a kingdom unto itself, even though it sits in the middle of my empire? I am the Holy Roman emperor, yet Pope Gregory is not a subject of my empire."

"He is an enemy combatant, Your Grace."

"I do not lay siege to Rome. I lay siege to the Vatican. I lay siege to the pope."

"I understand the distinction, Your Grace," Ezzalino said.

Frederick pondered his comment for a moment. He was laying siege to the pope. On the surface, it seemed like the actions of a monster. Even though he felt justified, this action troubled him greatly.

"I have been Holy Roman Emperor for twenty-five years," he said to Ezzalino. "I have assembled the greatest fighting force since Richard the Lionhearted, Julius Caesar, or Genghis Khan. I could attack and defeat any army on the face of the earth, but this is what I'm using it for?"

"These are the people that threaten you Your Grace," said Ezzalino. "This is where your great army should be."

Pope Gregory had labeled Frederick the antichrist and ex-communicated him, attempted to have him assassinated, and called on the armies of Europe to fight against him, giving them crusading credentials for joining the holy war.

What choice did I have but to answer the pope militarily? Frederick thought. *Still, isn't this exactly what the antichrist would do?*

Francis of Assisi had counseled Frederick to hold the pope in high esteem, if not for the person who was elected pope, then for the office itself; after all, he was the judge for God on Earth.

But how could Frederick maintain esteem for an office that called for a crusade against him and separated him from God?

Frederick passionately believed that God had ordained him to be the king of Sicily and the Holy Roman emperor. How else could he account for the obstacles he'd overcome?

The pope had declared war on him . . . on his own emperor. Frederick took excommunication and a crusade against him very seriously; it was more than just a symbolic gesture of disrespect. As such, Frederick brought his massive army to the gates of Rome and surrounded Pope Gregory and the Vatican to illustrate just how seriously he had taken the declaration.

But Francis's words still rang in his mind. *You must respect the pope. He is the mediator for God.*

Francis had fought battles against religious leaders, religious armies, and even against his own father in Assisi, yet he always respected the pope.

Would Francis approve of my actions?

The answer would not come, for the man who'd started the Franciscan Order was now with God. Frederick could only attempt to make sense of this situation on his own, or pray for guidance . . . perhaps for a sign.

How did it come to this?

A messenger wearing the uniform of the Vatican Guard approached the exit gate and delivered a scroll with a Vatican seal emblazoned on its tie. Frederick dismounted his horse, took the scroll from the guard, broke it open, and read the short message.

Frederick put the scroll into a bag on his saddle and turned to Ezzalino.

"The pope is dead. The cardinals request an audience with me. I will go with this man to meet them."

"How many guards will you require, Your Grace?"

"None," Frederick said.

He removed his armor and called for his crown. His fiery-red hair was now mixed with gray, but his deep blue eyes were just as bright as the day he was born. His armor hid a gangly frame that never seemed to be comfortable wearing the regal clothing of an emperor. The Saracens in Egypt decades ago had commented that if he were a slave, no one would bid a single dinar on him. But Frederick was not a slave. Despite his unimpressive physical stature, he was every inch a king.

"Emperor Frederick, we are at war with these people. They have called for the armies of all Europe to fight against you. It would be prudent to take guards along."

"Even at war, the Vatican is a holy place. I will go as an emperor, not as a warrior," Frederick said.

"If they harm you in any way, I will let loose every siege weapon we have, and then set fire to Rome . . . and then the Vatican!" Ezzalino said defiantly.

"This meeting is not about that, my friend. This is about the selection of the next pope. I will meet with the cardinals, and then they will retire to a dark room and vote. We will know their decision when smoke comes from that chimney." Frederick pointed at a Vatican building that was visible from their vantage point. "We will talk again upon my return."

Ezzalino nodded his understanding, and Frederick followed the guard past the gates and into the city.

Frederick and the Vatican guard walked along the familiar streets of Rome. A city once steeped with historic buildings and an almost carnival-like atmosphere of merchants and activity was now a desolate fort stocked with men in Vatican Guard uniforms and weaponry. The energy and excitement of Rome had been changed into a military outpost.

The Vatican guard turned to Frederick. "Have you ever been here?"

"I lived here when I was a child."

"In Rome?"

"In the Vatican."

The guard was stunned. "How does an emperor at war with the pope come to live at the Vatican?"

"So you know I'm your emperor, but you do not respect me by using my title?"

"I'm sorry Your Grace. The cardinals told me to treat you as I would any person. They see you as an enemy to Christianity."

"I understand. It was not by choice."

"Not by choice?"

"I lived at the Vatican as a child after my parents died. It was not by choice."

"And with all due respect, my lord, why are you—a Holy Roman emperor—attacking the Vatican?"

"What is your name?"

"Phillipe, Your Grace."

"You have lived in Rome your whole life?"

"Yes, my lord."

"My question in response to yours, Phillipe, is why does a pope find it necessary to call for a crusade against his own emperor? Shouldn't he be more focused on mediating God's word and less on European politics?"

Phillipe said nothing.

Frederick looked down the road and saw horses leaving a building.

"Do you have access to the Vatican stables?" he asked.

"That is where I am typically stationed, Your Grace. I am of the Equestrian Guard."

"Why do you wear the uniform of the Vatican Guard if you work in the stables?"

"We are all in the Vatican Guard when the Imperial army is at our gates."

Frederick smiled.

"I pray you can come to a peaceful solution, Your Grace."

"I do too, Phillipe."

I

Jesi, Italy

December 26, 1194 AD

The quiet town of Jesi sat tucked away in the foothills of northeastern Italy near the Adriatic Sea. It was a small, inelegant, insignificant village nestled amidst nothing spectacular. Not a single noteworthy event had taken place in the centuries of its existence, except for the occasional sacking by invading armies every couple of centuries.

But that insignificance was about to change.

The sun ascended into a gray overcast sky. The harsh trade winds, blowing in from the coast, had mercifully mellowed overnight, providing unusual warmth.

"I'm hoping this is a sign of an early spring," a fishmonger said to a fisherman as she set up her cart for the day's business. "The day after Christmas is usually colder."

"It's probably just a warm front moving in to overtake the frigid conditions we've endured these past months," the fisherman responded. He lifted a basket of fish for her cart.

"The sea has been unbearable. I nearly froze to death out there."

Fog slowly lifted above the frostbitten fields beyond the ancient town walls. Gradually, through the icy mist, images appeared on the wet clay road leading to Jesi's gated entrance.

Guards patrolling the top of the wall were the first to see the riders approaching at cantering speed. Their vivid orange-and-yellow uniforms quickly revealed their identity as Sicilian cavalry.

"Surely, this isn't an attack," Ricardo Librizzi, captain of the Jesi militia, said. "But what would they be doing so far from their kingdom?"

"King Henry has long threatened the communes of northern Italy," said another militiaman nearby.

"But we have always favored Henry's family," Librizzi said, "even over the pope. They wouldn't invade us."

"Here they come!" another militiaman yelled. "Their riders breach our defenses without response."

"What response would you recommend?" Librizzi shot back.

The horsemen galloped through the open gates, each one riding a black Frisian stallion. The horses' pace shook the ground. Forewarned by the thunder of hooves, the town's citizens quickly retreated and scattered away from their apparent destination in the town square.

Without explanation, the soldiers cleared the remaining onlookers away and created a perimeter in the shape of a large half-moon. Rolando Cortano, the leader of the Sicilian cavalry, rode in front to meet the frantic guards coming down from the wall.

Donning a dusty, old-fashioned uniform far too small for his overweight frame, Captain Librizzi struggled mightily down the ladder to meet the Sicilian soldiers.

"State your business here, Master Sergeant!" Librizzi yelled; trying to muster all of the importance he could from his winded voice.

Wearing the tailored armor of a knight, Cortano shouted, "I am Rolando Cortano, leader of the Sicilian cavalry. This town is needed for official business by Queen Constance of Sicily. Nothing more needs to be known."

Librizzi attempted to protest, but Cortano quickly cut him off. "Consider this a royal emergency," he said dismissively. "And there is no such rank as master sergeant."

Obediently, a bit embarrassed, and completely perplexed, Librizzi stepped back, yielding to the visitor's commands.

Cortano turned to briefly address the gathering crowd. "Your town will never be forgotten for this service throughout the history of mankind," he said, walking back toward his soldiers. "Now make way this town square, as Queen Constance approaches swiftly."

"Royal emergency?" Librizzi muttered to the soldier next to him.

"Never forgotten throughout history?" the soldier whispered in reply.

"What service? What exactly is approaching our town?" Librizzi asked Cortano. Not gaining a response, he looked through the open gate for his answer.

II

The Birth of Frederick

The royal carriage transporting Queen Constance trudged down the soggy clay road leading to Jesi. Behind her were the remaining cavalry, infantry, and her servants. The villagers of Jesi gawked as the spectacle passed by; a mundane morning had taken a turn toward that of storybook fable.

The ornate but weather-beaten coach came to a slow halt between the horsemen in the town square. The door opened, and an old man dressed in all white stepped out. He motioned for the servants to secure the steps at the opening of the buggy. Queen Constance then emerged, struggling to navigate the tiny stairs while carefully expressing a pained smile. She wore a long, flowing blue dress that matched her eyes. A cape covered all but a small hint of her long blonde hair. She wore no jewelry, except for a crucifix necklace around her neck.

A small but growing crowd politely applauded; some bowed, others curtsied. Most guarded their feelings for her, unsure of her motivations for this unannounced visit.

Constance was clearly in the final stages of her pregnancy. She frowned at her physicians, now organizing in front of the tent that was being assembled in the town square. They assured her that she could make it to Sicily to see her husband Henry crowned king of Sicily before the birth of their child, but several delays and an unforgiving winter storm had caused them to lose too much time and miss the coronation.

Now, several hundred miles from Sicily, it became clear that the birth of her first child was imminent and would wait for no schedule, destination, or coronation. Her journey down the eastern flank of Italy would have to come to a halt in this small, insignificant village. She could go no further until the birth of her baby.

Constance walked the short distance into the tent, and silently scowled at Bertoli de Apulia, the physician in charge. Knowing her disapproval, he tried to break eye contact with her and looked across the tent, but he was unsuccessful in avoiding her vision.

"Come here, Bertoli," she said sternly. "I need a word with you."

Bertoli summoned all the diplomacy a physician could muster, knowing he was dealing with a pregnant queen hours away from giving birth. This was not the first queen Bertoli had served; in fact, he had been one of the physicians present when Constance was born almost forty years ago. He knew there would be potentially unreasonable demands voiced impatiently and impolitely.

"Yes, Your Highness?" he said as he bowed. "How can I be of service?"

Bertoli's condescending tone irritated Constance. She had every right to be frustrated with him; after all, he was disobeying her request on how she'd planned to give birth. She held her anger, though, so as not to seem like a frantic, spoiled princess.

"We agreed on a public birth, Bertoli," she said, looking at the closed tent and frowning. "I haven't changed my mind."

Bertoli knew this would be a difficult birth without the drama of a crowd looking in on his progress. He'd hoped she would let that order dissolve once she entered the large tent and the birth pains began to ensue.

"Very well, Queen Constance. I will have this side of the tent opened for all to see," he said with the slightest hint of sarcasm. "Our only motive in closing the tent was to protect and care for you to the best of our abilities."

"I understand your concerns, but there can be no doubt about the lineage of this baby," she said, smiling warmly at Bertoli, then raising her voice for all the nursemaids, midwives, and other physicians to hear. "We will all have to get through this together. I trust you all in this, my time of need."

Bertoli nodded, bowed, and began the revision of the birthing area. It was not often that a male was allowed to be present at a birth. Midwives and nursemaids usually handled the birthing of a baby, but Bertoli and Constance agreed that with her advanced birthing age, it would be prudent to have a physician present.

As a queen, Constance was attuned to setting the scene for historic events. She knew the image of this tiny town would change. The crowd still seemed perplexed and confused about the events that were about to unfold. Constance abruptly gathered her composure and walked outside the tent toward the town square to address the growing group of villagers. Respectfully, a path opened for her as she approached. Quickly, silence replaced clamor.

"Please feel free, all, to witness the birth of my first child, a future king or queen of Sicily," she exclaimed loudly so everyone could hear. "Let it be known with certainty that this baby is indeed of the family of Constantine and Staufer."

The proclamation echoing in their humble ears, Constance turned and proceeded back to the tent. Now open in the front for all to view, she hesitated. She was not an outgoing person, and she would have preferred a private birth in her palace behind closed doors. Something much more modest was her style; however, her sensitivities had to give way to this historic situation. Doubts, rumors, and speculation dictated this action. Many thought Constance would not be able to carry this baby to term, and others whispered she might attempt to bring in an imposter. Dismayed and determined, Constance demanded to disprove this notion. If her modesty must be sacrificed in the process, so be it.

Despite being married for over ten years, she had never been pregnant. The assumption was that she was unable to conceive.

The audience began to murmur. Some of the residents ran off to tell others, while some stayed for a better view. This was truly a unique opportunity for the citizens of Jesi to witness a queen deliver a future monarch before their very eyes.

"Perhaps this is a blessing of sorts," she said to Bertoli. "Now no one will doubt this child's birthright. And with you involved instead of just midwives, it is not a traditional delivery anyway."

Bertoli shrugged his shoulders and agreed with her half-heartedly. He knew how rare it was for a middle-aged woman to have a child, many believing it to be impossible. As the trusted physician, he would leave no medical options open to chance, but here he stood with a crowd of onlookers up against the birthing tent. He swallowed the lump in his throat.

"Relax, Bertoli. God has willed this birth. He watches over us and over this baby. Just as he watched over Sarah and Rebekah."

"Those are mothers in the Bible, Your Grace?"

"Yes, Bertoli. Forgive me, I forgot you are a heathen when it comes to matters of Christianity."

"You have enough faith for both of us Your Grace."

"Yes I do, Bertoli. God will keep us safe. Fear not."

By mid-morning, the entire population of Jesi had surrounded the royal tent. The nervous Sicilian guard attempted to keep them at a safe distance, but there were just too many bewildered and excited towns-people vying for the best vantage point to hold them back.

Bertoli and his medical staff were even more nervous, becoming more and more uncomfortable with this public birth. As the delivery progressed and the crowd pressed closer, Bertoli grew more anxious. The procedure was not simple under perfect conditions, and in this precarious setting, the prospect of the baby dying during delivery was very real. Even more haunting was the prospect of Constance struggling during a public display and dying in childbirth. He could not bring himself to allow that thought to linger.

This was difficult enough without dealing with the noise of a crowd and the unfamiliar setting of a tent.

"Focus on the task at hand!" he yelled at a nurse who was distracted by the noise. The order was as much for him as it was for the nurse.

Hours passed, and the mystified and voyeuristic inhabitants of Jesi began to quiet down. The medical staff had grown so used to the clamor that they hardly noticed the subtle change from noise to calm. Gradually, the crowd thinned, with the few remaining spectators watching the final stages intently.

Despite the distractions, speculations, and fears, the delivery was flawless. Constance worked in unison with Bertoli, queen mother and royal physician working in perfect harmony. Bertoli breathed a heavy sigh of relief, smiled gently, and assessed the newborn and mother-to-be in perfect condition.

"Congratulations, Queen Constance. You have a son."

Constance was delighted with the baby and pleased the birth was over. Exhausted, she looked to Bertoli in appreciation and anticipation. Bertoli placed the child in her arms, and she smiled as the remaining crowd cheered wildly.

"He is the second coming of Christ!" an old woman yelled who was standing near the front row. "The child was born the day after Christmas in a tent. Jesi is the new Bethlehem."

The townspeople cheered wildly at her assertions.

Some, however, seemed intent to cast derision. "He is the antichrist," a tall, dark man, who was standing at the back of the mob, whispered. "Look at his fiery-red hair and deep blue eyes. Even from a distance, I can see that his eyes are that of Satan's."

The newborn prince would be a polarizing figure his entire life.

Immersed in her joy, Constance cradled her new son and fell in love with him immediately. She stared, overwhelmed by the baby's bright red hair and strong blue eyes. Never had she felt such joy.

The boy had an unusually focused look on his face, as if somehow he could draw conclusions about his surroundings. Constance knew he was special.

As she gazed upon her baby, she saw the future of Sicily.

III

A Father Meets his Son

T he rumble of galloping horses shook the tent and awoke Constance and most of the servants. Her startled nursemaid peered out an opening in the tent to see what it might be.

"No need to be nervous," she said, laughing and placing the baby back in his small bed. "I know who it is."

King Henry and his men rode into Jesi, storming past the Sicilian guards in front of the tent as if they planned to take it by force. It was the only speed and direction he and his German soldiers knew—fast and forward.

"What are all these Italians doing around my wife?" Henry joked while pushing the flap of the tent open. His stature and broad shoulders towered over everyone. His men now at his side, he pushed his long brown hair out of his face and bellowed, "Where is my son? Show me my boy!"

Constance looked up at her husband—arrogant, brutish, unsophisticated, and somehow charming all at the same time. She outstretched her arm toward the child.

"Here he is, Henry. Here is your son."

Constance beamed when Henry cradled the boy in his massive arms. She was at her happiest. Although not one for public displays of emotion, she was nearly giddy from the day's events.

Henry looked down at his son with evident pride. For once, he was awestruck and silent, if only for a moment.

"If you are not a German, get out of this tent," he said with authority.

"You know neither of us were actually born in Germany, right?" Constance said.

"Being German is a state of mind, Constance," he said, then yelled once again in German at the people in the room.

"Henry, you are the Holy Roman Emperor, King of Germany, King of Italy, and now the King of Sicily. Try to act a little more regal in front of so many strangers, my dear."

Placing the baby in Constance's arms, Henry smiled, trying to be kingly in this tender moment. Meanwhile, an unofficial translator softened Henry's tone, using less scolding words for the Italians as they filed out of the tent.

Henry's hulking men closed ranks around the couple to get a better look. One of them even made cooing noises at the boy.

Henry frowned at the man, stunned that such noises could come from such a huge and hardened soldier.

"All of you, out!" he yelled. "Give us this room."

His guards left the tent, and Henry continued his rant.

"Constance, what are you and my son doing in a tent in Jesus, Italy?" he asked.

"It's not Jesus, it's Jesi," she said, forever playing along with his sarcasm. "And I am too tired to explain further. Ask Bertoli why we are here. But are you not pleased with your new son?"

"Oh yes. You've done well this day, Constance."

"Thank you, Henry," she said softly, and closed her eyes for a moment.

Henry looked proudly upon the new baby while Constance attempted to sleep. He could not get over the baby's blazing red hair; it was the same color as his father, Frederick Barbarossa. Each characteristic seemed destined from the royal lineage, but for royalty, a name must be carefully chosen. They had agreed beforehand to name him Constantine II in honor of the great king from Constance's side of the family.

Still, Henry couldn't dismiss the full head of red hair. "It must be a sign," he reasoned. He impulsively declared, "The boy shall be named Frederick II, in honor of my father." Constance began to protest, but

Henry interrupted her. "God has willed it," he said with absolute certainty. "Look at the boy's hair. He is the image of my father."

She smiled and closed her eyes again, knowing Henry would never relent after such an inspiring thought, and this had been too great a day to debate the politics of naming a royal baby.

"Whatever you say, Henry," she said with a smile.

IV

Waiting on a Pope

H enry remained with Constance and Frederick in Jesi for the next several days. Constance was drained, so she took this time to rest and recuperate from the toll childbirth had taken.

Henry checked in with her and Frederick occasionally, but the import of his energy was in composing a letter to Pope Celestine. This would be a letter without precedent.

Henry asked the pope to baptize his son at the Vatican, as well as to bless him as king of Germany. It was an attempt to supersede the princes of Germany who had always elected their own kings. Henry wished to choose his successor and use the pope to lend credence to his plan. He knew this went against the custom of German princes electing their own king, but Henry felt he should be able to choose his son as successor if he wished it. Further, he thought the pope would support this action, given that the pope should have far more say in the electoral process of a Holy Roman emperor that he ultimately crowned.

While the request for baptism seemed innocent enough, Pope Celestine did not miss the subtlety. Even though he felt tempted to choose the king himself despite the prince's electoral process, he knew this would benefit Henry's plans more than his own.

Days passed, causing Henry to grow impatient while awaiting word from Celestine.

"How long does an emperor have to wait for word?" he asked the Italian stable boy in his thick German dialect. The boy looked away nervously, continuing to brush down Henry's horse. "How long will I have to wait in this godforsaken village for a reply from Celestine? I could have ridden to Rome by now and gotten my answer!"

Not understanding his words, but fully understanding his rage, the boy ran from the stable without finishing his duties, convinced Henry was going to kill him.

Henry shrugged his shoulders, picked up the brush the boy had abandoned, and continued to groom the horse and stare out of the stable.

"What could possibly take him this long?" he said to himself.

—◊◊◊—

The following evening, the rider that Henry dispatched to the Vatican rode back into Jesi and carried a letter with the pope's seal emblazoned on its cover. Henry quickly tore through the seal to get to its contents.

"Careful, Henry," said Constance, now out of bed and approaching him. "You'll tear right through the words you've waited so long to read."

Henry began to read, his eyes quickly showing disappointment at the pope's words.

Celestine congratulated Henry on his coronation as king of Sicily and Constance on the birth of Frederick. He went on to decline the request for baptism at the Vatican or to be a part of the ceremony at all. His reason was to guarantee the impartiality of the Papacy toward potential political offices. "It would look as if I were trying to influence the princes of Germany in their choice of king," he stated in the brief letter. "It is best for the pope to remain neutral in these matters at this time."

He wanted Henry to know he fully understood his less than subtle attempt to bring him into the process. Celestine had long hinted about the pope being a part of the election, but Henry was not the ally he wanted to advance his effort.

After carefully reading each word, Henry placed the letter down on the table. Constance picked it up and began reading. Without waiting for her response, Henry ordered his aides to send a messenger to the room.

"Any word for the pope, Your Grace?" the messenger asked.

"No," Henry said firmly, "but ready your mount. I will have a dispatch for the Bishop of Assisi forthcoming."

He looked down at Constance, still seated at the table reading the pope's letter.

"Assisi has an appropriate cathedral for my boy's baptism. We shall have it there on our way back to Sicily. We shall present Frederick to the princes of Germany in the traditional manner. They will not reject an emperor's wishes."

"The pope doesn't want to show partiality," Constance said to Henry, who seemed oblivious to her response. "He should be partial. If not a pope, then who should make recommendations to the princes?"

Her rant continued to her nursemaid, who was attending to Frederick after Henry walked out of the tent.

"After all I have done for the church," Constance continued. "The funds I raised for that man. For God's sake, I spent nine years in a convent. Who better to show partiality? Politics keeps my son from receiving a holy baptism from the pope?"

"Why not talk to your husband, Majesty?" the nursemaid suggested. "Perhaps he can convince Pope Celestine to reconsider."

"No, Henry's mind is made up," she said, putting her arm around the maid's shoulder, and looking down at Frederick in his crib. "And I think the pope's mind is made up, too."

V

The Baptism of Frederick

Pietro Di Bernardone sat with his wife and eldest son in the very last row of the packed Assisi Cathedral. Several steps behind them, his younger son, Francis, slid across the pews to be nearest to the only clear window in a church filled with stained glass. While almost everyone in the cathedral watched the door for the arrival of the emperor, the queen, their baby, and the bishop, Francis watched the window.

The town of Assisi was small in stature and population, but home to one of the most spectacular cathedrals in all of Italy. Upon getting word of the arrival of the royal party, they went to work making Assisi worthy of such an event as the christening of a future king. Everyone seemed a part of the preparation.

The Bishop of Assisi took Henry's hand in his and welcomed the royal family to Assisi and his cathedral. He led them past the crowd to the front of the church where the ceremony would take place.

While not Rome, Assisi was still one of the richest towns in the region. The cathedral was their pride and joy, and this event only made that pride swell.

"We are both honored and pleased that you chose Assisi for this event," the bishop said loudly for everyone to hear. "Congratulations on your first child," he said to Constance.

"Thank you, Father. We are happy to be here."

Henry smiled at the bishop. *At least we are closer to Sicily than if we were in Rome*, he thought to himself as the bishop began the ceremony.

The congregation watched in awe. The bishop christened Frederick to an adoring assembly; Francis, however, was more interested in the windowsill. He watched as two birds worked diligently on a nest in a tree beside the church. One bird flew off and returned with hay or twigs while the other bird stayed and organized the materials.

Kind of early in the winter to be constructing a nest, Francis thought. "Perhaps it's a sign of an early spring. Sometimes birds can sense these things," he said inadvertently.

"I present to you, Prince Frederick of Sicily," the bishop said at the moment Francis was talking to himself about birds.

"Shhh!" his father warned, hissing at him with his index finger over his lips and an angry glare. "No daydreaming in church, Francis. Not when there is royalty present."

Francis nodded with a conciliatory gesture, then turned his head to watch the birds' progress. He was still more impressed with the nest than the procession coming down the aisle. His brother laughed, having witnessed this behavior many times before. His mother frowned at Francis, then winked and smiled at Francis.

Frederick awoke while being carried down the aisle by the bishop to be presented to the city. He seemed to look Francis in the eye and smile. Francis smiled back, and then turned his attention to the mother bird pecking on the window.

VI

Life at the Palace

Lucera, Italy

1197 AD

Frederick's infancy passed by quietly. Constance took the role of primary parent while Henry went off to conquer lands not already a part of his empire. It was not unusual for a king to be absent from his family for years at a time. Royal children like Frederick were often raised by servants or moved to another relative's castle. Constance, however, took on motherhood as her life's calling.

By the time he could walk, Frederick spent every waking moment with her. Henry left Constance as Regent of Sicily, but that title was secondary in her mind to the duties of raising her son.

They lived in a small country palace called Foggia. It was near the town of Lucera in southern Italy, which was a part of the Sicilian kingdom. The palace was built on a small hill overlooking the Adriatic Sea. Many boats and ships passed by on their way to Sicilian ports. As they did, Constance told Frederick where they came from by the style of the craft and its flags or markings. Frederick enjoyed the sea and the ships that sailed by, but his true love was on the opposite side of the palace.

To the west, north, and south was the great Royal Forest, which spanned several thousand acres. Hunting was allowed only for the royal family, guests, and servants employed by the king. Because of this, the forest was filled with all types of animals that were essentially unafraid of human beings. Many animals could be approached without running off, especially if Constance and Frederick brought food.

They went into the woods nearly every day, and never failed to see animals and birds of numerous varieties. Constance told Frederick everything she knew about the species they observed, taking as much time as Frederick needed to understand fully.

That evening, they played a game in which he would become the animal or bird and talk to Constance. He would explain what it was like to be that animal using the information Constance had taught him, and his own imagination. He discussed how it felt to fly or walk on all fours. Sometimes, he would give names to the animals and birds he imitated.

The game stimulated his imagination and gave him a better understanding of the wildlife around him. It was also popular with the palace servants and tutors, who looked forward to his show each night.

When he was outside, Frederick played on the grounds or wandered into the woods if the servants didn't watch him closely. Frederick was always curious about anything that caught his eye; he wanted to understand how things worked.

As time passed, Frederick's observations went from a curious child to artist, and from an artist to chronicler. He sketched the animals and their movements, and his mother would record his observations on the animals' mannerisms, diet, and even drinking patterns.

Birds fascinated Frederick. He watched every type with amazement, from sparrows to eagles. His favorites were the falcons and hawks that frequented the Italian sky. Their speed in flight and patience on the ground or in a tree astonished young Frederick. He drew pictures of the hawks and falcons, as well as their spectacular display of movement in flight.

Constance wanted Frederick to understand nature, how all creatures and the environment were tied together, and how a seemingly small occurrence could affect everything in that environment. By understanding nature, he could better understand the links of society and the flow of an economy once he was king. She knew if he could grasp nature, he could grasp the nuances of running a kingdom.

For now, it was about observing a bird patiently hunt for a worm and bring it back to the nest for its newborn, or watching a deer silently glide into a stream and drink, only to catch the scent of them and scamper off.

Sometimes Constance would shirk her duties as regent and spend more time with Frederick than her aides felt appropriate to govern Sicily, prompting her frantic staff to besiege her upon her return from the forest. Often, she would answer their questions and make the decisions a regent was to make while walking from the lawn to the palace. She relied on her staff to handle day-to-day matters, but making Frederick love and understand Sicily was a far more important task.

Constance also taught Frederick about horses. The palace kept a small stable for servants and guards to use for transportation and security, and Frederick was trained to ride, care for, and groom the horses. Frederick had a natural connection to them. Despite their overwhelming size, he never feared them. He walked freely throughout the stable grounds, as if knowing he would not be trampled or harmed in any way. Frederick became a talented and intuitive rider, as Constance felt that a king should ride with the confidence befitting his crown.

Frederick's interests in more scholarly subjects were just as passionate as his interest in nature and animals. It was as if his curiosity knew no boundaries, and Constance did everything to keep that curiosity piqued. She introduced him to art and poetry. She also read Aristotle and other Greek philosophers to him.

Although Frederick was too young for these subjects, he seemed to grasp everything put in front of him. His recall of these subjects at later times was phenomenal.

One night, Frederick couldn't sleep, so Constance agreed to read to him if he would go to sleep afterward. She had read Frederick stories, fables, parables, which included illustrations and pictures on the adjoining pages to the text. Frederick had heard most of these stories many times.

She lit a candle and began to read. After a while, an open window allowed a draft to pass through Frederick's room. The breeze extinguished the candle, leaving only limited light and shadows to see the words. Constance was too tired to relight the candle, so she continued reading by memory; however, as she struggled to see the text, her story became more and more abridged.

Soon, Frederick stopped her.

"You're leaving out parts, Mother," he said to her in a small, curious voice.

"It's hard to read, dear, when there is no light, and I'm too tired to get up and light the candle," she said patiently, yet wanting her son to know she would prefer being asleep.

"I can finish the story, Mother," he said, looking up into her squinting eyes with innocence.

This surprised Constance, especially since Frederick had said it so confidently. He couldn't read, but she wondered if he might be able to make up an imaginative story. She thought it would be an opportunity to test his imagination.

"All right, Frederick, you may finish."

Frederick read nearly every word on the page, stopping on the exact word where the page broke. After several pages, she realized Frederick had memorized the text of the page by the corresponding picture on the facing page. After Frederick had finished, Constance turned to a page in the middle of the book and lit the candle again to make certain what she was witnessing. Frederick read the entire page without a single mistake.

Constance had never seen anything like this before. Despite her limited exposure to children, she knew this was unusual. It was clear that Frederick was a gifted child, probably more gifted than she could even comprehend. His memory was nearly flawless, but that was only one quality she wished to nurture in her son. To make him well rounded, he would need many others.

Not long after, Constance began to employ tutors to teach Frederick more advanced subjects that would not normally be taught to such a young child. Constance felt Frederick needed to be challenged, and teaching him at an appropriate pace would leave him far ahead of the subject matter. Soon, the subjects would become simplistic and Frederick would lose interest, so staying ahead of Frederick's capacity would keep him stimulated.

She read to him every night, and his interest in books became notorious throughout the palace. As soon as Frederick could grasp reading on any level, books were found all over the palace—both inside and outside. Servants were often seen with handfuls of misplaced books on their way to the palace library.

Despite Constance being a very religious and spiritual woman, she wanted Frederick to be well read and well versed in all subjects. She wanted him to understand all cultures and religions that he might encounter as a king. She introduced him to Judaism, Islam, and Buddhism, as well as Greek philosophy and mythology. When he was older, she brought in tutors to train him in rhetoric, science, mathematics, and Christianity. The Papal tutor objected to many of the other disciplines taught to Frederick, especially the religious ones, but Constance did not heed his objections. She considered these lessons to be of vital importance to his ability to govern Sicily and understand the world around him, not just the small box that was a Christian education. She would not let the Papacy dictate Frederick's education; after all, they were unwilling to baptize him.

Finally, she requested a new tutor from the Vatican.

Cencio Savelli was the treasurer of the Vatican under two popes as well as vice chancellor of the church. However, when he heard of Constance's request, he asked for a leave of absence in order to be Frederick's tutor. Cencio always had a heart for teaching and was more than anxious to tutor Christianity to a future king. He respected Constance's wishes for Frederick to have a diverse education, but he was able to teach Frederick creatively within those parameters. He amazed Frederick with tales of Rome, as well as saints and many exciting stories from the Bible.

He quickly became Frederick's favorite.

VII

An Impala Named Roger

One day, a tribe of impalas emerged from the woods and walked quietly onto the palace lawn. Frederick and Constance watched from the window upstairs.

"This must be the African tribe of impalas that were a part of your grandfather's animal collection long ago," Constance said. "I'm surprised they are still in existence after so long."

"My grandfather had an animal collection?" Frederick asked.

"Yes."

"King Roger?"

"Yes, Frederick. He had animals from all over the world. But there was a fire in the palace that spread to the forest. King Roger ordered the gates open rather than risk the animals harm. He recovered many of them, but not all. The impalas were long thought to be extinct, but apparently they were able to survive all these years in the wild with relative anonymity."

"What's anonymity, Mother?"

"It means that no one saw them for a long, long time, Frederick."

They watched in amazement as the tribe assessed the grass bordering the forest and leading to the palace; they were somewhat cautious, but with enough trust of the grounds to venture even closer. A young impala trotted up to the lower window and looked inside, directly below Frederick and Constance. It seemed he was the bravest, and even at his undeveloped age and stature, he had taken the leadership role.

As the rays of the sun fell upon the young impala's coat, it shined as red as the breast of a robin. He was only as big as a cat, with large, inquisitive eyes that looked up at his royal audience. His long, spindly legs did not fit his small body. His ears were as smooth as silk, and tufts of fur grew out of them like a fox. His nose was as black as the night, shiny and wet. His small, cloven hoofs dug into the ground as he walked or clicked as he stepped clumsily on the brick path leading to the palace.

For several days, the impala tribe visited the palace grounds. Servants began leaving food and scraps on the western lawn near the forest. While the impala nibbled on corn or carrots, Frederick approached them.

Constance warned Frederick that these were wild and unpredictable animals, but Frederick had a sense about this one; he knew there was a connection with this small impala.

He smiled and waved to his mother. "It's all right, Mother," he said calmly.

The tribe watched Frederick closely, then ran back into the shallow part of the forest and turned to see if he followed; all of the tribe ran, except for one.

The young impala had stayed to eat a large carrot. When he looked up, his eyes focused on Frederick, who was crouched only a few steps from him. Then he looked back toward the forest; his tribe was visible, but safely in the woods.

Both boy and animal seemed to have a sense about the other. Frederick offered the impala another carrot from his hand, which it accepted. Soon after, Frederick had the young impala in his arms. Constance smiled in wonder at her son. It was quite a rare experience to hold an authentic and alive part of nature in your arms.

Frederick named the impala Roger after his great grandfather who originally freed the tribe.

On the strength of his great bravery, Roger quickly became a palace favorite.

"Can you imagine if Henry ever saw a wild creature in this palace?" Constance asked one of her servants.

"I guess it's a good thing he is rarely present, Majesty," the servant replied.

Constance smiled at her and walked off. She missed her husband, despite their vast differences in culture and personality.

—⚏—

Henry was the son of Frederick Barbarossa, one of the great warrior kings of his age. Henry was destined for greatness and conquest, and he did not disappoint that destiny. He succeeded his father as Holy Roman Emperor, King of the Germans, and through battle, he claimed the Italian and Sicilian crowns.

Constance was the daughter of King Roger. He was less the warrior that Barbarossa was, but still an effective king. He had brought lands together through negotiation, and formed a strong centralized government.

Constance spent her adult life in a convent before marrying Henry in an arranged marriage. Unlike Henry, she was studious and favored intelligence over brute force.

The marriage made sense for the two powerful families, but Henry and Constance shared little more than friendship as a common bond.

It was in the battle for Sicily that his love for Constance was bonded, and her love for him as well.

During the conflict, Constance was taken prisoner in Naples and held for ransom against Henry. Pope Celestine saw an opportunity to keep Henry out of Sicily and brokered a deal that would free Constance if Henry agreed to withdraw his claim on Sicily. Instead, Henry attacked the captors and freed Constance by force.

His attack on her captors bonded the two together in love that lasted beyond any sort of personality conflicts over the years.

—⚏—

The impala tribe came and went as if the palace and its grounds were a province of the forest. They usually visited just before sunset, moving in against the trees like dark silhouettes on the green grass. When they stepped out to graze on the lawn in the light of the afternoon sun, the brilliance of their shiny red coats against the green grass was a sight that stopped the entire estate, as if it were a natural event like lightning, a sunrise, or snowfall.

Roger would often take the next step in nurturing the relationship by coming in from the wild to show he was on good terms with everyone, and he made the house one with the landscape so no one could tell where one stopped and the other began. It was the same with Frederick, who wandered into and out of the woods every day.

They were young ambassadors to each other's habitat.

VIII

Falconland

For a long time, Frederick's childhood passed by quietly and peace-fully. He continued to impress his teachers more and more each day. The palace of Foggia had become a learning academy with only one student. Tutors outnumbered servants in attending to Frederick.

On his occasional visits, Henry let it be known he disapproved of this environment.

"You are turning the boy into an Italian intellectual," he bellowed at Constance in German. "It will soon be time for him to learn the ways of a king."

Constance disagreed with Henry. Was this not exactly what a king should be taught? But she always kept her tongue and agreed with him, knowing she would win the war of attrition and he would leave Sicily soon. Time was always on her side.

Henry would use these short visits to reconnect with Frederick as best he could. Frederick loved his father, but he barely knew him. Soon after his arrival, Henry would leave and things would go back to the way they were.

"Have someone teach him something not contained inside a book, Constance," Henry said as he mounted his horse. Constance nodded and waved good-bye. Deep down, she agreed there was more for Frederick to learn, but these studies would form the foundation of the child's thought process. He could learn to be a man and a king later in life.

"When he is older, you can turn him into a German," she said to her husband.

Soon after Henry left Sicily, Constance decided it was time to stimulate Frederick's imagination in a more practical matter; there were indeed elements to being king that Frederick would not get from books. So, she told Frederick to create a kingdom in his own mind and for him to be its king. The first day, he was to name it and draw pictures of its land and its people and how they lived their lives. The project excited him, and he drew pictures all day.

He named the kingdom Falconland.

The next day, she had Frederick write down the types of work the people did in Falconland. What goods did they produce? Whom did they sell these goods to? Did they keep the goods for their own kingdom? Did they trade for other goods from other kingdoms? Within two days, Frederick had dozens of pictures and lists about Falconland.

Each day, Constance would add elements for Frederick to include in his kingdom. As the days passed, Falconland grew. Frederick added castles with motes, dragons, defenses against the ogres and trolls, farms to feed his citizens, trade routes, and other kingdoms to trade with Falconland. This imaginary kingdom soon became Frederick's primary focus. He began adding to the kingdom without suggestions from Constance.

A royal navy of pirates would defend his shores and the important trade routes of the Mediterranean. A royal zoo would be his prized possession, with wild, exotic animals from all over the world, like his grandfather's. A court of international wise men would advise him and live in an Oriental palace.

After a long while, Constance asked him about the economy of Falconland. Most of the riches would flow through him. He decided it would be fair for him to disperse the wealth better than the lords or barons or whomever would normally disperse it. Frederick would want the riches to flow through everyone like the water of a stream—there for all to drink.

With the treasure, he would build roads and docks that would make life easier for everyone and allow merchants from other kingdoms easier access. People would be paid a fair wage, goods would flow into and out of Falconland, and the kingdom would prosper.

Each day, the kingdom became more complex. Constance told him to name the officials who would help him govern his kingdom. He named several, some human, some antelope, and some birds. Frederick also started a school to train others to help him run the kingdom. He named Constance as the head teacher, along with a sparrow who built a nest outside his window as her second-in-command of the school.

Within a few months, Frederick filled his room with pictures, charts, and stories of his fantasy kingdom.

But as he got older, Falconland took a less prominent role in his day-to-day life.

Constance eventually took every single writing, chart, and drawing about Falconland and saved it in a wooden box. She put the box in a secret closet inside a forgotten room within the palace for another time. Frederick moved on to matters of mathematics, science, and Aristotle. She accepted her son's natural evolution to other challenging subjects, but she would miss Falconland.

She became more focused on being the regent of Sicily. For practical application, Frederick would spend half the day in studies and the other with her as she governed. She feared Frederick was so smart that he could easily be lost in books, studies, and theory. She wanted him to see how to apply these studies and theories in real life. She wanted him to learn how to deal with people of all types—from kings to peasants.

It was her belief that a well-educated, well-rounded ruler could create a grand kingdom all on his own talent and energy, no matter the other elements or obstacles put in front of him. Even without warfare, he could prosper and add land to his kingdom. It didn't have to be at the tip of a sword, but through negotiation and prosperity. Although a rarity for kings of this age, she felt it could be done.

She saw her son as this potential king.

IX

Crusade

Rome, Italy

1198 AD

It took the death of Pope Celestine to bring Henry, Constance, and Frederick together after a long interval between visits. Henry's quest to expand the boundaries of the Holy Roman Empire had kept him in northern Italy for some time. The funeral of the pope had all of Europe in Rome.

"I wonder if this will raise the interdiction of my lands and my excommunication," Henry sarcastically said to Constance.

"You aren't ex-communicated, Henry," Constance said, not wanting to entertain his humor at the pope's funeral. "He lifted that after you freed Richard. You should have never taken him hostage. That is beneath a king."

"That ransom paid for almost everything we have been able to accomplish in the past years. Do not get self-righteous with me. This is the way of European politics. If it had been me, Richard the Lionhearted would have held me for a hundred years to fund his wars. Look at the taxes he levied against his own people. Celestine would have done well to stay out of it."

"Perhaps the next pope will focus on God," said Constance, "not on kings and crusades. I pray that it is so."

After the burial of Pope Celestine, Henry requested an audience with the cardinals before they went into solitude to elect the next pope. He made it clear to all that he favored a German as Celestine's successor.

"The Italians have had far too many popes for far too long," he said. "It's time Germany was better represented at the Vatican."

"Maybe it's time for an Italian emperor," one of the cardinals joked while one of the German cardinals smiled but said nothing. "For too long, Germany has controlled the Holy Roman Empire."

"The next emperor will be Italian," Henry said. "My son Frederick has been born and raised here." He put his arm around Frederick.

Seeing no point to the discussion, the cardinal got up from his chair, causing all the cardinals to follow.

"It was good to see you again, Emperor. Sorry that it was under such circumstances. Our Lord works in mysterious ways. We shall inform you as soon as there is a new pope," the cardinal said.

"You put no value in my opinion as to the next pope?"

"Emperor, did you know that Pope Celestine attempted to resign as pope so that he could name his successor?"

Henry remained silent.

"We denied his request, because it is the tradition of the Vatican for the cardinals to elect each pope. It isn't that we don't value your opinion; it is just that not you—nor even a pope—can be a part of this decision. God speaks directly to us and we convey His will."

The cardinals then took their leave.

"Let's go, boy," Henry said to Frederick, leaving the Vatican and Rome on their way back to Sicily.

Later that day, the cardinals cast their first round of ballots for Celestine's successor. After several rounds, a frontrunner emerged. Clearly, the next pope would not be German, or even Celestine's hopeful successor.

Lotario De Signi was a young Vatican attorney who had worked in the church since he was twenty-nine. He was from a powerful family and rose in stature in the Papacy at a meteoric rate. He was a talented attorney of church law, a noted orator, and a man who understood the political climate of Europe quite well. He was a man of limitless ambition.

Not the typical qualities one would expect from a pope, but qualities that could certainly change the job description. He chose the ironic name "Pope Innocent III."

Pope Innocent had a vision that would elevate the Papacy above kings and emperors alike. He felt that church law gave him that distinction, and in his opening speech before the cardinals and aristocracy, he said as much.

"God has instituted two great dignities—a greater one to preside over souls as if over day, and a lesser one to preside over bodies as if over night. These are the pontifical authority and the royal power. Now, just as the moon derives its light from the sun and is indeed lower than it in quantity and quality, the royal authority derives the splendor of its dignity from the pontifical authority in position and power."

The cardinals were taken aback by this speech. It shocked the royalty of Europe, too; however, Pope Innocent believed that these kings, if left unchecked, would ravage Europe with endless wars and taxation to finance the wars. Given unlimited powers, these kings and emperors would wreck the fragile European society that had emerged after the Roman Empire.

Innocent felt an obligation to be a governor to the aristocracy for the good of the people. There was a need for regulation, and only the Vatican could provide it. It had long been discussed and sometimes tested by previous popes, but to no significant avail. Innocent, however, was a pope with the talent to make this proposition a reality.

He started his career at the University of Paris, where he tested his oratory and legal skills against the best and brightest in Europe. Despite being from a prominent family, he was not of regal stock and could never be a king; so, he turned instead to the church.

"The church is the only place where talent and performance can propel a man to a place of power," he once said to friends. "Otherwise, it's about lineage."

Not exactly the calling most had to enter the church, but Innocent did have a profound effect on the Vatican. He reorganized the day-to-day management into a finely tuned bureaucracy. Within months, the Vatican doubled its business throughout Europe as more priests ventured into rural lands to start churches with the pope's blessing.

Innocent worried that Henry would unite all of Italy with Sicily and Germany, thus surrounding him and limiting his power. He needed smaller kingdoms with smaller leaders, such as counts and barons who would be easier to control. This would allow him to be the power broker he felt the pope should be.

However unusually calculating Innocent was for a pope, he understood the human condition. He understood the mind of a king, particularly Henry's.

He understood the strengths and weaknesses of the Papacy, so he would not wage war on Henry, either literally or politically.

Not yet.

Instead, he would attempt to send Henry and his army to a faraway battleground, hopefully with other armies and other kings.

The Crusades!

For a century before, popes had called for kings and countries to take up the cross and fight for their religion against the infidel Saracens of the Middle East. Innocent would play to Henry's ego for battle, as well as his pride for Germany and family, to promote the idea of a crusade.

In a letter to Henry, Innocent pointed out that no German knight or king had ever completed a crusade. Henry's father, Frederick Barbarossa, went with Richard the Lionhearted on the third crusade but drowned before reaching the Middle East.

"It should be Henry's task to right this obligation for Germany, his family name, and Christianity as Holy Roman emperor."

A crusade would take two to three years; during that time, Innocent could control the region without any threat. The chance to wage a war of this scale was too tempting to Henry and the other kings. The vision of eternal glory was too valuable for him to turn down.

The letter from Pope Innocent surprised Henry, but it triggered something within him, too. He knew it was bait from the new pope, but in a way, it was exactly what he wanted.

After his coronation as king of Sicily, Henry had turned his sights to northern Italy. He fought with the towns of the Lombard League in an attempt to unite Italy with the Holy Roman Empire and the Kingdom of Sicily; his success was limited.

He knew Pope Innocent (as did every pope) preferred the Lombard League of small rulers and small regions to an empire that would surround Rome. He knew this would delay the prospect for years and give Innocent a political foothold.

Still, the prospect of a crusade intrigued him.

It was always Henry's goal to go on a crusade after his northern Italian campaign. He was a proud German and wanted to lead a European army into the Middle East in honor of his father. His plan was to battle-test his German knights in northern Italy before venturing into a crusade, but the temptation to crusade at the request of a pope with his German knights as the spearhead was enticing.

"The letter is inappropriate and insulting," Henry said to his top general, Markward Van Anweiler. "It insults my intelligence."

He showed the letter to Markward, hoping to get agreement from him.

"My Lord, if the pope calls on us to take back Jerusalem, let us ready ourselves and sail for the Middle East," he countered with certainty. "There is no higher calling."

"But don't you understand his motivation? He baits us into this crusade. He wants northern Italy to stay as it is. He has no interest in our progress in Jerusalem except to rid himself of me."

"You speak the truth, Lord. Every word you speak is righteous and with good council. But history will not recall the motivations that sent us to Jerusalem. History will only record our success there. We will be the army that reclaimed Jerusalem. You will be the leader who returns the Holy Land to the Christians. Everything else pales in analysis."

Henry agreed with that logic to a certain extent. He also knew why he kept Markward near him; he would always bring a fresh and candid perspective to any issue. It was a rare quality for an emperor to find in someone advising a king.

Henry understood the logistics and cost of a crusade. It would take a year of planning and fundraising to make this a worthwhile endeavor. Henry was a great warrior, a good king, but he was a poor planner. He was hesitant to leap immediately into this before he was ready. He squinted at the letter again, with the fire as sole provider of light. He groaned and put a hand on his stomach.

"My Lord, we must go back to Sicily and have a physician look at your stomach pains. That ailment has lingered with you since we left Germany weeks ago."

"Perhaps if there was a German doctor in Sicily, I would feel better about my prospects. But there is only Bertoli, and he is the man who let Constance deliver a baby in a tent inside an Italian village of idiots. He will probably want to treat me on the docks of Palermo. He is a senile old Italian."

Markward laughed at the mental picture.

"On the other hand, we could start planning the crusade while we are in Sicily and I could see Constance and Frederick. It's been so long since I saw my boy."

"We shall leave for Sicily in the morning, my Lord."

"Won't the Lombards be surprised when we are not on the battle-field?" he said, laughing and rubbing his stomach as he retired to his quarters.

By the time Henry had arrived in Sicily, his stomach pain had escalated. He struggled to ride his horse the last few miles and masked his agony at dismounting.

"Bring a physician to the emperor," Markward ordered the first servant to approach, as two of Henry's men helped him past the palace doors and into a private room. Once inside, Henry sat down on the floor.

Constance rushed into the room with a worried look on her face. "What's happened? Was he injured in battle?" she asked, holding Henry's hand.

"It's his stomach, My Lady," Markward said. "It has gotten worse in these past few days of our journey."

"Your stomach pained you at Celestine's funeral months ago, Henry. Surely, this is not related," she said with fury in her voice. "Surely, a physician has seen you since then."

Henry groaned a non-responsive reply, but Markward defended Henry's inaction.

"It has only worsened in these past few days, Queen Constance. King Henry thought this to be only a sour stomach."

"For several months?" she yelled at Markward, then turned to Henry and took his hand again. "There is no point in this debate. Where is Bertoli?"

She looked down at her husband, who was writhing on the floor in quiet agony. "Is there anything we can do for you, dear?" she asked, wiping tears away from her eyes.

"No," he said stoically, measuring his words, knowing any additional effort would cause him pain.

A loud voice echoed down the corridor until Bertoli stepped into the room. "Where is he?" Bertoli asked.

"Here he is, Bertoli," Constance said. "It's his stomach that ails him."

Bertoli looked down at Henry, and his inquisitive look turned grim.

"Give us this room, please."

"What is wrong with him, Bertoli?"

"I don't know yet, Majesty. Please, leave us now. Allow me to examine him."

For about an hour, Constance and Markward waited in the adjoining room and watched the door. Neither spoke a word as they watched the medical staff yell orders to servants, rushing in and out of the room, with no one giving them any indication of what was happening.

"Should you let the boy know?" Markward asked.

"No," Constance said as tears dribbled down her cheeks. "This would be too much for him to understand. I pray Henry survives this so that Frederick can see him at least once more."

Finally, Bertoli opened the door and walked over to Constance, his head bowed. He took her hand and looked into her eyes.

"I'm sorry, my lady, but Emperor Henry has died. We did everything we could, but his condition was far too advanced."

Constance stood there in shock.

"What condition?" Markward asked. "He complained of stomach aches for months now. No one sensed it to be anything more."

"It probably started as an enlarged spleen," Bertoli said, almost relieved to speak in medical terms. "The condition deteriorated over time, and the physical activity of riding probably caused the enlargement to rupture."

"And neglect," Constance added.

"Excuse me, Queen Constance, but we were at war. Emperor Henry showed no ill signs except a small stomachache. As soon as his condition worsened, we rode here to seek medical attention. This cannot be—"

"Henry neglected the ill spleen for months," Constance interrupted. "He complained of it at Pope Celestine's funeral. Had he sought medical advice anytime between that interim, it would not have ruptured."

She looked at Bertoli for confirmation.

"That is correct, My Lady. An enlarged spleen is treatable."

Markward slammed his gloved fist into the stone wall. Constance smiled in a somber way and walked into the room to see Henry. She turned to thank Bertoli and Markward but was overtaken by emotion. She closed the door to Henry's room behind her.

X

A New Sicily

Palermo, Sicily

1199 AD

After Henry's funeral, Constance became the most popular woman in all of Europe, for with her hand came the Kingdom of Sicily.

But Constance had no interest in marriage.

Her only purpose was to protect Frederick's future and Sicily. She wrote the princes of Germany and withdrew his name from consideration as king of the Germans; instead, Frederick became the king of Sicily, with Constance as regent. This cleared the way for Henry's brother, Philip of Swabia, to ascend to the throne. Since he had already been appointed the regent for Germany, Philip was the logical and likely candidate to succeed Henry as king of the Germans and Holy Roman emperor. On the surface, it seemed to be a wise arrangement, seamlessly transitioning from one brother to the next; however, it did not consider Sicily's defenses.

With Henry gone, the tiny kingdom was without any military presence. Not being part of the Holy Roman Empire, Sicily would be defenseless because the German knights protecting it would be recalled to their homeland. As regent, Constance had to consider either the potential attacks from the Middle East or a greedy king from Europe. Given its lack of military support, any attack would be likely to succeed.

Markward had amassed a great deal of land, knights, and prestige in central Italy and had made many offers to Constance. He knew a marriage proposal would be quickly rejected, as was the fate of many who'd previously offered. He didn't, however, request the role of king; instead, he offered to become the protectorate of Sicily in exchange for part of the kingdom's riches. This seemed a fair trade to Markward, a wise business arrangement for both sides that was endorsed by Henry in a letter given to Markward prior to Henry's death. This seemed to be an ironclad agreement that was in everyone's best interest.

However, Constance had another plan in mind.

"I do not doubt the authenticity of this letter, General," she said after much deliberation. "And I do not doubt your sincerity or ability to protect Sicily, but I do not want a German presence in Sicily, even if that was Henry's wish. I have denied the Staufer family and even my own family from helping because I don't want the Kingdom of Sicily to feel as if they are being ruled by Germans or any Europeans."

Her resistance to Henry's letter stunned Markward. He saw no other viable option for Sicily outside of a marriage she refused.

"What is your plan, Queen Constance, to protect this vulnerable little island?"

"God will protect Sicily, General Markward," she said dismissively. "Now, please take your knights and leave Sicily as soon as possible, unless it is your intention to occupy Sicily or take it by force."

Markward was both surprised and offended by her remarks, but he kept his anger within him.

"It is not our intent to occupy or take by force your son's kingdom, My Lady; I fought alongside his father for years. We shall cross the Straits by first light tomorrow. I pray to God for your safety."

Before she could respond, he turned his back and walked away.

—◌—

After all of the would-be protectorates and suitors had finally acquiesced, Constance wrote the pope and requested an audience at the

Vatican. Pope Innocent complied quickly, and she traveled immediately with Frederick to Rome.

She was surprised to see that the pope was around the same age as her. His jet-black hair and eyes gave definition to his long serious face. He was tall and thin and wore the Papal robes even in casual settings.

I guess he doesn't want anyone to forget he is the pope, Constance thought to herself.

"Your Holiness, it is my hope that we can come to an agreement for the Papacy to become the protectorate of Sicily and guardian of Frederick in the event of my death," Constance said. "Above all others, I trust the pope to keep my son and his kingdom safe."

Pope Innocent smiled with surprise and pleasure at her unexpected proposition. He had wanted the breakup of Sicily and Germany as a union; now he would have his wish on incredibly good terms.

"Queen Constance, it would be an honor for the Papacy to be the protectorate of Sicily and guardian of King Frederick. I had prayed we might be of service to you in your time of need. Given your background as a nun for those many years before your marriage to Henry, we felt this would be a natural progression."

"Thank you, Your Holiness. I did live in a convent for almost ten years and served God in every way that was asked of me. It was then that I learned much about the Vatican, the church, and its commitment to its parishioners and the aristocracy. I came to appreciate the pope as a mediator between God and man, just as you stated in your speech to the cardinals; however, please note that I was not a nun while I was at the convent since I never took vows of chastity."

"Queen Constance, it would be my honor to show you and Frederick the Vatican. Would you like a grand tour while our advisers sort out the terms of this arrangement? Would you honor me?" he said, holding his arm out.

"Frederick and I have longed for that very tour with Your Holiness, but I cannot accept until the negotiations are final."

Constance surprised the pope with her resistance. This was a woman he held in slight regard. First, she came to him and handed him Sicily without pre-conditions, voicing her trust of him. Then as terms were to be set, she became a very interested party, a detailed negotiator. He was a savvy leader, priding himself on reading other heads of state, but Constance was difficult to understand. Was she naïve or shrewd?

Those who knew Constance knew she was far from naïve; rather, she was an intelligent leader and an engaged mother who sensed a unique opportunity to keep her kingdom and her son safe. This arrangement, while seemingly overly weighted in the Vatican's favor, would align the Papacy with Sicily for defense. This would allow her to avoid incurring a costly military presence that predictably would end in either a coup or another army invading Sicily. With the Papacy as protectorate, she effectively had every European knight in her defense without having to pay any of them. Her only charge would be a larger population of priests and churches in Sicily, along with a tithe of revenues from Sicily that she was likely to pay the pope anyway.

Constance was careful not to ignore the pope's unique talents and aspirations. She was well aware that the pope, especially this pope, was as much a political figure as he was pontiff; his expectations for the Vatican were more about power than spirituality. It troubled her that he could use politics as leverage, but it was clearly the lesser of two evils. She would set aside her reservations and trust her rationale, a decision she hoped she would not regret.

Negotiations flowed smoothly, and both sides were eager to secure the beneficial deal as the final terms were agreed upon. Constance, ever the protector of Frederick, made him a ward of the Papacy, specifically naming Pope Innocent as guardian. This, she felt, would guarantee that Frederick would not be kidnapped for ransom or killed in the event of her death. And making Frederick the Pope's protectorate would give him a seamless claim to the Sicilian crown once he came of age.

"I believe all terms have been discussed and met, Queen Constance. Do we have an agreement?"

"Yes, Your Holiness, we have terms."

XI

Alone

The Foggia Palace

1201 AD

The arrangement between Constance and Pope Innocent went well for years. She oversaw the kingdom's business, and Innocent stayed out of the affairs of Sicily, except to bring priests and new churches to the kingdom. The result was of great benefit to the smaller regions of Sicily, as Constance welcomed the pope's expansion efforts and the Vatican received increased donations collected by the priests. As agreed, Constance also paid a tithe of ten percent of all the kingdom's profits to the Papacy. It was an arrangement she gladly paid. No security issues arose, and the cost was minimal.

Meanwhile, she was still spending a large amount of time with Frederick, although the tutors were playing a much larger role. As regent and mother of the king, the public and private burden of her position was taking a toll.

Constance had lived quietly with illness, suffering in silence for years, unwilling to call attention to her pain, but the rigors of being regent were beginning to drain her of energy. Each day, she would end work a little earlier. Within a few weeks, it was down to half-days. Before long, she was too weak to get out of bed.

Frederick spent that time with his mother in her room. He started reading to her, much as she had read to him for so many years. They talked about everything a mother and son, monarch and heir, could possibly discuss in the short time left, with her trying to compress every lesson she felt he needed into the short timeframe.

But Frederick didn't fully understand the concept of death. No one had explained to him how his father had died because he was too young and he didn't attend the funeral. It was perhaps the only thing Constance did not expose her child to, but possibly the most important lesson for him to learn.

Even though he knew his mother was ill, he never fully believed she would die. She was always alive, full of energy, and a central part of his life. Each day he woke up, and so did she.

Maybe this is how it will always be, he thought to himself each day.

One morning, Frederick awoke before Constance. Arising, he rattled around the room, wanting to wake her but without being too obvious. He made lots of noise until she finally opened her eyes and struggled to sit up. Her breathing was short and forced, and the color had left her face.

She silently motioned for Frederick to come to her. Fear began to grasp him as he walked to the side of her bed.

"Your father and I are so proud of you, Frederick," she whispered faintly. "Soon, you will be a king."

Frederick said nothing as he fought back tears. He didn't want her to see how scared he was. He tried to smile as she spoke, but he sensed the worst.

"I want you to go to your old room and open the closet. There is a surprise for you in an old box. Go there now and open it while Bertoli and the nurses look after me. Can you do that, Frederick?"

He nodded his head, unable to say anything for fear his emotions would overcome him. She kissed him and said good-bye, her voice barely audible and her breathing now too strained to continue the dialogue. He kissed her and said good-bye, trying as best he could not to cry.

Constance watched him slip out the door. Bertoli, accompanied by other physicians and servants, stayed by her side and comforted her.

There was nothing left to do. Finally, her labored breathing stopped, and she died.

"Should we tell the boy?" one of the servants asked.

"No," Bertoli said. "She wants Frederick to go to the playroom before we say anything to him. Leave him alone until he returns."

On his way, Frederick stopped to look out at the forest that he and his mother used to explore every day. He thought of how much he enjoyed that experience, reminiscing about many of the fond memories. He noticed the shrubbery moving at the perimeter of the grounds and, like many times before, watched it for a moment. Just as he was about to walk away, an impala suddenly burst through and onto the green grass of the grounds. Frederick watched closely as it walked regally toward the palace. Before it had made it to the doorway, he recognized it as Roger.

It had been a long time since the young impala made an appearance at the palace, and as Frederick looked down on him, he realized Roger was now fully grown. Even though he was much bigger and it had been a long time since his last visit, Frederick knew this was that same impala, his old friend. He stared out the window, and Roger looked back at him. Then as quickly as he arrived, Roger looked away and scampered off, jumping the shrubbery and disappearing into the forest. Frederick smiled for a moment and walked the rest of the way to the playroom.

Inside the closet, he discovered the old wooden box his mother had instructed him to find. He dug it out from amidst a stack of books, struggling to pull it through the doorway and into the middle of the room. There, he carefully opened the lid and found a cedar chest. With curious abandon yet careful appreciation, he opened it and found dozens of drawings, sketches, maps, and journals. The memories flooded his mind. The chest contained everything he had ever written or drawn about Falconland. Frederick lingered to inspect each of these items until he found his way to the bottom of the chest. There he saw a letter with Constance's seal molded into it. Frederick opened the letter and began to read.

My dearest Frederick,

If you are reading this, then I have started my journey to heaven. Don't be afraid or sad for long, my dear. It was an honor to raise you. It was my greatest joy in life. You are all a mother could ask for.

I saved Falconland because soon you will be a true king, and a king needs a plan for his people. Falconland was a creation in your mind, dear boy. On these pages, I was given hope for Sicily's future.

It made me proud to know my son has the imagination to create such a place. It would be my wish that you use it as a guide to rule over Sicily when the time comes.

Make Sicily as wonderful a place as you made Falconland, and I will be a proud mother looking down on you from heaven, dear boy. No matter what your future holds, remember you are the son of an emperor and a queen, and the rightful heir to the throne. God ordained you to be king, even before you were born. We will always be proud of you, Frederick, as long as you do what is best for family and kingdom.

My love always,

Your Mother

Frederick put the letter down and cried uncontrollably. He had gone from the heir of two thrones to an orphan whose destiny was very much in doubt, but that was nowhere in his thoughts.

He was all alone.

XII

Life at the Vatican

A few weeks after Constance's death, Frederick watched as riders approached the Palermo castle. It was decided that Palermo was safer than a small palace in the forest, and it would be harder to kidnap him from an island castle in Sicily. Frederick didn't mind the move; the new location didn't have the constant reminders of his mother, and he couldn't look out and see the forest. Palermo was boring, but that was better than the sorrow he felt at Foggia.

Frederick recognized the riders as German cavalry. A tall, blond man confidently dismounted his horse. Even from a distance, Frederick knew he was of royal blood. Constance had taught him how to recognize a regal by the uniforms or clothing they wore, and that knowledge served him well in this occasion. The man walked the length of the courtyard to meet with the sergeant on duty. Frederick noticed that the man's mannerisms and attitude revealed that he was indeed a monarch. He had seen so many at his mother's funeral.

After a while, the man and several other German knights entered Frederick's room.

"Hello, boy," he said in a husky German dialect. He sounded like Frederick's father, with a slightly softer tone.

"I am Philip of Swabia. I was your father's brother. I am your uncle."

Frederick looked up at Philip but said nothing. He looked a lot like Henry. He was taller and leaner, but they shared the same face and same strong blue eyes. Philip knelt down to be at Frederick's level.

"I see why Henry named you after my father," Philip said, smiling and rubbing Frederick's thick red hair. "Give us the room," he said firmly to everyone, but still smiling at Frederick.

"No fun here, is it, boy?" Philip asked.

"It's okay," Frederick said.

"It's probably better here than at Foggia. No children to play with. At least here you have some companionship."

"Not really," Frederick said. "They don't allow anyone around here. They think people want to take me. But that's all right. I didn't play with children at the palace anyway. I have my books. I'm fine."

"Who did you play with?"

"I didn't play with anyone. I spent time with my mother mostly."

"You read books and spent time with your mother? I don't think I've ever met a boy who did only those two things. What else did you do?"

"We went into the woods and watched animals and birds. We watched the ships coming in, and I learned how to tell where they came from. We rode horses. We did a lot of things."

"I noticed you said 'we' a lot. Your mother was your best friend, wasn't she?"

"Yes. She was my only friend."

"I know you must miss her, Frederick. I'm sorry for your great loss. You're too young to lose both your parents. I'm sorry I wasn't able to make it to your mother's funeral. We started out as soon as we got word. It was just too far to make it in time."

Frederick looked down and nodded his understanding. He went back to reading his book.

"What are you reading?"

"It's just something I wrote a long time ago when I was a kid. I'm finished with it now."

Philip sat down on the floor and picked up one of Frederick's drawings of a hawk. The detail in the sketch surprised him.

"Did you draw this?"

"Yes," Frederick said.

"This is very good," Philip said. "You have a true talent, boy. Did your father teach you falconry?"

"No," Frederick said inquisitively.

"One day, I will take you hunting."

Frederick looked at him and pulled out another sketch—this one of the pirate fleet.

Philip laughed and asked more questions about the drawings and Falconland.

"Is there a lion in Falconland?"

"Not yet."

"Not yet? I thought you were done with Falconland?"

"I may add more characters."

"I see. Well, there are three lions on the Staufer banner, so maybe you could find a place for them in Falconland."

"I'll do my best."

Philip and Frederick talked for hours. He told Frederick more about his parents, Germany, and his grandfather. It was the longest conversation he had had with anyone since his mother. In a few short hours, Frederick felt closer to Philip than he did to his usually absent father. He felt closer to Philip than anyone in the world.

Philip explained to Frederick that he would be taking him to Rome, where he would stay with Pope Innocent for a while. This was what his mother had requested.

"What do you know about the pope, Uncle Philip?" Frederick asked.

"I'm surprised you didn't meet him at the funeral."

"I saw him, but we didn't speak. And I saw him once when we went to Rome, but I don't remember him."

"Uncle Philip, what kind of man is Pope Innocent?"

"Well, Pope Innocent is a man of God. The pope is the mediator between God and man here on Earth. I once studied to be a priest myself, and I have heard what great work Pope Innocent is doing at the Vatican."

Frederick was asking what life would be like living with Innocent at the Vatican. Philip knew what he meant and understood his apprehension;

however, he chose to answer diplomatically and evasively instead of putting preconceived notions into Frederick's mind.

Philip found Innocent to be a cold and calculating man, and had no idea what it would be like for a child to live with him at the Vatican. He could not imagine that Frederick would enjoy the experience.

"Sometimes God tests us," he said, as Frederick looked deep into his eyes.

"In those times, things may not seem to be as we want. But in time, we realize it was for the best. We learn from these tests, and we grow. It's called experience."

Frederick was grateful for Phillip; his father had never spoken to him like this.

"Is this going to be a test? Me living with the pope?"

Philip smiled at the boy, feeling he understood his message entirely.

"It will be a test. You will grow, and I'm sure you will leave the Vatican a great deal more experienced. Now get some sleep. We leave for Rome at first light."

Frederick climbed into his bed and closed his eyes. He heard Philip shut the door. It was the safest he'd felt since his mother read him stories to fall asleep.

The journey to Rome started at first light the next morning. Frederick exhibited an excitement over the trip that he had not had since his mother's death.

"How long will it take to get to Rome, Uncle Philip?"

"A few days. Will you be all right on that horse?"

"Oh yes. I will ride it all the way to Rome."

"The carriage will be there just in case, boy."

Frederick took it as a challenge. He knew Philip was testing him, and he not only accepted the test, he embraced it. There would be no carriage rides.

For most of the trip, Philip seemed to stay inside his head. Since the death of Henry, Philip had fought a civil war against Otto of the rival Welf family for control of Germany.

Otto was one of the seven electing princes of Germany. He was from an important family in northern Germany called the Welfs. There were German kings crowned from this family.

Despite Philip being elected by a majority of the princes, Otto rebelled against the decision, because he saw an opportunity to seize the throne after Henry's death. It was his opinion that northern and southern Germany should be two different kingdoms, and that the south had too much power. A successful campaign against Philip would end that power.

It began with the Welf family and its knights fighting against Philip's Staufer family and their knights. This was not a rare occurrence. For generations, these powerful families had fought for various reasons. But in this case, the family feud became a civil war—northern Germany against southern Germany.

Philip pushed back hard on Otto's rebellion. This was the first time the seven electing princes' choice was not being respected, and it brought the entire kingdom into the conflict. After about a year of battles, the result had been a stalemate.

Nothing won, but much lost.

Now, it was transitioning into a political rather than military result. Because a winner did not emerge, it was Pope Innocent's turn to create a resolution. Through a series of letters sent to the princes of Germany, as well as Philip and Otto, Innocent made his case that a civil war between families for the crown of Germany had negated the powers of the princes to elect a king. If a strong family such as the Welfs or the Staufers disputed the election, it could simply resist the decision made by the electors and plunge the kingdom into war. It was time to allow the Papacy a selective voice. With Germany on the brink of ruin, the princes agreed. Otto and Philip had begrudgingly gone along with their decision.

They agreed to halt the fighting and allow Innocent time to resolve the conflict. After all, the king of the Germans was also the Holy Roman emperor; it only made sense that the Papacy should play a role in that selection, Innocent argued successfully.

This was exactly what Pope Innocent wanted, a symbol of the pope's superiority to kings and emperors. Innocent's success involved his making Sicily a protectorate, its future king a guardian of the Papacy, and potentially selecting the next Holy Roman emperor. Certainly, this gave him new powers no pope before had ever enjoyed.

On the same trip, Philip was requested to deliver Frederick to Innocent, and then sit with the pope and discuss his qualifications and plans for Germany and the Holy Roman Empire.

"It was all theatre and symbolism," Philip said to his aide, who was riding alongside him, in reference to Otto and his large army of German knights. "It's a big show to illustrate Innocent's dominance over Germany. Perhaps we deserve it, though, fighting a bloody war over a crown."

"But why would Otto bring an army of knights into this holy city, my lord?" Philip's aide asked.

"He does not understand the distinction between military and diplomacy," Philip said. "Otto has no concept of negotiation without a show of force. Even in front of the pope, he must be Otto."

Philip turned and looked at Frederick, who was listening to every word of his conversation.

"I see you managed to ride your horse all the way to Rome without once being relegated to the dreaded carriage."

Frederick smiled but said nothing.

Philip patted him on the back. They rode the last part of the trip into Rome side by side. He was proud of his nephew for showing inner strength, despite a somewhat sheltered life and the tragedies he had experienced.

"When we get to the inn, gather your things from the carriage, and take a room. We will rest now and meet Pope Innocent for dinner at the Vatican."

Instead of finding a room at the inn, Frederick chose to explore Rome. The very sight of the wide streets, tall buildings, and colorful markets were overwhelming. He had never encountered such a multitude of people. The sights and sounds fascinated him. With people and places abounding, his curiosity piqued. It was unprecedented and exciting. It was no wonder Frederick didn't make it back to the inn until darkness overtook the city.

As awed as Frederick was at Rome, the Vatican was even more impressive. The last time he was here, Frederick had not noticed how large and old it was. Fascinated, but slightly intimidated, he would need his tutor Cencio to act as liaison for the transition to life in the Vatican. Cencio was wise in taking Frederick and Philip on a tour of the grounds and building, orienting them to the surroundings. To no one's surprise, Frederick was most interested in the Vatican's library.

"I hope they will let me spend a lot of time here," he said, smiling up at Philip.

Cencio seemed a bit uncomfortable at Frederick's comment being uttered so near to the library staff. He looked at them while they shrugged at Frederick's presence.

"This isn't a place for children," said one of the library staff to another. "This is the Vatican Library. The boy should not be here."

"I will always try to accommodate your reading needs, Frederick," Cencio said.

For once, Frederick didn't pick up on the subtlety of his comment; he seemed too mesmerized by the multitude of books in this incredible room, more than he had ever seen in his life.

The dinner was attended by the pope, Cencio, most of the cardinals in residence at the Vatican, and other priests who would be tutoring Frederick. Philip and his knights were also part of the dinner guests. Frederick sat next to Innocent at the head of the table.

It was clear to Philip that this would not be a happy stay for Frederick. He wondered if Constance had ever met this man before she agreed to give her son to him.

Innocent had long held the Staufer family in low regard. For generations, they challenged the authority of the Papacy, and when Innocent looked at Philip and Frederick, he simply saw two more generations of that legacy. Nothing Frederick could say or do was likely to change his mind. Innocent saw exactly what he wanted to see: a future rival.

Despite Pope Innocent's chilly reception, Frederick was able to impress most of his future tutors, thanks largely to Cencio. Frederick was an optimistic child. He was looking forward to his days at the Vatican, but Philip was skeptical. He saw Frederick's prospects as poor, and his own even worse the next morning.

—m—

"Philip, we have met already with Otto, and his concessions to be emperor are vast," Pope Innocent said as they sat at a large table in his meeting room. "It will probably be difficult for a proud man like you to meet those concessions."

"It's not difficult to agree to terms you don't intend to keep, Your Holiness," Philip said with contempt. "Otto has never been a man of his word."

"The Welfs are every bit as honorable as your family, Philip—probably more so."

Philip paused, not taking the personal bait set down by Innocent.

"Your Holiness, this isn't about two families," he said calmly. "This is about which man is better qualified to lead Germany and the Holy Roman Empire. Otto is a warrior. I have acted as regent and king of the Germans for some time now. I am the choice of the majority of the princes. I should be your—"

"Perhaps a warrior is exactly what I need as emperor," Pope Innocent interrupted. "After the civil war you put Germany through, perhaps I need a strong emperor to keep the peace."

"I do regret the hostility that Otto and I put Germany through these past years, but if you install Otto as emperor, ready yourself for blood the likes of which this empire has never seen."

"Is that a threat, Philip?"

Philip paused for a moment to hold back the rage he felt for this wasted journey. He considered taking Frederick with him but understood that it could be perceived as kidnapping, considering Constance's wishes.

"It is not a threat, Your Holiness. I will not be the catalyst of this violence to come; it will be your emperor. I am going to leave now. I can see this decision was made before I arrived."

"Nothing has been decided," Innocent said as Philip headed toward the door. "Your insolence for the Papacy has been noted, Philip."

Philip turned around to face the pope. "And your arrogance and narrow mind will be noted for centuries, Your Holiness."

After Philip and his knights slammed the door behind them, the discussion between Innocent's aides became more candid.

"Your Holiness, Philip has a point," one of his aides said.

"That I and the previous popes are arrogant and narrow-minded?"

"No, sir. It's very possible Otto did concede too much to the Papacy and may not intend keeping all of his promises."

Pope Innocent looked down the table at the young priest and laughed.

"It's an absolute certainty Otto will not keep his promises—save one. He will not attempt to take land in Sicily, and that is the only concession I am interested in."

"What makes you so certain of that, Your Holiness?" asked the young priest.

"Otto is a German. The Welfs never leave the North Country. This is probably the first time he has ever seen Rome, or even Italy for that matter. Of course, Philip is right. Otto is a warlord, but his ambition reaches only as far as the German crown. The Holy Roman Empire is beyond his abilities and motivation. Otto will ride back to his homeland and bask in the glory of being king of the Germans. In the meantime, the Papacy will control the empire as a whole, specifically Italy and Sicily, its kingdom ruled by the Papacy as protectorate and its future king trained by us as his guardian. As long as Otto is emperor, the Vatican will not be boxed in by this empire."

The aides to Innocent did not speak a word. Some stared blankly at him. Others looked down at papers or the ground.

One advisor spoke. "Your Holiness, in your letter of recommendation, you will have to reference Frederick. Even though he resigned his intent to be emperor, some electors still nominated him."

Pope Innocent nodded his understanding and left the room.

—⚏—

Philip walked out of the building and into the Vatican courtyard, where he saw Frederick and his men at the stable. Frederick was watching one of the squires wash his horse.

"Let the boy do that," Philip said to the squire. "He rode in on him; he can wash him down."

Frederick, overjoyed to take over, grabbed the cloth from the squire and started in on the wash.

"You rode him well, boy."

"Thanks, Uncle Philip."

"Maybe we should leave him here for you to take care of," he said, pausing and looking at his men. "It would be good for him to learn."

"Or maybe I could ride him back to Germany with you," Frederick said, beginning to sense his time at the Vatican might not be as pleasant and exciting as he once thought. "I bet I could ride him all the way there."

Philip smiled. "It will be too dangerous a journey. You must stay here in the safety of the Vatican for now."

Frederick attempted rebuttal, but Philip cut him off and continued.

"You will be a great king someday, Frederick, just as your mother predicted. I can see it in you already. Use this time to learn. Learn about the pope and what he does. Learn about the Vatican and how it operates. Learn about the people and places of Rome." He stood and looked around as he continued. "It will serve you well to learn all about this place."

Frederick knew Philip would be leaving soon. *I will not get emotional this time*, he thought to himself. He would show his uncle that he was strong.

"I will learn about everything and everyone here," he said as his voice choked up. "And I will report it all to you when I see you again."

Philip mounted his horse and turned to Frederick. His knights awaited his lead.

"You have a responsibility to destiny, boy—a responsibility to history. God has willed it so."

Frederick never forgot Philip's words, but he never saw his uncle again.

XIII

On the Road Back to Germany

Philip began the journey back to Germany knowing he would not be king. He knew he was the rightful heir—the majority vote of the princes, and the most qualified candidate. He also knew Pope Innocent would never select him and that the princes would honor the pope's recommendation.

It mystified Philip that the pope could not see how his abilities far exceeded Otto's and that the politically savvy leader did not catch on to Otto's disingenuous concessions to the Papacy. Otto was a warrior and should not be trusted. He had no diplomatic or political skills. How could the pope not understand that he only relied on brute force to bend men to his will?

Phillip contemplated other plans to fill the time while they rode back to Germany. He knew that continuing the civil war was a far worse scenario. He knew he had agreed to allow Innocent to choose between them and, to his dismay, the pope had chosen Otto. He knew he had no choice but to honor the pope's decision.

"Maybe that is the reason. Maybe it is my allegiance to my word that cost me the throne," he said to himself. "Perhaps Innocent had chosen Otto knowing I would not contest his decision. Otto inevitably would." That was the only logical explanation Philip could imagine.

The painfully slow ride back to Germany had allowed Philip's mind to resolve the matter. Now he could set that aside and look ahead, not at what might have been. He smiled and looked at one of his men.

"I'm going back to Germany for a time, and then I am going to bring Frederick back to Sicily and be his guardian and regent of Sicily."

The man looked over at him in disbelief. "This doesn't sound like something Innocent is going to get behind. What makes you think he will give up his receivership of Sicily to you and give up his tutelage of Frederick?"

"When the time is right, I will convince him of the merits. Innocent wants the kingdoms of Sicily and Germany never to be ruled by the same person, and having rival families ruling in each will almost guarantee that result. It would be logical for him to understand the merits."

"But Innocent controls Sicily as its protectorate. He has the young king of Sicily as his ward. Why would he give that away for your proposal?"

"Because one day Innocent will see that he doesn't control Sicily. There are no knights. There is no naval presence to defend attacks from the sea. There are no walls to protect Palermo. Innocent is relying on his reputation to defend Sicily. Soon enough, Sicily will tempt an army, because of its vulnerability, and attack. Deep down, Innocent knows this. He will come to terms on Sicily soon enough."

"I'm not sure Pope Innocent will see it in those logical terms, my lord, but I defer to your thinking and pray to God that this be His will. It would be best for all concerned if it came to pass."

The men rode slowly down the narrowing path toward another blind pass.

Philip continued. "Frederick will be one of the great kings of Europe. I can see it in him already. His development at such a young age is astounding. His mother brought him along well, but I can take him the rest of the way. I will make sure he becomes the king he is destined to be."

"And what shall you do once he comes of age?"

"I will make a seamless transition from honored regent to dignified advisor and elder statesman to the king."

They both laughed a little, as well as the other riders in the group. All of them were happy Philip had bounced back from such a staggering blow as losing his kingdom.

"Look at that, I've planned my life's career in only a few minutes."

Upon turning into the pass, Philip saw a patrol of men on horseback dressed in black waiting at the upcoming hill. Behind him, another patrol came out of the forest to block the way.

"My lord, we are ambushed!" one of his advisers yelled.

Philip had limited knights in his entourage, but he had to defend himself as best he could.

"Form a tight column," Philip said to his men while the riders began their galloping descent down the hill. "Swords at the ready."

The surge of the anonymous black cavalry was brutal. They pounded at them with axes and long swords, taking down most of Philip's men in the very first wave of violence. Philip was hit hard by two different assailants but managed to stay on his mount; he plunged his sword into one of the masked riders galloping past.

Philip and his surviving men turned their horses just in time to defend themselves against the next wave coming from the opposite direction; the other riders disappearing into the forest. Philip and two knights were the only survivors of the next attack.

Philip stabbed another rider, attempting to hit him with an axe. He looked down at the man and screamed, "Who are you?"

The man rolled over and groaned, but Philip didn't understand what he was trying to say.

Silence overtook the path as the second wave of riders also disappeared into the forest.

"Show yourself, Otto!" Philip screamed. "I know this is your cowardly attack."

He pulled on the reins, causing his horse to step on the fallen rider; the man screamed in agony from the weight of the horse, which broke every bone in his hand.

"Who is the leader of this attack?" Philip seethed.

The man moaned in pain and mumbled something; the accent sounded German. He passed out before Philip could interrogate him further.

"My lord, I believe the road ahead is clear," one of the knights said. "Perhaps we have an opportunity to ride out of this attack."

Before Philip could respond, a volley of arrows flew out of the trees from both sides, hitting all three men. An arrow struck Philip in the back, missing his shoulder blade, and piercing his heart.

He died instantly.

—⁓—

Not long after Philip's death, a letter arrived from Pope Innocent to the prince-electors of Germany and to every German church and public square.

"It is the business of the pope to look after the interests of the Holy Roman Empire, since the empire derives its origin and its final authority from the papacy. Its origin, because it was originally transferred from Greece by and for the sake of the papacy . . . its final authority, because the emperor is raised to his position by the pope who blesses him, crowns him, and invests him with the empire.

Therefore, since three persons have lately been elected king by different parties, namely the youth (Frederick, son of Henry VI), Philip (of the Staufer family, and brother of Henry VI), and Otto (of Brunswick, of the Welf family), so also three things must be taken into account in regard to each one, namely: the legality, the suitability, and the expediency of his election.

Far be it from us that we should defer to man rather than to God, or that we should fear the countenance of the powerful. On the foregoing grounds, then, we decide that the youth should not at present be given the empire. We utterly reject Philip for his manifest unfitness, and we order his usurpation to be resisted by all.

Since Otto is not only himself devoted to the church, but comes from devout ancestors on both sides, we decree that he ought to be accepted and supported as king, and ought to be given the crown of empire, after the rights of the Roman church have been secured."

XIV

A Frozen Hell

F rederick's life at the Vatican was like a frozen hell. Even the death of his father and mother would turn out to be less traumatic. Pope Innocent played the role of guardian exactly as expected: distant, icy, and detached. Contempt and scorn overtook any emotions he showed toward Frederick. Innocent saw all the similarities he had to his family, and he was not about to help him develop, especially knowing what his aspirations would be for his adult life.

"This child shall be no different from any of his family," he often told Cencio. "They will always turn out the same, considering themselves above the Papacy."

"I have seen no evidence of that, Your Holiness," countered Cencio. "The boy shows us nothing but respect, save the endless questions on our every subject. He has a curiosity for everything."

"He has contempt for everything, Cencio. Once he begins to understand your lessons, his familiarity will breed contempt, just as all his regal family does. It has always been this way with them."

Fortunately for Frederick, Innocent usually focused on other matters and was more of an observer to the boy's daily routine. The Vatican staff fed and tutored Frederick. There was little else he was allowed to do. Pope Innocent's rules for Frederick were vast. There were rules for when he woke up, rules for his lessons, rules for his meals. No running or yelling in the Vatican. No exploring. No access to the many libraries in the Vatican. To Frederick, it was like a prison sentence.

He had free time after his lessons to play in the large courtyard outside, but even the free time was regulated with more rules. Frederick was able to endure all of this without disobedience, except for one: he was not allowed outside the Vatican walls—ever. He wasn't allowed into Rome even if the Vatican guards accompanied him.

Rome!

The most exciting city in the world was right outside the walls, but it might as well have been on the other side of the world. He could hear the merchants yelling prices of their goods in Italian, occasional speeches in Latin . . . so many diverse sounds he didn't fully understand. Occasionally, he could glimpse the outskirts of Rome in the hills on a clear day, but he never saw the heart of the city, despite living in the middle of it. He was a caged bird yearning to fly.

Pope Innocent would not risk the possibility of someone kidnapping Frederick, as the Vatican guard was ill equipped to defend against a large, planned attack. Innocent saw no reason to risk a trip into town for the boy, and every reason why it was a bad idea. Innocent was not concerned about Frederick's unlimited interest and curiosity. He would have to adapt to life in the Vatican.

Frederick resided primarily in his own head, a lonely place for a child who had lost both his parents. Imprisoned within the Vatican walls, his only freedom rested in his imagination. He was a ward of the pope, but not a guest—a prisoner yearning for freedom.

Had Pope Innocent taken the time to know Frederick, he would have realized his plan was shortsighted. His efforts for security yielding a lasting contempt in Frederick that would actually threaten the safety Pope Innocent tried to create.

It was only a matter of time before Frederick found ways to stay connected to nature, as he did in Sicily. His love for animals led him to explore the stables where he found the horses for the Vatican's small army. This became his sanctuary, his freedom. Frederick soon was celebrated in the stable and the army barracks, endearing himself to both the horses and their riders. He watched the soldiers perform their drills on horseback, studying the horses closely. Upon his request, he fed and groomed the horse Philip had given him. His observation and study led to note taking and sketching. Each day he would return to the stables, journal in hand, pencil sharp, eager to record the shapes, movements, and personalities of both man and mount. This reminded him of those idyllic days in Sicily, happily spent with his mother. He recollected how eager he was to show her his journals; now his eagerness was to show them to another relative.

"I can't wait to show Uncle Philip these drawings," he told a Vatican guard dispatched to the stable. "He will love the horse sketches."

The guard smiled uncomfortably and walked off.

Frederick's love of nature and animals could not be contained. He enjoyed the tales of a few of the soldiers who hunted in the woods outside Rome. There, near the stables, they kept a team of falcons, specifically to aid them in the hunt. Ever since Philip had mentioned the sport, Frederick was interested.

It was here Frederick was first introduced to falconry. Although he didn't go on the hunts, Frederick's passion was unbridled. He was fascinated by the falcons and eagerly volunteered to help feed and care for these majestic birds.

His introduction to falconry led to a growing appreciation for all birds. He began to notice many different types even within the confines of the Vatican walls. He became more aware and mindful of birds that seemed to come and go with some consistency throughout the grounds. One day, he noticed many birds that had landed in a walled area where he was strictly forbidden from entering: the pope's private garden.

Starving for knowledge, interaction, and experience, he couldn't help himself, or simply chose his own action. It was time to fight for his freedom.

This was to be the beginning of Frederick's plan of defiance. It happened so quickly, the details obscure but the result profound. Quietly, but strategically, Frederick plotted, planned, and persisted. He could tell no one because his freedom, his sanctuary, lay in the balance.

Secretly, the pope's garden became Frederick's freedom, and he frequented it often. Its complex paths, tall shrubs, and towering trees reminded him of Sicily and seemed to stretch to infinity. To his amazement, he was there alone. Gardeners were absent while he frolicked and explored. Frederick observed the seemingly endless varieties of plants. Amidst the foliage, he discovered countless birdfeeders tucked into coves and atop tall poles.

This explains why so many birds landed over the fence, he thought.

The garden became Frederick's hideaway, where he could wander and remember those days with his mother.

If only she were here to share this garden with me.

But she wasn't, and he was particularly aware that he was trespassing on the pope's space. He used the strategies he had learned, growing stealth in the garden, eluding the occasional gardener, and ever mindful that Pope Innocent could look into the garden from certain parts of his office and see him frolicking about; however, Frederick knew that Innocent rarely walked away from his desk.

Frederick's boldness grew, and his joy increased. He visited the stables, the barracks, and the falcons. He sneaked into Innocent's garden, and returned before sunset to eat dinner with the servants and go to his room. Once things were quiet, he would sneak out of his room and into the library. He took books back to his room, sometimes without even seeing what they were about. Frederick read the Bible from cover to cover without any instruction from his tutors, who felt it was far too advanced for him. Their tutelage focused on parables and stories while his questions became complex. It astonished them that he was always more advanced than they seemed to know, always in command of the subject matter more than he let on.

—⚀—

For the first time since he'd arrived at the Vatican, Pope Innocent summoned Frederick to his office. Frederick entered, and was startled when the huge wooden door closed behind him. It was the loudest sound he had ever heard. It shook the floor when it finally shut completely.

"Sit down, Frederick," Pope Innocent said from across the room. He sat upright in his chair behind his desk.

Frederick felt uneasy at the whole situation—the slamming door and the pope's booming voice. He took the long walk on the dark red carpet runner that led to Innocent's desk. He sat down in the chair opposite and felt small in comparison to the massive desk, which seemed to be raised from the floor.

"Frederick, I have some bad news. Philip of Swabia is dead. Philip was the man who brought you here. He was your uncle."

"I know who he was," Frederick snapped. His heart pounded.

"You will not use that tone with me, Frederick. I was not aware of your knowledge of Philip."

"I'm sorry, Pope Innocent. I did get to know him well on the way here. He was the only relative left that I knew at all."

"That is true enough, Frederick. And the death of Philip essentially ends the line of potential succession of the Barbarossa men. The Staufer family has been dealt a very damaging blow . . . a blow that affects you as well. Any claim you have to Germany in the future is probably futile. I doubt you could even make a claim on Sicily, given the weakness of your family at this time. Your only hope of a crown will come at my recommendation."

"A crown is the furthest thing from my mind."

"That's a childish attitude, Frederick. I was told you were advanced for your age. What *is* on your mind?"

"My father, my mother, and my uncle."

"They are gone, boy. You would be wise to look forward, not into the past."

"When did Uncle Philip die?"

"A few months ago."

"Why didn't you tell me then?"

"We wanted you to get accustomed to the Vatican before we told you this news. There is nothing you could have done. You are a child."

"How did he die?"

"It's not important."

"My mother and father died of illness. Did Philip have an illness? Is that how I will die, too?"

"No, Frederick. Stop these questions immediately. Philip was killed on the road to Germany, and before you ask, we do not know who killed him. Do not jump to conclusions about a rival family. I have seen enough bloodshed between the Staufers and Welfs. This feud is concluded."

"May I go?"

"You are dismissed."

—⟋⟍—

No one at the Vatican tried to explain death to Frederick, deeming the topic too dark for a child. Meanwhile, his three closest relatives—mother, father, and uncle—had died within a few years of each other. Because there was no one to mend these emotional wounds, they became scars that stayed with Frederick for years and manifested in greater form later in his life.

Frederick's emotional growth was stunted by the news of Philip's death, and the select Vatican tutors who might have been intuitive enough to sense this were blinded by his intellectual skills, which were dramatically advanced for a child. Their experience with children was, of course, limited. Frederick began to act out, and matters only regressed.

He rebelled against everyone at the Vatican. This included Innocent, his tutors, even Cencio and the Vatican guards.

Innocent took on the role as disciplinarian, but only after a long period of time had passed. With no experience in raising children, and after stepping in at a later date than he should have as the authority figure, he predictably overreacted. Innocent beat Frederick with a paddle more and more when Frederick misbehaved, the results of which only made matters worse.

Not knowing what to do, Innocent escalated Frederick's punishment to more severe beatings, plunging Frederick's state of mind deeper into depression and rage. He started to miss his lessons with tutors and hid in the gardens, in the back of the stable, or somewhere in the Vatican buildings. One day, after another beating by Innocent, Frederick ran behind the stable and found an opening in a fence that led to a pathway into Rome. His rebellion was about to increase.

For the next several weeks, Frederick went only to Cencio's lesson, and then missed the rest of his classes. He escaped through an opening in the fence and spent the rest of the day in Rome. Some of his tutors wondered where he was, but most were happy to have the free time to catch up on other matters. Pope Innocent had more than doubled the workload of the Vatican staff, and while he did bring efficiency and success to the Vatican, the priests and bishops were not used to this rigorous workload. Over time, Frederick expanded his visits from Rome into the forests outside the great city. Finally, they caught him.

While Pope Innocent didn't pay much attention to Frederick, having him sneak into Rome and then into the woods was unacceptable. He decided to punish Frederick even more severely than before. Once again, he gave little consideration to the consequences and overreacted.

He began by forcing Frederick to stay in his room for thirty days. He also removed all of Frederick's books and sketchbooks from the room. Absent of any "distractions," his tutors came to teach his lessons. His meals were brought to his room. No other contact was allowed. Frederick was given a sentence of solitary confinement typically reserved for the most offensive of adult criminals. His freedom was squelched; his prison was reinforced, which made matters much worse.

Frederick became more rebellious. He had nothing to do in that room except consider the contempt and rage he felt for Innocent. Within a day of being let out of his room, he left the building and escaped again into the woods just outside of Rome. There, he found his freedom, secure in the woods and memories of his mother. No penalty, even the harsh ones created by Innocent, could stop him. He had nothing to lose.

After several days missing, Pope Innocent dispatched a search party that found Frederick in the woods near Rome. Frederick knew the punishment would be severe. Innocent let his anger do the disciplining. He beat him with a belt and sent him back to his room for another month. He added personal insults about members of Frederick's family. He beat him physically and emotionally and told him he wasn't worthy of a crown. As was the case before, Innocent missed wildly on what was important to him.

Frederick began to recede into a very dark place, into the crevices of his mind. Alone, he had no one to talk to except Cencio. He had no friends, largely due to the fact that there was no one his age within the Vatican walls. In fact, it had been a year since he had even spoken to another child. Left alone, his dark thoughts took him to evil places. He was growing hateful of life, specifically the Vatican and Innocent. For such a young child, Frederick was growing into a bitter critic of the world, with no friends, no trusted allies, and no loving parents or relatives.

The month finally passed, and Frederick, at the first opportunity, ran away into the woods for days. When they finally found him, Innocent beat the boy so severely that the Vatican priests on hand had to stop the pope from his own anger, and from causing permanent physical damage to Frederick.

The emotional damage would probably never heal.

Innocent had had enough of Frederick. He decided to send him back to Sicily to live with foster parents. He would make it so Frederick would live in anonymity with barons or counts until he was irrelevant to European nobility. His claim to the throne of Sicily would be forgotten. He would never stand for him being a king. He would wash his hands of this problem. He hoped he would never see Frederick again. For Frederick, the feeling was mutual.

XV

An Unhappy Return to Sicily

There was no ceremony or good-byes when Frederick left the Vatican. Pope Innocent was not even in attendance when he bid farewell.

A rotund man rode into the Vatican on a smallish horse, with five knights and a carriage in tow. This comical scene elicited private joking from the Vatican guards.

"That poor horse," one of the attendants said. "Maybe he should be riding atop the man."

"I am Gentile, Count of Manipolo," the man said to the guards. "I am here to collect Frederick."

The guards looked at the count but said nothing.

"The boy is ready," Cencio said as he squeezed Frederick's shoulder. "I will accompany him and be his tutor in Sicily."

"This was not agreed upon, or even discussed. We have no need of a tutor. We have our own teachers at my castle."

The count pulled the reins tight when his horse tried to circle about in the tight quarters of the Vatican courtyard. Cencio approached the count, leaving Frederick a few steps behind.

"Pope Innocent has agreed to this arrangement. Why is this of issue to you, Count?"

"No issue . . . no issue at all. I just wasn't informed. I made no accommodations for you."

"I have lived the life of a monk. I need no special accommodations."

"And I won't pay you. I have to pay my children's tutors. Pope Innocent will have to meet your salary."

"My needs are met. There is no need to be troubled. My responsibility is solely to the boy."

"May I ride my horse to Sicily?" Frederick asked Cencio.

"No," the count quickly said. "He must ride in the carriage out of sight. I will not risk him being taken by some upstart."

"We will travel together in the carriage, Frederick," Cencio said, glaring at the count. "We will continue our studies on the way there."

"I can't ride the horse Uncle Philip gave me?"

"We will take good care of him," one of the Vatican guards said. "He will be in perfect shape when you come back for him."

"We must leave now," the count said. "Collect your things and get into the carriage."

"Cencio?"

"Yes, Frederick?"

"What is an upstart?"

"An upstart is a lesser nobleman trying to make a name for himself."

Frederick paused for a moment to consider the definition. Then he said, "Doesn't that describe the count of Manipolo?"

"Yes, Frederick, it does," Cencio laughed.

On the way back, the count stopped at the Villa of Markward Van Anweilerr—the German warlord who Constance had rejected as protectorate of Sicily. Since then, he had carved out a substantial fortune in treasure and knights just miles from the Sicilian border in southern Italy.

Frederick did not remember Markward, but Markward remembered the boy quite well. The tall, thin German with black hair, dark eyes, and a muscular frame looked down at Frederick when he walked toward the count. He forced a wicked grin at the boy without saying a word. He then turned away from Frederick and greeted the count. Frederick did not give Markward a second thought.

The count's castle sat just outside Palermo. Frederick was introduced to the family, and within days, he knew everyone on the property, including the peasants who lived just outside the walls of the castle and tended to the crops, the servants who lived inside the castle, the knights, and the castellan, who was in charge of everything at the count's castle. Frederick greeted all of them and always offered up a potential conversation if they would allow it. He seemed to get along with everyone, and all were fond of him, except the count.

Frederick soon settled into a routine of meals, studies, and play. Slowly, he began to break out of the bitterness, anger, and dark regression created by his Vatican beatings and isolation. He enjoyed the count's children, and for the first time, Frederick had peers his own age. To his immense pleasure, the castle bordered a forest in which Frederick was welcome to explore. He needed no encouragement or invitation. It all seemed to be the perfect tonic for Frederick's trauma.

The count's wife was a loving mother to her children, dedicated to their development. She reminded him of his own mother. She was also cordial and decent to Frederick, despite her guarded feelings in his presence. The count, however, remained cold and detached.

After a few months of this routine, the count and his family went on a trip to Messina. Frederick was left alone, accompanied only by Cencio, the servants, and the castellan.

Suddenly, riders stormed into the courtyard and burst inside the castle. There were no knights present to stop the attack; all of them were either with the count or away from the castle. Frederick and Cencio looked through a window and saw what was happening. Understanding the implications, Cencio took Frederick downstairs into the cellar to hide.

Within minutes, they could hear the castellan's voice nearing, and the sound of many boots. Cencio thought the raid was probably orchestrated by the count. He had taken his family and knights away, and the castellan was clearly the leader of the search party, taking them right into their hiding place.

Frederick felt foolish for trusting this family and even feeling a connection to them. It would be the last time he would feel anything for a very long time.

The cellar door broke open after several hard kicks, and Markward Van Anweiler stepped over the splintered remains of the door and assessed the room. He peered into Cencio's eyes as if to gauge his reaction as Cencio stood in front of Frederick.

"Escort the tutor from this room," Markward said to his men. He himself was unwilling to handle a representative of the Vatican and potentially a future pope.

"This is wrong, Markward," Cencio said as two men grabbed his arms and pushed him out of the room. "The boy is a ward of the pope, and Sicily is a protectorate. You cannot do this without a price."

Markward said nothing. He put his hand on Frederick's shoulder and tried to pull him from the room. Frederick punched him in the stomach and kicked him in the leg. Markward then picked the boy up off his feet and into the air without much effort. Frederick was oblivious to the futility of his counterattack. He struggled and resisted all the way out of the room and through the castle until he was thrown into a carriage and locked inside.

Frederick's spirit impressed Markward. He meant no harm to the boy; he simply needed him to negotiate terms for Sicily with Pope Innocent.

"Send word to the pope that we have Frederick and wish to discuss the terms of his release," Markward said to Cencio.

"And what shall I tell the pope of you attacking a Papal protectorate, Markward?"

"It is as God and Emperor Henry have willed it. His last wish was for me to rule Sicily until the boy came of age."

"I wouldn't call on God to justify your actions here today, Markward, but I will bring your message back to Pope Innocent."

"No harm will come to this boy—I swear it to God—but Sicily will be mine, as Henry willed. I have his document proving my words," he said, waving the scroll at Cencio. "Take the terms back to Rome. The pope cannot protect Sicily, and he is a bad guardian to the boy, too!" he yelled.

Cencio mounted his horse and sighed.

"You know this, Cencio."

Cencio said nothing in reply.

XVI

The Fight for Sicily

1205 AD

I nnocent did not respond to Markward's terms in any way that would please him. He did not pay a ransom; instead, he ex-communicated Markward and called for a crusade against him. He was furious that anyone would attack his protectorate. The safety of Frederick seemed a distant, secondary thought, the pope's primary concern being the loss of Sicily.

"Shouldn't we negotiate for the safe return of Frederick, Your Holiness?" Cencio asked. "A crusade will take months to set in motion, and the boy will be of no value once Markward realizes your intent."

"I cannot base my response around what is best for Frederick," Innocent said contemptuously. "I have to consider Sicily—the tyranny to the people of Sicily by this madman."

"You will not lose any ground in paying Markward's ransom for your ward, Frederick, and still calling for a crusade against him for invading your protectorate lands. But you are his guardian, Pope Innocent. You must attempt to protect him now."

"I will not give an inch to Markward. If Frederick's family wishes to pay the ransom, so be it, but I will not use one ounce of Vatican gold to deal with Markward. All of our resources will go toward crushing him."

Cencio suspended his lobbying for Frederick, seeing it as pointless. "What word shall I return to Markward?" Cencio asked.

"Tell him to leave Sicily immediately or face excommunication and a crusade with all the knights of Europe against him."

"Shall I also include the return of King Frederick in this message, Pope Innocent?"

Innocent stared at Cencio coldly. "Yes."

—⁕—

"The pope has no regard for Henry's letter," Markward said to his lieutenant. "This is the letter and seal of an emperor! His terms are to leave Sicily and give the boy back? Those are no terms at all. It shows a lack of respect for me, and for Henry's legacy."

"Yes, my lord," the lieutenant said

Markward had completely misjudged the situation; Pope Innocent had no regard for Frederick. This revelation put Markward on the defensive, not knowing how many knights might answer the call for the pope.

"A crusade against a German army in Italy without a Saracen in sight," he said sarcastically. "What proud knight would be a part of such a dishonorable endeavor?"

"Knights who do not want to take two or three years to travel to the Middle East to fulfill their crusading vows would jump at this opportunity, my lord," the lieutenant said. "Pope Innocent is giving them full crusading credit and benefits without ever leaving Europe. We should prepare for a large force."

"Name the kingdoms that would participate in this attack. France? England? Germany?" He laughed. "No. There are no kingdoms of merit who would endorse this venture."

"It will not be major kingdoms, my lord," another advisor said. "You are correct. It will be independent knights not attached to any king. It will be militias and mercenaries . . . maybe lesser kingdoms or city-states wishing to impress the pope. This is all unprecedented, my lord. A pope has never called upon knights to crusade against a Christian army with a valid claim on a kingdom. It will be difficult to gauge the size of the unit, but it will likely outnumber ours."

"Very well. If we are to defend against a massive surge of knights, let it be in southern Italy. We cannot wage a battle here on this island. Ships can easily surround us, and an army can stage itself from anywhere. To win, we must choose our battleground carefully."

—m—

During preparation for the battle, Frederick watched Markward closely. He could see he was a determined warrior. After a few days, he got up enough confidence to speak to him.

Markward was more than happy to talk to Frederick.

"We would have crusaded together if your father hadn't died. Your father was a great warrior, boy—a great German," he said empathetically.

Frederick liked Markward. In a way, he almost wished he did rule Sicily. It would have been better than living under the apathy of Pope Innocent, or at least he heard many Sicilians say such things. Still, he was a prisoner and was without his books or freedom. He silently vowed to escape at the first opportunity.

While Markward's men prepared their camps and battlefields, Frederick became more of a child running free than a prisoner. He often found himself unguarded and wandered throughout the countryside. One day, he came upon a clearing where he noticed an abandoned building. As he approached, a strange familiarity overtook him. Looking closer, scrutinizing what he saw and felt, he realized it was the palace where he grew up. A sudden and pleasing feeling swept him off to endearing memories. It was Foggia!

But he quickly refocused, noticing the palace was in use, claimed by Markward's men, who had discovered it for themselves. It was now their headquarters, a perfect venue for their purposes.

The royal forest provided cover for the majority of his army while permitting defensive views of the Adriatic Sea. This venue would reveal invading ships. Perched atop a hill, this property provided the high ground necessary for any battle, particularly if outnumbered. Roads and trails were built, connecting camps and battlegrounds for resupply and reinforcements.

It delighted Frederick that this old palace would once again be his home, even for only a short time. Here, he would stay for most of the time leading up to the battle. In a welcomed flashback, he investigated each of the rooms. He found the most comfort staying in his mother's room, finding little need to leave. There in the palace, his heart leaped when he found a few of his old books. They were like old friends to him, forgotten but welcomed back quickly.

Not long after that, scouts spotted crusading knights, signaling the impending battle. Once the fighting started, Frederick was forgotten in the palace.

He decided it was the perfect opportunity for escape.

Frederick packed a bag filled with food, water, and a few books and fled into the woods he knew so well. He tried to avoid the battle, but he also watched closely while knights fought on the battlefield near him in the forest. He darted carefully from tree to tree. He heard arrows sizzling through the sky, some striking their intended target, others sailing overhead. It was hard for him to fully understand the fast-paced conflict. Who was on each side? It all began to blur together and overwhelmed his untrained eyes. Eventually, he stopped watching and made it down the hill unseen. He thought he was free of the battle until he heard a horse galloping toward him.

"What are you doing here?" the rider asked as he slowed his approach.

Frederick said nothing and tried to walk past the rider into the forest. He looked up and realized the man was young; he probably wasn't even a knight. He wore a uniform, but certainly not the armor of a nobleman. He was thin and pale and looked scared. The young man rode in front of Frederick and turned to him.

"Who are you?" he asked again. "Are you Frederick?"

"Leave me alone!"

"You are Frederick, aren't you?"

Frederick seemed unafraid of the man, maybe even at ease with him. Still, he would not speak to him or answer any questions. He turned and walked in the opposite direction.

"We are here to save you, Frederick. This whole battle is to deliver you. And here you are. Come with me, and I will bring you back to your guardian."

When he mentioned the possibility of going back to the Vatican, a trigger went off in Frederick's head. This young man represented all that was wrong in Frederick's life.

"No!" he screamed, and ran off.

"What's wrong with you? We are all here to save you."

He rode in front of Frederick again, still watching the road in both directions.

"I don't want to be saved. I want to be left alone. I won't go back to the Vatican. I won't!"

He pushed the horse's side, and it reared and tried to buck. The young man was able to settle it and dismounted. He then chased Frederick into the brush just off the trail, catching him and holding him.

"Talk to me, Frederick. If you want to go afterwards, I won't stop you."

Frederick struggled with him for a moment, then stopped.

"I do not want to go back to the Vatican. I spent a year there, and it was horrible. I will not go there with you."

"I won't take you anywhere you don't want to go. I was under the impression that you were kidnapped."

"I was, but I would prefer being kidnapped to living with the pope."

"Then why are you running away?"

"I just want to be left alone. This war is for Pope Innocent to reclaim Sicily. It has nothing to do with me. I heard many soldiers discussing it."

"But you are the king of Sicily . . . or you will be one day when you come of age. You are Sicily."

"I am not. I will never be king, and I don't want it. Pope Innocent told me so while he was beating me one day. He said my family is all in hell, and I would join them there one day, and that I don't deserve a crown. If I were the king, I would have to deal with the pope, and I don't want to talk to him again."

"That doesn't sound like something a representative of God would say."

"I don't care if you believe me or not. You promised to let me go. So let me go."

"I will not break my promise, Frederick. I was misled into thinking we were on a mission to save a future king, but I see now it's about treasure and property. You may pass freely. I pray for your safety."

An older soldier might have disagreed, insisting that the forest was no place for a child to wander. A more opportunistic knight might have brought Frederick back for a reward or perhaps ransom, but this young soldier was neither. Although not a knight, he was honorable.

"Would you like my horse for the journey you are about to begin?"

"No, thank you. Won't you need the horse for the battle?"

"I think the battle is over for me."

"What is your name?"

"My name is Francis of the Assisi militia."

"I want to get deeper into the woods now."

"I understand. I wish you the best, Frederick. I hope we meet again under better circumstances."

"Me too," Frederick said, and quickly retreated into the woods.

For several days, Frederick lost himself in the forest, safe from the battle that raged. Once it ended, he was nowhere to be found. Most people thought he was lost during the fight, killed, or taken hostage.

XVII

The Street Rat

The Docks of Palermo

1208 AD

S arah and Rachel stood by the docks taking a break from their job at the inn just down the road. They watched the ships coming into port and speculated on the mysterious boy talking to one of the crewmen from a craft that departed from the Middle East.

"How does he know that language?" Sarah asked.

"What language?" Rachel responded.

"Saracen, Muslim, or whatever that infidel speaks."

"I don't know. I wonder who he is."

"Just some street kid—there are so many of them—but he sure is cute underneath all of that dirt. I've never seen such bright red hair and blue eyes. No one in Sicily looks like that."

"Maybe he isn't from Sicily."

"He is from Sicily, but his parents were German," an older boy said as he walked up to the two girls. "He is the boy who lived in the woods for months after the War of Sicily."

"When did Sicily have a war?" Sarah asked.

"A few years ago. Well, the war was in southern Italy, but it was for ownership of Sicily . . . or something like that. You girls are too young to remember."

The girls laughed.

"No, really. A man named Markward tried to kidnap him and take Sicily for his own. The pope sent knights to fight him. Eventually, they killed Markward but couldn't find . . . Frederick. I think his name is Frederick. Then months later, he shows up in Sicily. The people were amazed a kid his age could live in the wilderness for so long."

"Why would they kidnap him?" Rachel asked.

"His parents were royalty," the boy said. "He was supposed to be king of Sicily."

The girls laughed again.

"He's too short to be a king," Sarah said. "Kings are always tall."

"He may be short and dirty," Rachel commented, "but he sure is cute."

The girls laughed again.

"I'm serious. He has lived with every nobleman's family in Sicily! He keeps running away from them. He is hopeless, but he does have royal blood in his veins."

"We are in the presence of royalty," Sarah said, giggling. She waved at Frederick. "Hello, Your Grace," she said, but not loud enough for Frederick to hear.

Frederick scowled back at her and said nothing. He didn't wave; instead, he turned his attention back to the discussion with the Saracen.

"Some king!" Rachel said. "Let's get back to work."

Frederick had patiently listened to his two friends. Despite the distraction of the two girls yelling in his direction, he was now poised to tell the two Saracen sailors what had happened while they were off at sea. Usually he listened to their stories of the world, but finally he had news that merited his speaking. It was his greatest joy to be an involved member of a genuine adult conversation with the people that frequented the docks of Palermo.

"Three days ago, pirates raided the docks," he said. "There was no one to defend the village or the markets. They took almost everything."

"Are you serious, boy?" the sailor asked. "This place looks like it did the last time we were here. I don't see any damage at all to the village or the docks."

"That's because they didn't have to attack. They just sailed into the harbor and took what they wanted. There was no one here to defend against them."

"Where do you think they came from?" the other sailor asked.

"They came from Tunisia."

"How can you be certain?"

"He told me."

"You talked to the pirates?"

"I talked to one of them. His name was Jahagaddar. He told me they attacked ports in Sicily all the time. It is a short sail from their hideout."

"How does Pope Innocent allow this?"

"He isn't concerned with Sicily. All he cares about is his tithes from the noblemen. And the nobles only care about their little pieces of land. No one is concerned with the docks, or the coastline for that matter."

"Why would a pirate talk to you?"

"Because I am an invisible kid that no one fears or even notices. People will talk to me and do things in front of me without concern. I see everything that happens on this dock."

"For an invisible kid that no one notices, you sure do speak good Arabic," the older sailor said. "How is it you learned a tongue that lives nowhere near your shores?"

"I had tutors when I was a boy. I speak Greek, French, Italian, Latin, and Arabic."

"The kid speaks five languages," the younger sailor said, laughing. "I'm lucky to speak one."

"You have a quality far beyond your status on these docks, boy," the older sailor said. "I do not think you were born on these docks. Who are you?"

"I am no one."

"That is not true, boy. Do not try to hide behind the dirt and ripped clothing. I have traveled the world. I know an educated person from a peasant. I swear it to God, the world will hear from you one day."

—ɯ—

During the time he lived in Palermo, Frederick grew from a boy into a teenager. Every noble family in Sicily took a turn taking care of him, but none of them showed any compassion or interest in his life.

The Vatican still had a responsibility to see that Frederick was cared for, and paid each noble family handsomely to look after him. Despite their lack of interest in him, Frederick was still a member of the one-time powerful Staufer family in Germany. And the Vatican thought it was prudent to continue the agreement they made with his mother Constance years ago.

What these noble families did teach Frederick was how poorly the feudal system performed. With no king to keep it in check, the servant and peasant classes were relegated to the margins between poverty and starvation. One bad crop could be the difference between life and death for poor families.

Frederick watched closely as nearly every count and baron with whom he resided mistreated its peasants and serfs. Blinded by their small thinking, the noble class quickly reduced Sicily to a wasteland. Within a decade of neglect, Sicily splintered and quickly decayed.

The lower classes had little options. If they complained, the noble-man had his knights intimidate them. That was usually enough to squash an issue before it took root.

The nobleman also had judgment rights over their vassals, which meant the nobles acted as judge over any complaint brought against him or anyone on his property. If the peasants' gripes mounted, the nobles had the right to punish or fine them.

Frederick observed the knights compete in makeshift tournaments throughout the unchecked land. These tournaments were not a simple jousting match, but rather large-scale battles that destroyed peasant homes and injured innocent bystanders for the sole purpose of defeating another knight in a staged contest.

This all seemed completely unfair to Frederick. He remembered the servants and vassals who worked for his mother. They were never treated this way. These were all Sicilians and deserved much better. There was no need for the majority of the population to live so near to destruction in such a potentially fertile economic environment.

To make matters worse, the feudal system had no mechanism for economic growth except for the individual nobleman's well-being.

The docks of Sicily had no feudal structure at all. They were free for all to embark and disembark. No one was in charge, and the docks were falling apart. Pope Innocent coldly considered them too expensive to repair and far too little yield to compensate for the liability. It was a wasted revenue source.

The docks held a fascination for Frederick. He was thirsty for the stories of travelers and workers. Soon, he knew every weathered plank of the docks. He knew which one creaked and which one would crack. He listened to the many men, who arrived and departed, and how the docks used to be the biggest revenue generator in all of Europe; now it was the disgrace of the Mediterranean.

Most had forgotten that he was the rightful king of Sicily, including himself. His chances of ever claiming that throne were extremely remote, and his destiny was fading further into oblivion every day. He had no promise, nor did Sicily.

Despite the neglect, Sicily was still a major trade route and remained the largest port in the Mediterranean Sea. It was the perfect place for him to be exiled. The diversity ignited his curiosity.

Sailors and merchants from all of Europe, the Middle East, Africa, and the Orient embarked in Sicily. He met Muslims, Jews, Christians, and Buddhists traveling abroad. Knights coming back from the Middle East or monks and priests on their way to pilgrimage were often in Palermo. The streets and docks of Sicily were a melting pot of the entire world, and it was here that Frederick became an observer, a student, and the creation of all that he experienced.

While he was no longer studying the normal subjects of rhetoric, math, religion, and history, he was gaining insight into what made a society tick. Frederick saw firsthand the daily inner workings of life in Sicily. He saw it unvarnished as an anonymous, invisible teenager, not the inauthentic way a king might view his kingdom. No one was putting on any airs for him.

XVIII

Frederick Meets Hector

The day was fresh, alive with the sunrise and the cool breeze blowing off the sea. From the shadows of his favorite hiding spot on the docks, Frederick watched his newest foster parent, the count of Palermo, walk majestically down the dock. He advanced to the gangplank where he stood waiting for the large merchant ship to dock. This scene was familiar to Frederick. He assumed the count was looking for him, but it seemed as if his focus was on the approaching ship.

The count stared at the craft, intent on its arrival. Frederick sensed an opportunity, a time to be bold, and he advanced to a closer hiding place. If the count was not here for his capture, what was his purpose? He needed to get closer for a better view.

Several Saracens disembarked carrying goods from the Middle East. The count ignored them, waiting for something else. Finally, a light-skinned man with broad shoulders and fiery red hair walked off the ship and shook the count's hand. He towered above the Saracens, who were still waiting for baggage to be brought to them. He also towered over the count. The two spoke briefly. Frederick snuck closer to them in the hope of hearing the conversation, but by the time they became audible, the red-haired man walked away from the count.

Frederick was too curious to hide any longer. He gave up his secret location and approached.

"Who was that?" he asked the count.

The count glared at him. "Where have you been?"

"Who was that person you were talking to?"

"His name is Hector Mac Brae. He is back from the crusades."

"Back from what crusade?"

"The Third Crusade. He fought alongside Richard the Lionhearted."

"That was twenty years ago."

"He stayed in the Middle East after the crusade. The Vatican sent him. He has agreed to be your tutor; that is, if you ever come back to the castle, you street rat."

Frederick scowled at the count, turned his back to him, and headed toward the crowded town.

"Where are you going?" the count called after him.

"I'll be back at the castle soon."

"You better be, boy. He has business to attend to in Italy, but he will be at my castle in a week's time. Do not embarrass me."

Frederick was intrigued at having access to a crusader; he just didn't want the count to know his excitement level. The Middle East had always fascinated Frederick. He had heard many stories from crusaders and Saracens alike about the region. Not only did the crusades interest Frederick, but also the culture and history of the Middle East.

This opportunity is probably worth going back to the castle for, he thought with a smile.

Inspired by the well-traveled crusader he was about to meet, Frederick started thinking and speaking in the different languages he had learned over the years. He started in Italian, then French, Latin, and finally Arabic. He wanted to be at his best for his first lesson since there was no telling how well Hector Mac Brae spoke those languages. For the first time since returning to Sicily, Frederick was looking forward to something.

—m—

Frederick waited impatiently in his room at the count's castle for his first lesson. In anticipation of this day, he had re-read every book and studied everything there was to study.

Finally, Hector entered the room, leaving the door open behind him.

"Hello, young man," he said in a Scottish accent. His booming voice carried throughout the room.

Frederick nodded to Hector as the count entered the room and introduced them formally.

"Frederick, this is Hector Mac Brae."

"'Tis a pleasure to meet you, young Frederick. I have heard a lot about you."

He shook Frederick's hand firmly. Before Frederick could respond, the count spoke again.

"I hope you show this tutor more respect than you did—"

"My lord, will you leave me with this young man?" Hector interrupted. "We have a lot to cover today."

The count shrugged his shoulders, looked at Hector, and stepped out of the room.

"So, what will our first lesson be?" Frederick said with a smile. He could barely contain his excitement.

"Come with me, young Frederick," Hector said, walking out the door. "Our first lesson will be on horseback."

Hector led Frederick to the stable, where they both saddled their horses. This was the first time Frederick had handled a horse since his time at the Vatican. It was something he enjoyed doing but had lost an interest in since his return to Sicily.

Both of them mounted and walked their horses out of the castle grounds and onto the forest trail leading to Palermo. They rode in silence a long while until Hector spoke up.

"Tell me about yourself, young Frederick."

"Not much to tell," Frederick said weakly. "My parents died when I was young. I lived at the Vatican for a year, and now I live with the count of Palermo. Before that, I think I've lived with every nobleman in Sicily. But soon I will be too old to live with families, and then I will start my own life."

Hector knew all about Frederick's life before he ever met him. He realized how incomplete Frederick's response was. This was a young man with a big hole in his personality, and Hector was here to fill that void. It wasn't by chance that he had been sent. He knew it was best not to ask another question. There was no reason to lead him into a subject he was not comfortable discussing. He wanted to build Frederick's trust. This was not just another tutor, not just another foster parent. Hector committed himself to assuring Frederick that he had his best interest in mind, and that Frederick could trust him emotionally and in all future life matters. Hector's mission depended on Frederick's trust.

They rode in silence the rest of the way.

—⚉—

The next day, Frederick waited in his room until Hector appeared at his door.

"Let's go," Hector said.

Exactly as the day before, they saddled their horses and rode into the forest in silence. Hector seemed more interested in the scenery than in Frederick for the moment.

"Beautiful land," he said.

The fact that an authority figure was not judging or scrutinizing him was comforting to Frederick. He liked the idea of just riding a horse again, as well as enjoying the scenery. It was something he quietly missed all of those years.

"Tell me about yourself," Frederick blurted out, as if he had no control over the comment.

"Not much to tell," Hector said, smiling, as if needling Frederick for his response from the previous day. "I was born in Scotland. My family lived in a small house in the hill country near the town of Glasgow. My mother and father died when I was young."

Frederick turned to look at him, but Hector's eyes remained focused ahead.

Hector continued. "My guardian was the clan leader of the hill country. He was a good man, and because of my size, he trained me to be a knight. When King Richard came to Scotland to collect taxes for his crusade, he talked my clan leader into giving some of his knights to him. I was chosen, along with a few others, to reclaim Jerusalem for Christianity.

"We rode from England all the way to Sicily, right through this very forest, on our way to your beloved docks to charter ships to Cyprus. This was before your father was king of Sicily . . . before you were born."

Hector paused for a moment to let the story resonate with Frederick.

"We sailed to the Middle East, where we were supposed to meet up with your grandfather, Frederick Barbarossa. He drowned on the way to the crusade, and the Germans never made it to the holy lands. Most of us thought we would turn around as well, considering we lost over half of our knights when the Germans withdrew, but Richard was not about to leave without a fight. He had spent too much time, effort, and treasure to turn around. And the thought of matching up against the great Saracen leader Saladin was too enticing to resist.

"We fought in Syria and down the Mediterranean Coast for three years, in Lebanon, Acre, and finally Damascus and Jerusalem. We made progress but usually could not hold what we won for long. Richard and Saladin were the greatest generals of the crusades. It was almost unthinkable to believe one would emerge as the victor over the other.

"In the end, Richard agreed to a truce with Saladin in order to stop a revolt against him in England. The two never fought again, or even saw each other. Richard was captured and given to your father, Henry, and ransomed. Saladin died just after the crusade. Richard died in a minor skirmish in France a few years after Saladin."

"But you stayed in the Middle East?" Frederick asked. "You didn't go back with King Richard?"

"That's right, young Frederick. Many of us stayed in the towns we held in the truce. We were waitin' there for Richard to return. But of course, he never did."

"I notice that you have an occasional Scottish accent," Frederick said.

"I am from Scotland after all."

"But most of the time you speak without an accent no matter which language you are using."

"My accent seems to show up when it's an emotional topic."

Frederick nodded in understanding. His thoughts suddenly drifted to his mother's smiling face.

"We all have our emotions to deal with, young Frederick. And they all come out in unique ways."

"Yes," Frederick said. "After you received word of King Richard's death, why did you stay in the Middle East?"

"After so many years in the Middle East, I had become part of the European Christian society of that land. Under the truce, we were able to interact with the Saracens. We shared our cultures and knowledge with them, and they did the same with us. I studied with scholars, mathematicians, and philosophers. I became a knight of the Teutonic Order and learned the chivalric code. My life was more there than here. So I stayed."

Frederick looked over at Hector again. His face was aged and spoke like a man who had seen many hardships.

"What made you come back?" Frederick asked.

"The chance to teach others what I have learned," he said, turning to Frederick. "And those lessons will start tomorrow, young Frederick."

—ɯ—

That night, Hector wrote a letter and had it dispatched to the Vatican:

Father Cencio,

Thank you for your hospitality at the Vatican during my visit. Your assessment of Frederick is accurate. He is a gifted young man, and with proper focus and training he will make the great king we desperately need in Europe. Sicily in particular needs the leadership currently lacking from its protectorate.

At this time, I think I can do more good in training Frederick for his coming challenges than anywhere else in the world. It is an honor to be called upon to tutor this boy.

In sincerity,

Hector Mac Brae

—◊—

Within weeks, Hector had brought purpose and curiosity to Frederick's life. Hector was well versed in all disciplines of education, and he was also able to introduce Frederick to advanced swordplay and military tactics. It wasn't clear to the count of Palermo why Hector was teaching Frederick non-academic subjects, but he didn't dare ask him why. He, along with all of his knights, feared Hector. With every new lesson, the bond between them grew.

When they were not sparring with swords, Aristotle quickly became their favorite discussion. Frederick had heard many men quote the renowned Greek philosopher, but no one before Hector seemed to be able to go deeper. His understanding came from studying Aristotle in the Middle East, as well as from debating Saracen philosophers. Although studying Aristotle was still a controversial topic in Europe, sometimes running counter to the church, Hector knew it was still an accepted subject for tutoring a talented student.

"The Saracens called him the First Teacher," Hector said. "Cicero described his writing as a River of Gold."

Hector dedicated a great deal of time to the study of Aristotle. The storied philosopher had written on vast subjects ranging from physics to poetry, theater, music, logic, rhetoric, linguistics, politics, government, ethics, biology, and even zoology. Hector was probably the foremost expert on Aristotle in all of Europe. Frederick welcomed his expertise and teaching and quickly took to his theories and thoughts, hoping one day to have the same command on the subject as Hector.

"It seems he has a comment on every single thing that has ever been said, done, or thought," Frederick said about Aristotle. "How are you able to learn it all?"

"You never grasp it all, young Frederick. It's dedication to the philosophy you strive for. The Greeks said he was the last person on Earth to know everything."

Frederick excelled at all subjects under Hector's tutelage. He seemed to gravitate to the intellectual areas of study, but Hector insisted he also learn to ride well, fight, and understand military tactics. He stayed ahead of Frederick in every subject to keep him stimulated, just as his mother had done. They spent half their day inside with books, and the other half outside with horses and swords.

"This is how the Romans taught their children, young Frederick. You'll be a knight before I'm done with ye."

—◊—

Hector continued to correspond with Cencio for several months, reporting on Frederick's progress.

All was well until a letter from the Vatican arrived one day.

"Cencio says that Emperor Otto has started quiet negotiations with northern Italian towns and is amassing larger than usual armies in close proximity to him in Germany," Hector said. "He thinks this could be the beginning of a campaign to invade either Italy or Sicily or both."

"How certain is he?" Frederick asked.

"Cencio considers it a credible rumor, but knowing Otto as I do, I would consider it very likely. Otto attacks what he appraises weak, and Sicily by all assessments is weak."

"He would really attack a protectorate of his own empire?"

"Sicily is a part of the pope's empire."

"But the Holy Roman Empire is endorsed by the Vatican. Pope Innocent chose Otto to be emperor."

"That was a foolish choice, as the pope will soon learn. To Otto, this is a way of telling Pope Innocent that he is superior to him. He would far prefer taking a crown from an enemy king on a battlefield than have a pope endorse his bloodless ascension."

"Otto's logic eludes me."

"I know it does, young Frederick. You have been trained in logic and diplomacy. Even at your young age, you have better political skills than the emperor does. This is why I insisted on your training as a warrior, as well as the other skills. Sometimes conflict cannot be avoided."

"Will we be a part of this conflict?"

"It's too soon to know, but I see no clear path to avoidance with a man like Otto."

—⁘—

Within a month of Cencio's dispatch, Pope Innocent was warning the nobles of Sicily to begin defensive measures. Otto would be upon them soon, and the army the pope was recruiting would be behind his advance.

"You will be under siege from Otto within the year. Hold out as best you can. My army will be there to reinforce you," the pope wrote.

XIX

Otto is Coming

1210 AD

O tto's imminent arrival brought with it mass exodus from the Sicilian nobility, and barons, counts, and knights became the primary exports. No one felt the need to stay and defend Sicily. Only those not rich enough to flee remained.

"I don't blame any of them," Frederick said to Hector as they watched the ships depart one day at the docks. "This is the fourth invasion of Sicily since Innocent took over as protectorate, and each one has been successful. This time, it's an emperor and a massive army. These noblemen have no allegiance to Sicily. They may as well go to another kingdom that's more stable and secure."

"It's not the nobility that surprises me," said Hector. "'Tis the knights. They took an oath to protect the defenseless, but instead they go with their nobles to safe lands to fight in pretend battles!"

He raised his voice as two knights passed by within earshot.

"Running away like cowards . . . like the nobility they protect, they run away at the first sign of danger. I have never seen anything like it. Richard would have had their heads."

The count of Palermo did not surprise Frederick with his flight from Sicily; however, the idea that he would take him along did.

"There is nothing here for you, Frederick. You should come with us to northern Italy. We have another castle there. Otto is not interested in war with the Lombards. Here, you will surely be a primary target for him."

"If Hector stays, I will stay."

"Hector is under my employ and will go where I go."

"I'm sorry, Count, but that's not the case. I am honor bound to protect the defenseless people of Sicily. My duty supersedes any commitment I have to you. Besides, my duty was from the Vatican all along. They employed me to tutor Frederick."

"And if Hector stays, then so will I. Sicily is my kingdom and my home. This castle was rightly my family's to claim, and if you are going to flee, we will take ownership of it."

"Very well, suit yourself. Pope Innocent has left no instructions regarding you. Both of you are fools to stay here. There is no honor in staying and fighting an insurmountable foe. Hector, this is a fool's errand that will lead to your death, and you are putting your pupil right in the middle of it."

"Hector does not put me anywhere I do not choose to be. This is my kingdom, and I'll stay here to defend it as a noble person should. Just because the odds are against us does not make your flight any less cowardly. Oh, and I am aware of the Royal Treasury that you have been a good steward over these many years, Count. See that it stays in the castle's vault as it has always been."

The count took a step toward Frederick and outstretched his arm as if to slap him. Hector stood in front of Frederick, and the count stopped.

"'Tis best you move on now, Count. There is nothing to be gained by this conversation. You have a long journey ahead of you."

"All of a sudden you are qualified to be King of Sicily. It's laughable. You will die here Frederick. Mark my words! Oh, and your service to me is at an end, Hector. I will make sure to tell every nobleman I know how poorly you performed."

Hector took a step toward the count, backing him up to the edge of the dock.

"Best to move along now, Count. Nothing can be gained by stayin'. Every moment you tarry, Otto draws nearer."

—⁂—

A few noblemen and knights with lands not on the island stayed, believing they could negotiate with Otto. Surely, he would not attack a Papal protectorate when he was Holy Roman emperor. Surely, he would accept terms that would leave them as overlords of the region and he as ruler. They were not willing to leave their land and riches.

Hector did not expect Otto to bargain with these nobles, given they had nothing to bargain with that Otto couldn't take. He knew Otto better than any of them.

"Otto isn't a man to make deals when he has the advantage, and he will certainly have the advantage when he arrives. Otto only bargains with those who have an advantage of some sort over him."

—⁂—

As the days to Otto's invasion neared, his intent became clear. He sent word to Sicily that he was there to liberate the country from a potential foreign invasion. He would also move King Frederick to a safer venue. Just the fact that he was calling Frederick "king" was ominous. This was not an attempt to protect; this was the language of a kidnapper. He was calling for an unconditional surrender.

The nobility followed Otto's premise in agreeing to recognize Frederick as King of Sicily. Hector explained to Frederick what was happening. It was all a political ploy. It seemed Otto's plan was to invade Sicily, take Frederick as hostage, and leave the nobles alone. This pleased the remaining Sicilian nobility.

Hector scolded the nobles for throwing Frederick into the fire.

"You have no concern for Frederick," he said. "Ye would be happy to sacrifice him to Otto if it meant you could remain as counts and barons."

It was all starting to feel very real to Frederick.

"So, I am king of Sicily just like that?"

"Ye were always king, Frederick."

"But no one recognized me as such until there is peril."

"That is true, but it is in peril sometimes that opportunity emerges."

"I'm not ready for this. I need time to think in silence, and in solitude. I will be crossing the Straits tomorrow at first light."

"I understand, young Frederick. But don't be too long. We have work to do."

XX

Into the Forest

Frederick skipped his lessons and snuck out of the castle in the early morning darkness.

He stowed away on a ferry to cross the Messina Straits, just as he had so many times before. The fog was just beginning to lift when the ferry touched shore and Frederick hustled into the woods and out of sight. There, he would renew his vows to nature and the animals, an oath he would never break. He needed time away from this situation in Sicily, and this retreat was the perfect solution.

He was on a mission. Climbing over the foothills, he quickly ascended the landscape and disappeared into the secluded forests that had no need of a name. Once deep in the canopy of trees, where even sunlight was unable to discover him, he could relax and concentrate on what he came to do.

Here, with the forest as his hideaway, was his sanctuary. In an ever-shifting world, here he found the earth solid beneath his feet and precious in his heart. This was indeed hallowed ground. With towering trees stretching to the skies and framing the walls of his cathedral, he felt his mother's presence. Just being here brought him peace.

After a moment of analysis, he spotted the tallest tree and scaled it to the uppermost branch. Shifting to the middle, he could see the sky above, the ground below, and a hidden valley nestled inside the forest. It was the perfect spot.

From his perch, he observed the hawk's flight, watching one seemingly all the way from the Straits into the forest. As it circled the nearby clearing for an hour or more, Frederick watched intently, never losing sight of the majestic bird.

Suddenly, it curled its wings and swooped down toward the valley below, leveling off as it descended to the ground. The hawk's agility fascinated Frederick as it maintained its speed only inches from the ground.

This savvy hunter was the predator, and its prey, an unsuspecting field mouse, had disclosed its position. The hawk sprang into action, swooped down, and snatched the mouse, clutching it in its talons and carrying it off to somewhere above the trees and out of sight. This gave Frederick pause.

Nature usually did.

The forest, though brutal, was awe-inspiring. *The hawk was so patient. It had flown over the valley for over an hour,* he thought. *I wonder whether I would have given up.* Quietly, he vowed to master that quality someday.

He couldn't help seeing the lesson from the hawk and the mouse. Was he acting more like the field mouse or the hawk right now? Was he hiding from events in Sicily, only to be swooped up once they found him on the run? Surely, it would not be difficult to ascertain where he was hiding. For that matter, Otto's army might march right through this forest on their way to Sicily. This, too, gave him pause.

Breaking free from those thoughts, he determined not to be dissuaded from his purpose. *This matter is to be contemplated later.*

Glancing below, he sensed new activity near the tall tree. There were numerous animals that had appeared in the clearing to drink from a nearby creek. A large deer approached the tree and stopped to eat grass. Frederick sat silently. Suddenly, as if sensing Frederick's presence, it raised its nose, sniffed for a moment, and bounded off into the thicker brush. It amazed him that the deer could be so sensitive to such a subtle change in scent.

Frederick could spend all day in this forest. Comfortable in his perch, nestled in the rafters of his personal cathedral, he could stay balanced and comfortable for hours and not lose focus. Hunger or thirst wasn't a consideration. Although he was at peace, he was also pre-occupied with events back in Sicily. Was he wrong to be here? Did the people think he ran off, like so many knights and nobles? What did Hector think of him? The inner battle raged on.

A distant noise from deeper into the woods shattered the serenity and commanded his attention. Curious to the origin, he sat perfectly still on the branch, mimicking the animals he so admired. Then he heard it again. Soon he could detect more suggestion of the sound. Struggling to find any familiarity, he noticed a somewhat fluttering noise that became slightly more specific with additional consideration.

"Possibly music?" he whispered, not wanting to be heard.

Impulsively, he jumped to the ground, too impatient to climb down. He risked injury leaping from the high branch of the tall tree, but getting a quicker start on his sudden quest was worth the risk, at least initially. He landed hard with both knees bending deep, nearly buckling. Frederick smiled, knowing he got away with something he shouldn't have tried.

Back on the ground, Frederick straightened up and stood perfectly still. After a moment of silence, the mysterious sound started again. Frederick was able to determine a direction and started running toward it. He didn't know what it was, but he had to find out. He boldly headed in that direction.

It's music, he thought, hoping to convince himself to continue. *But who would be playing music in the woods?* Curiosity outweighed any fear he should have had while he advanced on its position.

Frederick stopped periodically to listen and make minor adjustments to the music's exact location until it was quite clear. *Possibly a small instrument, and perhaps a man's voice singing or chanting,* he supposed. Gradually, he sensed its location, likely at the bottom of the hill, in the next clearing. He moved ahead quickly.

As Frederick made his way down the hill, the trees began to thin. The winding creek came back into view, and he spotted the clearing. To his surprise and amusement, before his eyes was an odd-looking man playing a wooden flute, occasionally pausing to sing out . . . in French!

Frederick smiled cautiously as he watched for a few moments from a distance, seemingly safe as he hid behind a thin tree. He had been so engulfed in his quest that he failed to notice that he stood at the steepest point of the descending hill.

The man was as serene and happy, almost like a puppy at play. He danced and played his flute, singing, chanting, and laughing—all by himself. Like Frederick, who was equally unconcerned, the man was totally oblivious to his surroundings and completely in the moment.

Frederick found this to be particularly unusual, even though he shared that very same trait. The man was dressed in a brown burlap material made into a cape. A lighter brown cord rope tied to his waist held it tight. Although he was barefoot, Frederick saw a pair of worn-out sandals that looked too large for his feet sitting next to a burned-out fire and a large brown blanket. It didn't seem like the man had anything else with him.

He was tall and slender, but not underweight like so many peasants he had seen. This man was in good shape. Frederick initially thought he might be a hermit, as he'd heard that hermits sometimes lived in these woods.

But this man did not fit the description. He was too loud and too happy. Hermits were quiet and reclusive, staying near caves and hiding out. Certainly, a hermit would not dance and sing and speak French.

While Frederick briefly pondered, the man cried out what he thought was the name Mary in French. It startled Frederick, and he shifted his weight to get a better stance; instead, his foot slipped on the wet leaves, saturated with the morning dew, and he quickly dropped on the uneven ground. The wet leaves slipped beneath his shoe, but to compound the situation, the leaves found no traction on the moist ground. Despite shifting his weight to his right foot, his fate was sealed. In a comical flailing of arms, he tried to grab hold of the narrow tree, but missed. There was nothing he could do to impede his downward spiral.

Sliding all too quickly, he shifted his weight to miss a rock on the left, and then on the right. It all happened so fast. Fortunately, the wet ground kept him from tumbling head over heels. In the blink of an eye, he careened down the slope and was dumped unceremoniously into the man's makeshift camp.

Hearing the commotion heading toward him, the man instinctively crouched into a defensive fighting position, knees flexed and fists in near his chest. He stood up straight when he saw Frederick descending down the hill and into his view.

He ran to Frederick, not in an aggressive manner, but more like he was on an urgent mission of aid. He arrived at the startled boy about the time Frederick reached level ground and stopped sliding.

"Are you all right?" the man asked emphatically. Frederick said nothing; dazed, disoriented, and dumbfounded, he was unable to articulate a word. "Are you all right?" the man asked again, this time in Italian.

"Yes," Frederick said in a struggling voice. "I'm fine."

The man eyed Frederick in silence for several seconds from every angle. A sly smile crept across his face. Then, after a few more moments of careful appraisal, he broke out in uncontrollable laughter. His commanding laugh filled the air, saturating the clearing, and echoing back from the steep embankment. Frederick sat stunned. Here was this strange man, almost doubled over in hilarity without saying so much as a word. *What kind of man is he?* Frederick watched as he walked toward the creek, winding down the hill and into the clearing, laughing hysterically until out of sight.

Confused, Frederick checked for damages; everything seemed to work. He had no broken bones, and he was not bleeding.

Frederick would have been upset at this strange man, except he was fascinated by his big, crisp laugh. It was as sincere a laugh as he had ever heard, bringing a smile even though the levity was at his expense.

Soon the man appeared from the creek, holding a wooden cup filled with water. He handed it to Frederick.

"What's your name?" the man asked, clearly fighting the need to start laughing again.

"I am Frederick," he said, taking a long drink from the funny wooden cup. "Frederick of Sicily."

"That sounds familiar to me," the man said, but paused and did not pursue his curiosity.

"My name is Francis," the man said in a booming voice.

"Where do you come from, Francis?" Frederick asked.

Francis took a few more steps away from him, then turned and smiled at Frederick. "Assisi," he said.

Francis walked back to the stream and collected a pair of trout he was saving for dinner. He held them high above his head and called to Frederick.

"Would you like one of these, Frederick?"

"Yes, I would," he said, realizing he had not eaten all day. "How did you catch those? I don't see a pole or net."

"God provides."

The sun descended below the forest and out of sight. A charcoal fire was burning, and fish were frying above it. There was also bread and water from the nearby stream.

Francis was focused on the preparation of the fish, but talked to Frederick while he watched them cook.

"What are you doing in the woods?"

"I come here to think."

Francis smiled but did not laugh, still focused on the fish, but thinking to himself how funny it was to hear a teenager explain how he retreated to the woods to think.

"I used to live not very far from here and played in these woods every day. We are a long way from Assisi. What brings you to these woods?"

"I had a fight with my father," Francis said, turning the fish to the other side. "Staying in Assisi didn't seem like a good idea. I remembered these woods from a very long time ago and decided to come here to be alone and praise God for giving me a new life."

"You know this forest from before . . . from when?"

"I was here on crusade in a past life."

Francis's style of conversation sometimes confused Frederick, who thought he might be speaking in metaphor. There had been no crusade in Italy.

Then it occurred to him what Francis might mean.

"Did you fight against Markward?"

Francis looked up at him, diverting his attention away from the nearly cooked fish.

"Yes. How did you know?"

At almost the same instant, the two of them made the connection.

"You are the boy king of Sicily."

"And you are the knight that let me pass."

They paused and looked at one another as if to confirm the other's story. Francis turned the fish once more, smiling again, and breaking the brief silence.

"I never heard another word about you after that day. Where did you go?"

"I went back to Sicily and lived with the families of nobles. I was their foster child. I ran away many times and lived in the forest—this forest—and the streets and docks of Sicily, too."

"I knew it was wrong to allow a child to walk into the woods in the middle of a war. I should have taken you back to the Vatican to be with the pope, but I was having spiritual issues at that moment."

"No. That is where it all started. I was an orphan. The pope turned me out to live with these nobles as a foster child, but now they are fleeing Sicily and wish for me to be king once again. Emperor Otto is on his way to invade Sicily, so they fled and asked me to be the monarch Otto kills. This, they think, will save them and stop Otto from destroying their lands and castles."

The fish crackled in the fire, and the smoky aroma filled the air. As Francis took their dinner off the fire, Frederick broke the silence.

"How does a knight end up a hermit in the woods? How bad was the fight you had with your father?"

"I'm still a knight, Frederick. I'm a knight for Jesus. I've dedicated my life to His mother Mary, just as the chivalric code calls for."

"I have learned of the chivalric code, and it sounds as though you are bending knighthood and the code to its limits, shaping it to suit your own needs."

"No," said Francis, raising his voice sternly. "It was not my purpose to leave Assisi. That was thrust upon me. But I have made a vow to Jesus. I made a commitment to Mary. I've never stopped being a knight, and I believe in the chivalric code. I think all of it goes hand in hand. I've never been more certain of anything in my life."

Francis speared one of the trout with a knife and dropped it on a wooden plate. He then passed the plate to Frederick and did the same for himself. They ate the fish in silence.

Frederick regretted his flippant comment. Francis had clearly thought through his idea of chivalry, and Frederick's response had been more about Francis seeing him think critically and not like a boy. He didn't want to sound patronizing, but his observation was disingenuous and too strong. He feared he'd crossed a line.

"What were you singing before?" he asked, hoping to move past the comment.

"Before?"

"Yes, before."

"Before what?"

"Before . . . before when I got here."

"Oh, you mean before you slid down the hill and into my camp on your butt?"

Frederick smiled, knowing that this was Francis's way of moving past the previous subject.

Francis smiled and looked down at the fire, then moved a piece of wood to free a flame from its captivity under the smoldering log.

"It was my poem to Mary."

"Were you singing it in French?"

"Yes. My mother was French. Since I left Assisi, I have been singing and thinking in French. It is my preferred language. Although in the forest, the animals don't seem to care what tongue you use."

"I often do that, too. I speak to someone in Italian, and switch my thinking to French, German, Latin, or even Arabic. I've been doing that as an exercise. My tutor Hector taught it to me."

"He must be an excellent teacher if he has you speaking and thinking in so many different languages. That is quite an accomplishment."

"He is a great teacher. I have learned so much from him. Plus, he is a crusading knight that fought with Richard the Lionhearted in the Middle East. He is teaching me the tactics of warfare and swordplay, as well as riding a horse. Of course, he is also teaching me Aristotle."

"It sounds as if he is grooming you to be a king. What did he think of you leaving Sicily?"

Frederick contemplated that question for a moment. Was Hector grooming him to be king of Sicily? It had never occurred to him to consider such a notion. Was it possible that Hector had a larger plan in mind for him? He decided to answer the latter question from Francis and ignore the former observation.

"I didn't give him a chance to voice his opinion on my departure. It all happened so fast. The few remaining noblemen called on me to take my rightful throne, the same men who called me a street rat just a few months ago. Others were leaving the island as if it were plagued or on fire. Rumors are swirling of how close Otto is by land and sea. I needed time to think . . . time to breathe. I told Hector I was going, but I didn't wait to hear his advice. This is what I do when times are difficult."

"Did he say anything before you left?"

"'Don't be too long, young Frederick,'" he quoted word for word. "'We have work to do here.'"

Frederick looked away and took the last bite of his grilled trout. Francis finished his fish shortly after and threw another log onto the fire. The smell of cooked fish filled the campsite.

"What work is he referring to, do you suppose?" Francis asked.

"I'm not sure. I suppose he wants me to decide about Otto and the throne of Sicily."

After they had finished eating, they headed down to the stream to wash their plates.

"What was the fight about with your father that made you leave Assisi and live in the woods?"

"My father is a successful man in Assisi—the richest clothing merchant in all of Italy. I worked for him most of my life. I wanted to be a good son, but I knew being a clothing merchant wasn't my calling."

Francis cleaned off the plates in the stream and filled a very unusual wooden pitcher with water. He handed Frederick the pitcher while he brought back the clean plates and two wooden cups.

"Where did you get these?"

"I made them."

"When?"

"While I was here."

Frederick studied the cups and pitcher and was amazed at the craftsmanship.

"May I have a cup of water, Frederick?"

Frederick poured a cup for each of them as Francis continued.

"I went off to fight as a knight in two wars. One was here against Markward, and the other against a town near my home, next to Assisi. It was there that I learned the bitter lesson that some knights don't take their vows as seriously as I do. Unfortunately, I was taken prisoner and thrown in a dungeon, and held there until my family could pay a ransom. It was there in the dungeon that Christ first appeared to me."

"You mean He came to you in a vision?"

"Yes, in a way. He came to me and sat with me in my cell. As He was sitting beside me, He gave me a message. He told me to repair the church. Since that day, I have known my purpose, and it was not selling fabric."

Frederick was not totally grasping the implications of what Francis considered the obvious purpose God had given him. He remained quiet. The fire crackled, and a log broke apart, overwhelmed by the flames. Frederick drank the last of his water as Francis continued.

"Eventually, my father paid the ransom and I returned to Assisi. I was sick for a long time because of the conditions in the dungeon. Once I regained my strength, I went to a church on the outskirts of town, the structure long since burned down. I did what Jesus told me. I started repairing it. Since I had access to my father's silk, I sold some to buy materials for the church. Unfortunately, my work was not his work, and once he found out he punished me, but I didn't stop. He locked me in my room for weeks until my mother released me. Once I was free, I went back to the church and continued. My father decided I must be insane; he brought me before the town priest and accused me of stealing from him. I tore my clothes off and gave them back, wanting to be free of his debt. The priest, understanding my plight, gave me this robe, belt, and sandals. It was then that I left Assisi for the forest, knowing my purpose still stood before me. Like you, I needed time to think, and time to thank God for my new life and wait until He comes to me again to tell me my next mission."

Stupefied at his account, Frederick just stared at him. He barely knew what to say. He finally asked, "Has God come to you again?"

"His silence has made it clear to me. I must go back to that church and complete its repair. I was celebrating and thanking God for the renewal of His message when you spilled into my camp."

They both chuckled.

Is Francis insane as his father alleged? Or is this mission truly of God? Frederick thought. Francis was more convinced of his path in life than anyone he had ever met; surely more than he was of his own.

"When will you begin the next church?"

"As soon as I finish work on the church near Assisi, I will walk until I see the next church in need of repair. Then I will stay and do that."

"Maybe I will come with you until God makes known His plan for me."

"Your purpose is known, Frederick."

"But God has not come to me. I even spent a year in the Vatican, and God did not speak to me."

"Yes, He did," Francis said in a very soft tone. "Your purpose is clear."

Frederick sighed. "I may be young, but I would know if God came to me and told me my purpose. I have not seen Jesus. I have not had Him come and sit beside me. I know I am outside of God's favor."

Francis smiled and spread out two blankets near the campfire, then lay down on his back and looked up at the trees.

"God is with you now and always. You have your purpose, and it is an important one. Sometimes God sends a messenger we don't immediately recognize. In my case, He sent Christ Jesus, but then He sent silence."

"Who did God send me, Francis?"

"His name is Hector. He is waiting for you in Sicily. There is work to be done in your homeland. But now it's time to sleep."

Frederick lay down on the blanket and closed his eyes. He still smelled the smoky fish aroma and heard a distant wolf howl.

"Aren't you worried the smell will attract animals to the camp?"

"Nothing will harm us," he said with a content certainty in his voice that convinced Frederick. "If they do come, I will have a congregation to preach to in the morning."

Frederick smiled and drifted off to sleep. He knew exactly what would happen next. The stress of uncertainty had been erased from his thoughts.

XXI

The Return of the King

"No one is going into Palermo," the ferry attendant said. "My entire passage is outgoing from there. What is your business in Sicily, boy?"

"To save it," Frederick said.

The ferry captain laughed. "Well, good luck. If ever a kingdom could use saving, it's Sicily. I used to live on that side of the Straits, but I moved my family to the Italian side years ago. It's just too dangerous and unstable."

Frederick smiled and looked out at the oncoming landscape. He saw the dock filled with more refugees; some of noble birth at the ready for the captain's return journey to southern Italy.

Sicily's transformation was obvious. Palermo had changed from a heavily populated city into an isolated ghost town. Anyone who could afford to leave had left, and the only remaining inhabitants were Frederick, Hector, and peasants.

"Glad to see ye back, young Frederick," Hector said, as Frederick approached the lonely castle on foot.

"Glad to be back . . . I guess."

"Don't worry, boy, opportunity blossoms from the worst of situations. If invasion is what triggers Sicily into action, so be it."

Frederick believed that when Hector said Sicily, he meant him, and it was true. The threat of invasion had triggered him into action, but what could be done against Otto and his war machine, pointed directly at him and poised to attack? Frederick didn't know Otto's whereabouts. He didn't know if Otto would invade by land or sea—or both. Frederick had no army to defend Sicily, and the nobles and their knights had fled. Furthermore, Innocent's army was surely too far behind to aid against Otto. He saw few options, but he trusted Hector, who seemed somewhat optimistic.

"So what do we do first, Hector?"

"We establish you as Sicily's king. You are the rightful heir, and if you are willing to be crowned under these circumstances, no one should doubt your mettle."

"Won't that probably get me killed?"

"Possibly," Hector said with a sly grin. "A bold move like this is not without risk, but bravery in the face of imminent peril often brings with it unexpected benefits."

Frederick began to speak, but Hector interrupted.

"Young Frederick, you are king of this land, whether recognized or not. This is how Otto will see it. Embrace it for good or bad."

"All right, Hector. I must admit, I am the closest thing to royalty left in Sicily. You have convinced me. I will be king of Sicily."

"No, young Frederick. You cannot just say the words. You *are* the rightful king of Sicily. This has been your destiny from the beginning. You must accept your standing as rightful king of Sicily. Not just say it or act it out, like a player in a drama. This must mean something to you before it means something to others."

He put his arm around Frederick and smiled at him.

"And the next thing we do is gather intelligence on Otto's army. We need to know exactly where he is, how many men he has, how many are knights, and what his intent is. Send scouts down the coastline and through the whole of Italy to look for Otto and his army, and send a messenger to the Vatican announcing your decision to declare your throne now that you have come of age."

"You want me to do that?"

"Yes. You are the king. Find your scouts and order them to do their duty."

"Hector, have I actually come of age?"

"I surely hope so," Hector said with a grin.

XXII

The State of Sicily

O tto walked into the dark pub overlooking the Mediterranean Sea and surveyed the room. He towered over the other men, and his long black hair and beard made him look more like a rugged blacksmith than an emperor. He sat down across from an old man hidden by contrasting shadows and streams of light from a nearby window. Several of his aides, generals, and bodyguards sat at various tables alongside him. The old man looked down at his mug, paying little attention to Otto or his men.

"What news do you bring?" Otto asked.

"Good news," said the old man.

"What, then?"

"Sicily is in chaos. Men of wealth and title have fled. Knights have left to await crusades in the Middle East or shipped out north to Europe. There is no presence of military anywhere on the island. All that is left is the boy and his castle staff."

"That is not his staff," said an aide at another table. "That is the count of Palermo's staff. He wrote to us earlier describing conditions in Sicily. They don't belong to him. I'm not sure why they stayed. We had hoped Frederick would go with the count so we could collect him along the way."

"His tutor also stayed," the old man said. "A big Scottish man named Hector. He doesn't look like a tutor."

"Hector Mac Brae," Otto whispered as if speaking of a ghost. "He fought with Richard in the Middle East. He fought with me in the French Wars before the Great Crusade." Continuing, his incomprehension became evident to all. "I thought him long dead. How did Hector become a tutor to Frederick? I thought he stayed in the Middle East. I thought he was too stubborn to come home, even after Richard died."

"It's just those two, as far as I can tell," the old man said. "Them and the servants. No military force, and no plan of resistance."

"If Hector Mac Brae is there, then there is something you didn't see," Otto said, thinking aloud.

"But we are bringing too much force for whatever Hector has in mind. Our invasion will be too overwhelming for them to hold more than a day or so, and the fact that Henry's boy is on that island only makes this invasion more inviting. Let the men know we march for Sicily on the morrow. The ships follow the next day. The Lombards have agreed to free passage for our troops to the southern ports of Sicily."

"It should be very favorable terms," another aide said. "With Frederick and the pope at such a disadvantage, you should be able to name your price and—"

"There will be no terms," Otto snapped. "I have spent years building a political alliance in order to do this. I have spent years waiting for the perfect time. You know I hate politics and I hate waiting. We have the Lombards watching our backs from whatever knights come from Europe. We have England on our side. France is too occupied in Normandy to get involved. Pope Innocent is weak—he started his campaign too late, and he has most of the European knights tied up in that ridiculous crusade against heresy in France. There is no military presence in Rome. We can simply bypass it on our way to Sicily."

"But, Your Grace—"

"No, the victory is mine. Germany is behind me because I am Germany. The princes would never cross me. The time for diplomacy is over, and Sicily is too enticing a target for the Saracens to leave alone. We have to attack Sicily and liberate it for its own good."

Otto got up and left the tavern, leaving his aides sitting there dumbfounded.

"We've come all this way and just now understand Otto's motives," one of the aides said. "He's doing this to protect Sicily from itself and the Saracens."

"I wonder if the Saracens have even considered such an attack?" Said another aid.

The men laughed and slowly dispersed. The old man looked up from his ale and out the window.

"Sun's gone down," he said.

XXIII

An Unexpected Ally

Messengers arriving from Rome told the grim story: Otto was indeed in Italy. The next day, fishing boats in the Mediterranean spotted several warships with an imperial banner heading south.

"Otto is throwing all he has at us," Frederick said. "Whether Pope Innocent is protectorate or not, we both know the pope's support will not arrive here in time."

"Aye," Hector said. "'Tis up to us."

Palermo became the staging ground for the grim task of recruiting an army. There were very few knights left on the island, which meant there would be no cavalry and the infantry would be composed mostly of peasants, many without weaponry. Although they were able to raise about five thousand men, it would certainly not be enough to hold off Otto.

"Perhaps if Otto chooses a long siege strategy, we can hold until the pope's knights reach us," Frederick said.

"I wouldn't count on it. Otto will probably attack and not surround. It's not in him to wait . . . not if he sent men by land and sea."

"It's too bad we couldn't keep our knights and ships here. We would have had a better chance . . . if nothing else, at terms with Otto."

"Don't lose heart, young Frederick. There's an army on this island. If we convince them to fight with us, we will have a force of experienced light cavalry and a small fleet of fast ships that could hold off Otto for a long while."

"What army are you referring to, Hector?"

"The Saracens."

"The Saracens?"

"The Saracens in the hills of western Sicily."

Frederick stared at Hector for a long while, waiting for an end to the joke. Frederick would have already laughed, except for the import of the matter. He couldn't believe Hector was serious.

"The Saracens will not help us. They have always been against the ruling body."

"That's because the ruling body has always been against them . . . trying to eradicate them from what the Saracens perceive as their home."

"And if they weren't such gritty fighters, they would have been wiped out long ago," Frederick added. "They even helped Markward in his attempt at invading Sicily. They hated my father, and my grandfather King Roger. I'm sure they will not take my side—they have probably aligned with Otto."

"No, young Frederick. Otto will not accept nor request the help of a Muslim. He may not even be aware of their existence. But given the right motivation, the right mission, the Saracens will help you."

"And what motivation and mission will do that, Hector?"

"That they are fighting for their home and their efforts will give them a stake in the kingdom."

Frederick and Hector rode together to western Sicily to deal with the Saracens, who had inhabited those mountainous regions for generations. Along the way, Hector talked about his knowledge of them while he lived in the Middle East.

"Once we established ourselves in their land, they were willing to negotiate, trade, and even work with us. Their religion is important to them, but their leaders are well educated and their soldiers well trained in warfare. I don't know a lot about this group in the mountains, but the fact that they are Muslims shouldn't rule them out as allies."

"You don't think aligning myself with Saracens is wrong?"

"I know of no such rules of engagement."

"Not rules of war, but rules of Christianity. Are they not our sworn enemies?"

"Rules of that sort are for men nowhere near a battlefield. Men who are not pitted against an imperial army."

"I suspect Pope Innocent would disagree with you."

"You're right, he might. However, he did ex-communicate Otto."

"True."

"And how concerned are you with Pope Innocent's opinion on your allies?"

"I'm not at all concerned," Frederick said, laughing. "In fact, it only sweetens the deal for me."

—∞—

"What brings you to these hills, my lords?" a Saracen man said as he walked up to Frederick and Hector. He was tall and slender, and wore a black tunic and pants with a black turban. Behind him, twenty men on horseback surrounded them on both sides in the hills of western Sicily.

"We are here to speak with the leaders of your village," Hector said in Arabic. "This is King Frederick of Sicily. He begs a word."

"Kings do not beg for words. When was this boy made king? I had not heard of this."

"He has always been the rightful heir."

"It has been my experience that rarely does heredity claim a throne, particularly the European thrones. Power is what puts a crown on a man's head."

"Frederick has claimed his rightful throne in the wake of an Imperial attack. What better way to prove his rightful place?"

"Is Otto of the Welf family still the emperor?"

"He is."

"Why would a Christian emperor attack Sicily, which is controlled by a pope?"

"For more power, my lord," Frederick said in Arabic. "It is as you say, the powerful rule. Otto sees Sicily as vulnerable, even though his pope claims it as his protectorate. Even God cannot intervene."

"God intervenes as He pleases, but men and kings have a free will all their own."

"That is true enough, my lord, and Otto is exercising his free will. This is not God's will."

"Why does this boy call me 'lord'? And how does he speak a language so far from where he lives?"

"He speaks a lot of languages, and he has grown up with nobility," said Hector.

"I see your quality, my lord," Frederick said. "I do not need to be told you are nobility."

"Very good, young king. My name is Bashar al-Bistami. I am the Baron of Bistam. Now, tell me why are you in these hills all alone and so far away from your lands?"

"We came to offer you a stake in building Sicily, Baron al-Bistami. For too long, you have been a forgotten people in our lands. You have been attacked, and you have been isolated, but you have survived for generations. Maybe it is as God has willed that you remain in Sicily, even though you worship God in a different way than us. We come to you now to right the wrong that has been cast upon your people, but we also come to you in need."

"What is this need, Your Grace?"

"We need your light cavalry, Baron," Hector said.

"All of the knights in Sicily have fled with their lords," Frederick said. We have no military presence. It is our belief that your men are our best chance at repelling Otto. We need your help."

"And why should we do that, Your Grace? As you said, we have defended this land from many Christian kings, some of whom are your ancestors. Why should we come out of these hills and fight on the side of one Christian king against another?"

"Hector has told me great stories of the Middle East and its people. I understand the diversity of talents and skills that live in these hills. But this land is harsh and the ground infertile. Fight with me against Otto, and I will give your people a walled city with fertile lands and safe harbor. You will become artisans, farmers, and poets. You will no longer fear for your existence, and no longer scratch the Earth's surface for survival."

"Your king does not lack in rhetorical skills, my lord," al-Bistami said to Hector. "But can he back up his claims?"

"He can, and he will, my lord."

The baron smiled at them and looked back at his men. He dismissed his soldiers.

"Stay with us tonight, as our guests. We will discuss the terms of this agreement and decide after first light. Stay with us, Your Grace, and we shall feast in the custom of our people."

"We accept your gracious offer, my lord."

The baron clapped his hands and walked back toward his village. He motioned for Frederick and Hector to follow.

"Are we safe here, Hector?" Frederick asked wearily.

"We are," Hector responded. "When a Saracen offers you hospitality, you become a part of his family. Actually, a guest has better protection than his family. A feast is a sign of hospitality."

The terms that Frederick brought to the Saracens were for them to deliver five thousand light cavalry to bolster the Sicilian defense. They would also provide a blockade of small boats to slow Otto's warships, thus stopping their two-pronged attack.

In return, the Saracens would receive protected lands that would not be invaded by Sicilian armies. They would no longer be an unwanted race. They would be allowed to plant crops and trade with the whole of the kingdom. Their time would no longer be spent defending their lands.

Even though it was words alone as a bond, it was the first words the Saracens had ever heard from a Christian king. They trusted Frederick and Hector, believing a young king beholden to them would be more likely to keep his word. They also knew if Otto were to win, they would be in a fight with him. The Saracens accepted the terms.

Frederick and Hector rode back to Palermo knowing they had used every available resource of Sicily. They would have to prepare fast, then wait to see how big a force Otto would produce.

—⚏—

Not long after Frederick and Hector finished preparing Sicily for the upcoming battle, Emperor Otto arrived at the Messina Straits and set up camp. The number of knights and infantry Otto brought far outnumbered Frederick's, and the warships carrying more would make the situation even more overwhelming.

Hector crossed the Straits and approached Otto's camp under a white flag. He could see the emperor's force was much larger than the anticipated army, primarily the number of knights. As he drew closer, Otto rode out alone to meet Hector at the front of the camp. His men followed a few paces behind.

"You go from a crusader to a boy's tutor? What happened to you, Hector? I thought you were a warrior?"

"We all have our roles to play, Emperor."

"Did you come to surrender? Where is your student? Is he hiding in the basement?"

Otto's men laughed, but Hector seemed unimpressed by Otto's advantage, indifferent to the entire affair.

"King Frederick's terms are these: he will be acknowledged as the king of Sicily and allowed entry into the empire. He will also be a vassal and protectorate of the empire. For this acknowledgement, he will pay you a sum of gold today to withdraw from this ground and a monthly toll for as long as you are emperor."

"Is that all?" Otto asked, laughing. "How did Frederick come up with so much gold? How could he possibly pay a monthly toll? Sicily is in a shambles."

"He has a rich family, and left alone, Sicily will be the richest kingdom in all of Europe. What say you to those terms, Emperor?"

Otto smiled and looked back at his men.

"This is what I told you back in Germany. The Staufers are the most arrogant family in all of Europe, but you have to credit him with nerve. I thought for a certainty I would take Sicily unopposed. I thought he would take a fast boat to . . . well, a boat to somewhere . . . I don't know who would take him." Otto turned back to Hector. "But here you are, Hector, making terms with no power to enforce them. His family has always been an arrogant lot."

Otto laughed and continued.

"The idea that a Staufer is on that island only makes this invasion more attractive. I would prefer killing Frederick than not. And can you imagine how furious my knights would be if we came all this way and didn't fight anyone."

Otto's horse spooked at a distant noise and reared up. Otto pulled the reins to bring him down and turned the horse until he completed a full circle to face Hector again.

"Tell your student to stay in that basement until we find him and kill him . . . and everyone else who resists."

"Emperor, if you invade Sicily, you will surely win, but in doing so, you will lose at least half the men I see before me. Everyone on this island knows this is a fight to the death. All had ample opportunity to leave, and did not. The Saracen army has traveled this day out of the western mountains to stand with King Frederick. It will be a painful victory for you, Emperor; a victory steeped in blood."

"You've become soft, Hector. Teaching a boy does not suit you, and employing Muslims? How desperate you must be."

"Emperor, I swear to God at the end of this battle, Sicily will be left a smoldering battlefield with nothing for your bloodied army to claim. The riches of Sicily will die on this battlefield, just as your knights. I pray you will take King Frederick's terms. The monthly poll tax alone could fund a crusade."

"This is a sad state of affairs when a man of Hector's stature is reduced to begging for terms. You are not the man who once fought with the Lionhearted."

"Richard would see the futility in this conflict. Nor would Richard sacrifice the lives of half his knights to gain an advantage he could get for free. Richard was the fiercest fighter I ever saw, but he never fought for nothing. He was too smart for that, but no one has ever accused you of learning anything. Smart was never your strong suit, Otto."

Hector snapped the reins of his horse and rode off towards the Straits, turning his back to Otto.

"Your head will be on the end of a spear, Hector, right next to your pupil. Be ready, Hector; we attack at dawn," Otto yelled.

XXIV

The Battle of Sicily

With the sun rising, Frederick and Hector led their small army of knights, peasants, and militia onto the battlefield next to the foggy Straits of Messina. Hector formed two defensive lines of infantry next to the water's edge, with the knights in reserve but ready to react to whatever troops made it to shore. They would have to be flexible in their attack patterns.

The Saracens arrived shortly thereafter and lined up behind the infantry in two columns on the perimeters, with a very good look at the Straits. They would initially act as archers and volley arrows into the boats transporting Otto's men, then as light cavalry once the conflict began on land.

Al-Bistami rode to Frederick and Hector, concerned with the unknown power of Otto.

"Your Grace, the mist over the water gives us no idea of this army's plan," he said, pointing across the Straits. "And this army is quiet like a serpent about to strike. They could be spread out across the Straits, ready to surge from everywhere in small units. Or their archers could lead the attack from boats as they cross, and we would never know it until the arrows announced their arrival. This is no way to fight a battle. Perhaps we should withdraw this army inland."

"There will be no archers announcing an attack by Otto. You can count on the knights in heavy armor being first off the boats. I know this enemy. He will lead with his strength, as he always does."

"But how is it they are so quiet?" asked Frederick.

"That I don't know. Otto has never been one to keep quiet his arrival...'tis a mystery t' me."

Al-Bistami shrugged his shoulders and rode back to his men.

"Does he seem apprehensive to you?"

"He is a warrior, as all of these Saracens are," Hector answered. "When it is time, they will fight valiantly."

"But how will their skills mesh with our European style of warfare?"

"The Saracens have a balance of infantry and archers, along with the light cavalry, which will be the catalysts of the perimeter combat. With the infantry and the heavy cavalry in the middle of the battlefield, we have a diverse, formidable defense that could hold Otto on the other side of the Straits long enough for him to decide on a siege or accept terms."

Neither was likely, but it was their best hope.

As the fog slowly lifted, anticipation began to build in the Sicilian and Saracen armies. But as the water became visible, a surreal sight emerged.

Is this a trick? Is it an illusion? How could this be? al-Bistami wondered, then asked those at his side. They said nothing as they looked at the empty landscape. Where once there was an army, now there was none.

"We have lost this army?" al-Bistami asked, approaching Frederick and Hector at near galloping speed. "We have no scouts keeping eyes on him?"

"We had no reason to think Otto would be anywhere but in front of us," Hector replied. "We do have rear scouts, but this movement defies reason."

"Could they have boarded ships to attack from the other coastline?" Frederick asked.

"Our boats would have seen the ships," al-Bistami said. "There have been no reports from the sea."

"And Otto had no reason to employ risky tactics. He has superior numbers of knights, and he has the advantage. It's a very peculiar action."

"A rider approaches on the other side of the sea," a Saracen aid said to al-Bistami. "He is alone, carries no flag, and wears no uniform."

"He's a messenger," Frederick said. "He's been here many times with correspondence from the Vatican. I wonder how he slipped past Otto."

"Maybe he can enlighten us on the whereabouts of the emperor," Hector said.

The messenger crossed the Straits and rode to Frederick, Hector, and al-Bistami, and dismounted. Pulling a large scroll out of his saddlebag, he approached the men.

"King Frederick, a message from Germany," he said. "A message for you, my lord, from the princes of Germany."

"What could the German princes wish to tell me?" Frederick asked rhetorically. "And how did you get past Otto?"

"I didn't, Your Majesty."

"So Otto has read this letter?"

"I'm afraid so, King Frederick."

"Then how are you and this letter still intact?"

Frederick looked suspiciously at the messenger. Had he not known him from the previous Vatican letters that had occasionally made it to him during the preparation for Otto's invasion, he might have thought him a spy.

"Let's have a look at that letter," Hector said.

Frederick unrolled the breached scroll and began to read while the messenger further explained Otto's response.

"When I first approached Emperor Otto, he assumed this to be a bull of excommunication. Then after he read it, he dropped it on the ground and ordered his generals to break camp and depart for Germany."

"What does it say, King Frederick?" al-Bistami asked. "What could the German princes say to send Otto away from this battleground?"

Frederick stayed silent as he read. After finishing the document, he looked up but said nothing, as if to absorb the meaning.

"What does it say?" Hector asked emphatically. "Don't leave us in the dark."

"The princes have elected me king of the Germans."

"This was a reaction to the excommunication," said Hector. "This was a way of sending rapid aid that could not come in the form of an army."

"How did this help us?" Frederick asked.

"It took an unbeatable army off the battlefield. The princes knew Otto would return to Germany to take on the insurgency that elected you king of the Germans. They bought us time with this tactic."

"Tactic?" al-Bistami mused. "If the messenger was not captured by Otto, this would not have occurred. Only by falling into his hands did Otto even know of Frederick's election."

"I was not captured, my lord."

"Otto thought the message was for him," Frederick said. "The letter is not addressed to anyone. It simply announces my election. The messenger rode into Otto's camp and delivered this to him. Otto assumed I had already been informed and left. The princes knew both Otto and I had to see this for it to be effective."

The messenger smiled at Frederick. "I will wait for your reply, Your Grace."

The three leaders watched as the messenger rode toward the castle.

"What that messenger did, risking his life to ride into Otto's camp with news of that sort, and what those princes did . . . I have never seen such valor and bravery—not in the crusades, not anywhere, not ever," Hector said. "They have turned a poised army and treacherous leader away from us and straight at them. We must support them."

"Go to Germany and pursue Otto?"

"We owe it to the princes."

"But what can we do? Otto is still stronger. If we go to Germany, won't we lose?"

"These princes have saved us. They have put themselves in the way of a storm. They have elected you as their king. We must come to their aid. It is the noble thing to do."

Frederick shrugged and took a few steps away from Hector.

"I have known nobility all of my life, and what did they do when an army threatened their lands? What does nobility do to right the wrongs of a region? The nobles are self-serving and noble when it suits their needs. I do not need a lecture on nobility, Hector," Frederick seethed.

"You are confusing nobility with noble action. They are two different things, young Frederick."

Frederick looked at al-Bistami, who was trying to stay out of the discussion. He mounted his horse.

"As long as you are leaving, tell the messenger to stay the night," said Frederick. "We shall need this time to discuss the matter."

Al-Bistami saluted in a playful manner and rode off.

"My mother didn't want me to be king of the Germans. She withdrew my name from consideration when my father died. She wanted me to be king of Sicily, and nothing more. This was the land she loved. It's the land I love. I know nothing of Germany. How will I be able to rule there efficiently? How will I be able to defeat Otto in his own land? How can I help the princes when I can barely defend Sicily?"

Hector frowned for a moment, then looked down at the ground. He knelt and picked up a stone, surveyed it for a moment, and tossed it into the Straits. He watched the ripples from the water, and looked up at Frederick.

"Stay in Sicily, or go to Germany . . . either way, there is a fight coming. Accept the nomination or don't. Become the king of Sicily or don't. Either way, Otto comes."

"This isn't fair. I should be able to be the king of Sicily and live in peace. It's what my mother wanted for me. After all that has happened, it's what I deserve."

Hector smiled and stood up. He placed his hand on Frederick's shoulder.

"Fair or not, the fight comes. Your life will never be the quiet, peaceful existence you may want or deserve, not while Otto wants to kill you and take Sicily from you. You can wait here for him and try to defend Sicily, or you can prepare yourself and take this fight to him, with the support of the princes who saved you this day. But understand me, Frederick, no matter your choice, the fight comes."

"Am I ready for this, Hector?"

"You will be."

"Will you help me?"

"As long as you need me, King Frederick, I will be here for you."

The two men mounted their horses and rode back to the castle. The messenger was waiting for them on the castle grounds.

"Tell your princes I accept their nomination and that I shall see them in Germany as soon as possible."

"Yes, my lord. I will leave tonight and beat Otto back to Germany."

"Try not to get captured this time. This is a message that might get you killed if Otto intercepts it."

"Yes, my lord."

"Your bravery will not be forgotten."

"Yours won't either, my lord."

XXV

Preparing for an Imperial War

Sicily gasped a collective sigh of relief after Otto and his army had made their way back to Germany. The nobles, who fled in fear, returned to their lands, rebuilt their feudal establishments, and expected life to return to normal. They showed Frederick very little respect and treated him as a figurehead king.

The nobility of Sicily did not concern Frederick. He, along with Hector, knew the political climate of Europe, and it did not include the Sicilian barons and counts. They were of little regard, pretending to be more than they were.

It was clear that Pope Innocent would be unable to protect Sicily from Otto. Meanwhile, Frederick came to see that defending Sicily would give him the rightful claim to the throne, even if the throne were not of high value. Indeed, Innocent would bristle at the idea of Frederick being both king of Sicily and king of the Germans, but he, too, would have to live with this arrangement. Frederick's political savvy was beginning to emerge.

It was during this period of stress that Hector began seeing signs of Frederick coming of age. They resumed lessons, with military tactics, swordplay, and warfare taking the place of rhetoric, philosophy, and mathematics. Frederick learned from Hector with swords, on horseback, and in analyzing battles and stratagems used in recent and historical combat.

Frederick became a great warrior under Hector's tutelage, although untested. He could only hope Frederick would be ready under combat conditions.

Hector knew that Frederick would be regarded as the king in any action he fought, and therefore the leader of the army. Great leaders, Hector knew, did not merely delegate to their generals, but took the lead in peace and conflict. Hector began to build Frederick's competence and confidence as a leader of men.

"Richard was the greatest crusader of them all," Hector said. "His knights always respected him for being in front of every battle they fought. A leader should lead."

"Does that mean I should always be at the point of the surge, Hector?"

"It means you should always be leading, young Frederick. Whether in the rear commanding movement of the infantry or out in front of a knights' surge, let your men know your life is as invested in the outcome as theirs. Never let them think you value your life above theirs."

—⚏—

Weeks passed, and Frederick improved in the drills and sparring sessions. Each day Hector could see his growth, clearly mastering the skills he would need, particularly on the battlefield.

It was time. The moment had come to raise an army of knights to fight in Germany. Frederick was ready to lead.

However, in Sicily and southern Italy, there was little excitement for the prospect of following a teenage king into battle against a warrior emperor. The nobles preferred keeping their knights home to protect them and made it clear they had no faith in him and would not help. They did not see Frederick as their leader, even though he was the rightful heir to the throne.

Frederick was unfazed. He took note of the nobles' inability to rally around the kingdom's cause, knowing they would prefer to keep the feudal system active in Sicily. Dealing with them was for another day. It did not matter that they wagered he would never return. His focus was on Germany.

"These are not the knights we want," Hector said in frustration. "These are the vassals of small men. We will go to other lands and find knights worthy of this mission."

—ɯɯ—

"A month has passed, and we were only able to secure commitments from the Saracens of western Sicily and the king of Aragon, Your Grace," said one of Frederick's military aides. "We will need more than those commitments to stage a successful attack against an Imperial army."

"I am grateful for the Saracen support," Frederick said. "But they cannot fight alongside a Christian army in a European war if we want to have the support of anyone else. Ask them to stay in Sicily and protect our shared homeland."

This decision reflected Frederick's growing wisdom and stature. He was beginning to build a bond with the Saracens. They'd become allies, no longer enemies living in the badlands and hills of western Sicily.

Frederick had grown to appreciate the strategic, the political, and the unexpected. When a letter arrived from Pope Innocent requesting his presence to discuss his upcoming campaign against Otto, he recognized this previously unexpected gesture for what it was. Still, he was distrustful.

Although he wanted to formulate a plan and discuss knight recruitment with him, he could not forget the personal history they shared. Frederick did not want the pope's support; in fact, he wanted nothing to do with Innocent. The memories were still too vivid. He wanted no help from this tormentor.

Hector knew better and, as his mentor, appealed to Frederick's political and strategic senses. "We must include him. He can help build an army and raise funds from the whole of Europe. If he wanted, he could call this a crusade since Otto is excommunicated."

"He would never call this a crusade," Frederick said. "Otto may be excommunicated, but he's still Christian."

"Those who have been excommunicated are no longer seen as a Christian," the military aide said.

"Innocent has been considering this as a weapon for a while now," Hector said. "He wants the ability to call for a crusade to be fought in Europe against whom he judges to be an enemy. He's doing it right now in southern France to a group of people called the Cathars. He sent ten thousand knights to Beziers. It was a town of Cathars, Jews, and Christians. The knights besieged the town for less than a day, and then slaughtered everyone, Christians included."

"I thought the Albigensian Crusade was about eradicating small groups of heretics. I didn't know it rose to this level of killing. It sounds like a full-scale war."

"It is. The nobility that fight on the side of Pope Innocent are in it for land and riches. Pope Innocent turns a blind eye to that. He is just interested in eradicating the heretics, no matter the cost. Beziers is just the beginning.

"I understand the spreading of Islam, Judaism, and other pagan beliefs like Catharism concern Pope Innocent, but does he truly understand the loss of life and property that is going on over this?"

"Bishop Amaury sent a letter to Innocent bragging about killing twenty thousand men women and children. Then he plundered the town, and described it as divine vengeance."

"How did you hear of this letter, Hector?"

"I have my sources, young Frederick. He called his war against Markward a crusade to save you."

"Innocent wasn't trying to save me. He was trying to regain Sicily because of the tax revenue he was losing. Innocent's hypocrisy does have its limits. I think the crusades will be reserved for fighting Saracens in the Middle East, and heresy I guess."

"It would help our cause if he did, would it not, Your Grace?" asked the aide.

The emotion of the thought overwhelmed Frederick. He wanted no part of fighting in a crusade called on by the pope.

"I know Innocent all too well. I do not trust him. Who is your source of information about Innocent? Who is it that you trust above me?"

"I have my sources, young Frederick," Hector said.

"I wish he had nothing to do with it. I do not want to owe him anything once this is over. Did you see that he did not acknowledge me as the king of Sicily, or even as king-elect of the Germans in his letter? He still thinks I'm his ward. He thinks I'm a child."

"You shall have to show him otherwise, King Frederick. But in a war, we have to accept everyone's assistance."

Clearly agitated, Frederick paced, turning away from Hector, hiding his acknowledgement of sound advice.

"Tell the messenger we shall meet the pope in Assisi. I will not go to Rome."

XXVI

A Reunion with Innocent

J ust outside Assisi, Frederick saw a rundown church with several men on the roof and others going in and out of the missing doorway. As they neared, he recognized one of the men dressed in a brown burlap robe with a rope for a belt and worn sandals. It caused him to break from the lead rank and canter toward the church.

The robed man looked down the road when Frederick approached and smiled when he saw who it was.

"Frederick," he said, walking to him with open arms. "King Frederick of Sicily."

"How are you, Francis? I am so glad to see you well."

"Glad to see me well? I am not the one who has thousands of Germans out to kill him. I am glad to find you well, too."

Frederick dismounted and hugged Francis while Hector and the rest of the knights caught up.

"Hector, this is Francis, the man I told you about. The man I met in the woods near my old palace."

"I remember the story," Hector said, shaking Francis's hand. "Thank you for being such a great counselor to King Frederick at such a pivotal moment in his life."

"I should say the same about you, brother Hector. Your wisdom in this challenging time is invaluable."

"I am curious as to what you and your men are doing. Why are you rebuilding a church that is nowhere near anyone? Is there a village nearby that I am unaware of?"

"God told me to."

"God told you to repair this church?"

"God told me to repair the broken church. This was the first one I saw."

"When God told you to repair the broken church, I think He had more in mind than this," Frederick said. "God wants you to repair the broken church in Rome."

"I never presume to analyze the words of God. I hear His calling, and I go. When God says 'go,' you go! This is where God wants me. This is where God wants you. Otherwise, we would not be here."

"It is sometimes difficult to argue the simple logic of Francis," Frederick said, "and always pointless. I hope you are right, Francis. I do not feel as if I am in the right place. I do not think God hears me."

"God hears you, brother Frederick. He hears your every word and every thought. You are exactly where you are supposed to be . . . where God wants you. If it were not so, Emperor Otto would have overrun Sicily, as logic would have dictated."

"I see what you mean," Hector said to Frederick. "Brother Francis has an undying faith in God and worldly wisdom that is unexpected in such a holy man. He is a treasure, and you were fortunate to have met him."

"It was not fortunate, brother Hector. It was God's will."

"Well, when most men say that I cringe, but coming from you, I believe it is correct. I hope that we shall meet again."

"We must go, Your Grace," said one of the men accompanying Frederick. "Our meeting time with Pope Innocent grows near."

"He can come soon enough," Hector said in a stern voice.

"I will pray for you both on this important journey," Francis said.

"Thank you." Frederick smiled. "We shall pray for you as well, my friend."

Frederick knew Francis was convinced of his calling and confident that God would lead him in the right direction. It was a feeling Frederick wished he experienced.

"We will see each other again soon, my friend," Francis said, smiling while Frederick mounted his horse. "You are doing a very important thing, King Frederick. You are in God's favor."

"I will say the same of you, Francis. I will tell the pope of your work here and for his need of your authentic spirituality in the church."

"If God wills it, Pope Innocent will hear you. Until then, I will be doing His work right here."

They rode a short distance down the road to Assisi until Hector spoke.

"I am taken aback by him."

"By Francis?"

"Yes. He is a simple holy man, but his absolute certainty of purpose is that of a knight."

"He is unlike any priest, bishop, or pope I have ever met," Frederick said. "I feel a sense of divine purpose when I am in his presence, as if I am in the presence of Jesus Himself."

"He lives by a chivalric code," Hector said. "Is this not how the church is supposed to conduct itself?"

"The first time I met him, he said he was a knight for God. If we accomplish nothing else, let us make known Francis to Pope Innocent. We owe it to a church that has become as political and powerful as any king or emperor. The church needs a man like Francis to bring it back to its spiritual roots."

Frederick followed the road to Assisi with Hector and his knights. The thoughts of his last visit flooded his mind. He was far too young to remember it himself, but it still seemed so very familiar. His parents had recounted the event many times, telling him of his christening in this small town.

With that recollection came thoughts of his mother. It had been a long time since he'd thought about her, and years since he considered his father. It was a pleasant thought.

A smile crept over his face. He pretended he was riding into Assisi to meet his parents. This was one of the few places all three of them had ever been together.

Both in reality and in his imagination, Frederick could see a crowd lining the streets as they neared Assisi.

"I'm surprised to see them already lining up for us," he said. "I didn't know they were aware we were coming."

"They are waiting for the pope," Hector said, averting his eyes, looking down at the horse's mane.

"Oh, well that makes more sense," Frederick said. "I doubt Assisi knows me at all."

"They will know you soon, Frederick. But today we are not here for recognition or popularity. That is why Pope Innocent agreed to meet in Assisi."

"To establish his reputation in Italy for us to see?"

"Yes, but we are here to build an army. Stay focused on that goal, Frederick. Everything else is meaningless."

Frederick and his knights arrived in Assisi just after Pope Innocent's procession had completed its tour of the adoring crowd. He blessed them when he passed, and they cheered wildly. It had been a long time since the pope traveled to Assisi, and the people were hungry for his presence. Despite its wealth and prominent cathedral, it was a town of no importance given the current state of affairs in Sicily and southern Italy. Pope Innocent's presence that day returned it, if only in their memories, to its heritage of significance.

Meanwhile, Frederick rode into town in total anonymity. Even though he was king of Sicily (which included Assisi), the feudal system did most of the actual governing, and since Pope Innocent and the church saw the region as a protectorate of the papacy, Frederick was far removed from the thoughts of Assisi.

The crowd, still abuzz with excitement for the papal visit, hardly noticed when Frederick and his knights approached the cathedral. Frederick's ear caught a man who was acting as town historian to a small group of children.

"The last time royalty was in Assisi was about twenty years ago," he said. "But that was only King Henry, son of Frederick Barbarossa. He was a minor king in history. This is the pope."

"That was Emperor Henry of the Staufer House," Frederick said in a corrective tone, then laughed contemptuously at the comparison. "He was the Holy Roman emperor, not just a minor king in history."

The man shrugged his shoulders. He continued speaking to the group, but before Frederick could continue the debate, Hector interrupted.

"Frederick! Focus on the task at hand."

"Perhaps I should have just met him in Rome. Now he will look even more like a protectorate and guardian to the people of Assisi."

"Here we are," Hector said. "This is about waging a war, young Frederick. This is not a popularity contest."

"The popularity contest is over. These people believe that a pope is more significant than a king or emperor."

"They do now, but opinion changes like the winds, young Frederick. Focus on the task at hand."

Frederick barely recognized Innocent as the man he knew so long ago. The black hair was replaced by patches of gray. His slender physique was now rounder. His chiseled, serious long face was now defined with wrinkles. The pressures of the papacy had aged him beyond his years.

Still, images of that time in the Vatican assaulted Frederick's mind. Besieged by the torment, the change in venue from Rome to Assisi made no difference. Meeting his tormentor, the man behind his intense flashbacks, made the location irrelevant.

The pope, in all his majesty, sat perched high above on a throne, as if Frederick were his lowly subject coming to beg Innocent for his help. It was more than Frederick could bear.

The mere sight of him ripped open emotional scars. There was no way he could stand before this man.

In his arrogance, Innocent did not seem to realize that it was Frederick who was helping him defend Europe from the very tyrant that Innocent had endorsed as emperor.

That pompous attitude. That arrogant approach, Frederick thought, growing more enraged with each step.

Before they got any closer, Frederick stopped.

"I cannot endure this," he said to Hector. "I will not speak to this man."

"Easy now," Hector said, putting his arm on Frederick's shoulder. "Both of you are different people. We need this negotiation to go well."

"You will have to do this," Frederick whispered, looking away from Pope Innocent. "I cannot look upon this man without feeling rage. You have my proxy to act on my behalf."

Before Hector could stop him, Frederick turned and walked out of the room.

"Where is he going?" Pope Innocent asked. "Frederick, this meeting cannot wait."

"The king has given me proxy, Your Holiness," Hector said, walking toward him. "We may discuss this matter to its conclusion, and I will report its details to King Frederick."

"Very well," Pope Innocent said, smirking. "I hoped Frederick had matured, but I see he is still the rebellious boy I remember."

"With due respect, Your Holiness, King Frederick stood his ground in Sicily against your emperor when all other nobles left on ships for safer lands. He stayed and protected your protectorate when all other armies and knights of Europe lagged behind. King Frederick has proven his commitment to Sicily, and now he goes to fight a crusade against your excommunicated emperor. He has shown growth and courage in the years that you have . . . separated yourself from him."

"Are you calling this upcoming war a crusade on purpose, Hector? Or did you misspeak?" Pope Innocent asked.

"It is a holy war in my estimation, Your Holiness. Otto attacked your protectorate. What could trigger a crusade more than that?" Hector asked.

"I would hesitate to call this a crusade. It's within Europe, and it lacks a religious component."

"You have used the crusade label to fight heretics in France, and again when Markward attacked Sicily and kidnapped King Frederick. This would not be without precedence, Pope Innocent."

"I am well aware of my actions, Hector. But the Welf family has been an established house in Germany for generations. This will be a discussion for another day. It should not be a part of our negotiations and planning."

"Very well, Your Holiness."

—ɯ—

Frederick began to wonder if he were truly up to this task. Defending Sicily was one thing, but waging war in Germany against an emperor in his homeland so far away was another. Here he stood, not even strong enough to face a man who had tormented him in his childhood. How could he face Otto in Germany?

Frederick walked out of the cathedral. Crossing the street, he decided to check on the horses stabled nearby. Before he could cross, he saw an older man dressed in purple robes walking toward him. He did not recognize him and continued toward the stable.

"Your exploits in Sicily are the talk of Europe," said a voice from outside the stable. "A boy king and an outnumbered army stared down Otto and made him blink. The French, the English, even the Vatican has taken notice."

The distinctive voice penetrated Frederick's memory, striking a welcomed chord and breaking him from his tortured memories. It was Cencio, his treasured teacher. Frederick smiled and hugged him.

"How are you doing, dear boy?"

"I am well enough, Cencio."

"Are you?"

Frederick looked away for a moment, and then continued. "I feel alone and small. Men in that church—the church of my baptism—are negotiating my very future, and I am too small and too torn up by the past to participate."

Cencio empathized with Frederick, remembering all too well the treatment he'd received at the Vatican. He remembered what a gifted student Frederick had been and wished that his development were better handled. He also wished the streets of Palermo and a few detached nobles had not been his teachers for so many years. He wanted more for this young man who had showed so much potential.

"Take a walk with me," Cencio said. "Let's see what this town has to offer. We have plenty of time. They will be at this for hours. We will get back in time to see the conclusion."

"Hector is my proxy at the meeting. There is no need for me to be there."

Cencio let the matter go. He could see the experience pained Frederick.

"Have you been back to Assisi since your baptism?"

"No, not since I left Rome."

"Assisi has always been a town of merchants and travelers frequented for supplies. Her goods and silks are known throughout Europe. It is a rich town, but still obscure. I guess the proximity to Rome has made it insignificant."

"I suppose Rome has a way of doing that," Frederick said.

They passed by the many shops and flats of Assisi. Nobody gave them as much as a second glance.

"Enjoy this, Frederick."

"Enjoy what?"

"Freedom . . . anonymity."

"What do you mean?" Frederick said, turning to face him.

"One day, everyone in the land will know you. Knights will guard you. Servants will attend to you. Aides will counsel you. And you will look on these days as a freer, simpler time, and you will miss them."

"At this moment, I am doubting that I am prepared for this. I don't even have the nerve to face Pope Innocent."

"Old wounds are sometimes harder to heal than we know. But be assured, they are no indicator of preparedness. I have been informed that you have shown great promise and bravery in the last few years.

Meanwhile, Pope Innocent is not the same man he was when you knew him. You must remember at the time you knew him, he was a new pope. He definitely had no experience with children, and you were a curious child. Pope Innocent saw that curiosity as insolence, and in his insufficient knowledge, he treated you in the only way he knew. It was regrettable, and we tried to intervene, but the man in that cathedral is not the man you remember at the Vatican. Even more, you are not the child you were. You are a young man on the verge of greatness."

Cencio casually turned the corner back in the direction of the cathedral. Frederick followed him.

"You have been writing Hector, haven't you?"

"The Vatican likes to keep in touch with its protectorates."

Frederick smiled and looked up at the church. He knew he could go in now.

"Are you the reason Hector is tutoring me?"

"Hector and I have written for a very long time. I knew he would make a great tutor. But I think his tutelage of you has come to a close."

"I have had two great tutors."

They walked to the steps of the cathedral, Frederick taking the lead toward the door.

"I have to go in now. I have business to conduct. I hope I can prove I am worthy of my title."

Cencio smiled. "God has willed it, King Frederick. Do not forget, you are a king by divine order."

The negotiations between Pope Innocent and Hector had become cooperative and collaborative. Innocent respected Hector and was confident he could handle the management of a war. He was glad Frederick had him as an advisor, because his plans for Europe were linked to the success of the mission.

Together, advisers from both the Vatican and Sicily agreed that knights would be recruited by the Papacy and would travel to Rome and Sicily. The Vatican would raise war funds from churches throughout

Europe to pay the knights. These funds would also provide for weaponry, ships, and transportation—everything needed to wage war in Germany.

They discussed the idea of the kingdoms paying back the war debt to the Vatican, but it was ruled out.

"This war benefits everyone. Sicily and Germany will repay the debt in service to the war," Hector said.

Innocent did not dispute the point. The funds raised would be above and beyond the regular donations, and waging war in Germany would keep it far away from the Vatican.

Innocent rejected the idea of calling this a crusade. Hector initially made the point that fighting a rogue, excommunicated emperor was in effect a crusade; Innocent agreed, but he would not go so far as to label it as such. The idea did appeal to him on certain levels, but he knew this would relieve too many knights of their crusading duties. Innocent would reserve that label for Middle East wars against the Saracens, or spreading heresy, like in the case of the Cathars.

The final topic before the two men was a marriage between Frederick and Princess Constance of Aragon. Innocent would arrange the marriage, and with it came five hundred Aragonese knights, weaponry, and horses. Aragon was a tiny kingdom located in the northeast corner of Spain. Despite its small population, it was very adept at warfare. They would make a key ally.

"In matters of marriage, I will have to defer to King Frederick," Hector said.

"He is not a king until he is no longer my ward," Pope Innocent said. "The marriage makes sense. It will be more like a merging of Houses than a marriage. It is the only way I will release him from guardian status."

"And if I am to marry Princess Constance and wage war on your tyrant emperor, will you not withdraw your guardianship and protectorate status on me and on Sicily, Your Holiness?" Frederick said in a newfound booming voice as he stormed into the proceedings, surprising both Hector and Innocent.

"Where have you come from?" Innocent asked.

"I have been going back and forth across the earth, watching everything that's going on."

The pope looked at Frederick with a puzzled expression.

"Is that from the Book of Job?" Cencio asked, following behind Frederick.

"Nice to see a man of God knows his Bible," Frederick said.

"Nice to see you could finally join us, Frederick," Pope Innocent said, pausing to take a look at him. "I will withdraw my guardianship of you and name you king of Sicily. I will not release Sicily as a protectorate, and if you do become king of the Germans and Holy Roman emperor, you must relinquish the crown of Sicily or you will not be coroneted. No man must be allowed to rule both Sicily and the Holy Roman Empire."

Before Frederick could speak, Hector sensed the tension and quickly seized the opportunity to mediate a successful conclusion. No longer a proxy to Frederick, he was again the wise adviser to a king, helping him focus on the relevant matters.

"We have settled enough today. King Frederick will return to Sicily and marry Constance of Aragon. Both Sicily and Rome will accept the flow of knights, treasure, weaponry, horses, and ships until preparations are in order. At that time, we will meet again and plan the invasion of Germany in the war against Otto."

Both Innocent and Frederick seemed poised to return to their old ways, threatening the success of this negotiation, but Hector's wisdom and arbitration turned the moment and won the day. A preliminary plan was in place. Now there was just one small matter, though nothing that would negate the settlement.

"Before you leave Assisi, Your Holiness, you should go and meet a local priest named Francis. He is there at this very moment, rebuilding the church just outside of town. He is—"

"We are well aware of Francis," the pope interrupted, "and he is no priest. In fact, I'm sending Cencio to make sure he is not a heretic. The people of Assisi believe him to be a madman."

"In truth, I believe God protects this man, even from the Papacy," Frederick said. "But if it turns out that you harm this man or his mission, then we have no terms. I will not be a partner with anyone who would hurt Francis."

Pope Innocent and Hector looked at one another, neither saying a word; Frederick had surprised them both in the last few moments of the discussion.

"And one other thing, Your Holiness," Frederick said. "You cannot name me king of Sicily. I am rightful heir to that throne, as ordained by God. I have claimed Sicily's crown without your consent."

Pope Innocent chose to ignore Frederick's last claim and focus instead on Francis. "This subject will be in Cencio's hands. If he deems this man to be of sound mind and not heretical, then I will meet with him."

Frederick nodded in agreement but smiled inside. He knew Cencio would see the truth in Francis. He had won his point.

"That reference you made to Job was Satan," Innocent said.

"What?" Frederick asked.

"I have been going back and forth across the earth, watching everything that's going on . . . that is Satan talking to God."

"Well, I do have a summer home in hell, Your Holiness. Maybe one day I will build a hunting cabin there."

"You shouldn't joke about hell and Satan."

"Just ask the Albigensians, Your Holiness. Is that why you wage a crusade against them?"

"You are dismissed, Frederick!"

Frederick turned his back on the pope and walked out of the cathedral. He smiled at Hector, and they departed Assisi.

XXVII

Constance of Aragon

1211 AD

A small fleet of ships sailed into Palermo. The Aragon armada's red-and-yellow flags blew in the breeze.

"Quite an impressive display," Hector said. "Five hundred knights, horses, weaponry, and armaments are on board."

"So is Princess Constance," said a servant, nudging Frederick in the side, then backing away when Hector scowled at him.

Frederick, Hector, and the official delegation of Sicily assembled on the dock to greet the Aragon ships. While quickly inspecting the broken boards beneath him, Frederick realized its poor condition. He wished there was time to repair it, but of course, Constance was only minutes away from arrival. Frederick's mind raced between practical matters of no immediate consequence and the nervousness he felt at meeting a princess—his future wife!

It was all a haze to Frederick, a fantasy of some kind, but as the red-and-yellow flags grew larger and more vivid, he realized this was not a fantasy; this was present reality.

In a few days, he would marry this princess he had never met and become a husband.

It was happening so fast. First, he was facing the impending doom of Otto's invasion, and then the messenger announced he was the princes of Germany's nominee to be king of the Germans. There seemed no time to prepare.

No time to retreat.

Even an arranged marriage, decided by others for political reasons, was an overwhelming and emotional prospect. He had not chosen her for himself, but instead had to trust in his advisers. He tried to calm himself by returning to what he knew about the situation. He knew Constance was ten years older than he was and was previously married to the king of Hungary; unfortunately, that was all he knew. Otherwise, she was a total stranger. He had no idea how to act in front of her. After all, his only relationship with a female had been with his mother, and that memory had faded deep into his mind. He tried to calm himself, but he realized there was so much that he did not understand. He did not even know how to ask for help on such an intimate subject. It would embarrass him even to ask Hector.

There he stood, in front of the delegation, striking the pose he had learned, looking like the confident king ready to receive the horses, knights, and supplies. He appeared ready to greet his new bride.

The Aragon fleet crept slowly toward the docks, finally touching the wooden post of Palermo and dropping anchor. The moment lingered, suspended in time, eerily quiet. A lifetime seemed to pass for Frederick, suspended between a child and adult. Then, with a jolt, the gangplank lowered, revealing an unforgettable scene.

There stood Constance, stunning in her beauty. She moved forward, gliding onto land as if from the spirit world. Frederick stared in silence.

Behind Constance were her maidens-in-waiting—twelve of the most beautiful girls Sicily had ever seen, although Frederick scarcely noticed. Whistles from the crowd made the girls smile as they walked past in their identical dresses.

But Constance was all that Frederick saw. She was a statuesque vision in a long white dress with olive skin, flowing dark hair, and strong, dark brown eyes. She was an exotic beauty to behold.

His mind was racing as he stood there—so many thoughts, yet time seemed suspended. He noticed her eyes, striking him as intense but not intuitive. *What difference does it make if her eyes are intense or intuitive?* The conflict of thoughts raged as his brain fired off more thoughts than he could comprehend.

Fighting Otto can't be this challenging, he thought. He couldn't silence his thoughts, nor could he take his eyes off the princess as she approached.

"Easy, boy," Hector said, stepping up to him and tapping him on the shoulder. "Go to her and welcome her."

Frederick snapped out of his trance and looked back at Hector. "I don't know what to do," he whispered.

"Walk to her and take her arm, then lead us back to the palace."

Frederick walked the remaining distance to collect Princess Constance. He took her arm, and she smiled. Still nervous, he turned and led the contingency to the palace. The Sicilian crowd cheered, surprising Frederick; it was the first time a crowd had cheered for him, and the first time he had a girl on his arm. Life was unfolding quickly.

They walked together without incident, the Aragon contingency of servants and knights following behind in a very slow, deliberate, and loyal procession.

"*Bienvenue en Sicile,*" Frederick said, welcoming Constance to Sicily in French. "I hope you will like it here."

"*Merci,*" she said with a smile. "I'm sure we will."

He had forgotten anyone else existed while he considered the "we" part of her response. He looked back on the road to see the knights on horseback riding to the stables.

"They are quite impressive," he said to her.

"They are at your disposal, King Frederick," she said.

"And I am at yours, Princess."

Hector looked at one of the servants and smiled. "He learns fast."

XXVIII

The Franciscan Order

Francis looked through the open window of the church. He saw riders approaching with a coach in the rear and wondered who they were.

The riders stopped at the church, then one of them dismounted and opened the coach door. A man dressed in purple exited and walked toward the entrance.

"I'm looking for a preacher they call Francis," the man said.

"I am he," Francis said, wiping the sweat from his brow.

"My name is Cencio Savelli. I have been sent by the pope to speak to you."

"What does the pope want with me? What would I have to say that would be of interest to him?" Francis asked while several of his men wandered out of the church, curious about the conversation.

"The pope doesn't want to talk to you, Francis. He wants me to talk to you and to report to him the details of our discussion."

"Wouldn't it be easier for him to speak to me directly?" Francis said, smiling at Cencio.

"That would be easier, Francis, but the pope is very busy, as you might imagine, and he has asked me to take this meeting instead. I am his chief of staff." Pausing ever so slightly, he continued, "I do not rank high enough for you to talk to me?" He smiled.

Francis stared at Cencio, as if sizing him up. All twelve of Francis's men were outside of the church watching the verbal joust.

Francis gave a great laugh and put his arm around Cencio.

"Of course I will talk to you. I will talk to anyone, even the birds of the sky, and even the lowly chief of staff to the pope."

Cencio looked up at the decrepit church. Its roof was mostly missing. There were gaping holes in the walls. One entire wall had crumbled.

"What are you doing here, Francis?"

"God asked me to repair the broken church. This is the first one I saw after He spoke to me."

"Why do you suppose God asked you to do that?"

"I do not question or examine the wisdom of God."

"I'm not asking you to question or examine God. I am asking you to tell me why you think He would send you to repair an abandoned church that no one attends."

"God always puts us where we are supposed to be. This old church served its village well in its day. But it was never about this building, was it, brother Cencio? The village moved away after a bad crop season, and the building was of no value, but since I have begun work on this church, I have been visited by a king, a crusader, and a representative of the pope. Perhaps this church has a bigger meaning than you or I know."

"You think God sent us?"

"I would have no information on that. I just make sure I am always where God wants me to be, just as you are, my brother in Christ. God told me to come here, and I obey."

"Very well, Francis. Let's move on to the questions that brought me here. First, let me ask if you have an opinion on Pope Innocent."

"The pope is the mediator between God and man."

"That is the title of every pope. I asked you specifically about Pope Innocent. What do you know about him, and what have you heard said about him?"

"I do not know him, brother Cencio."

"Surely you have heard of him, Francis. Certainly you have heard stories about him and have drawn conclusions."

Francis turned to his men. "Have any of you met Pope Innocent? Have you heard stories about him or come to any conclusions about him?"

All of the men were silent.

"We do not know him, brother Cencio. We are not from Rome. The topics we discuss are about our Lord Jesus Christ, the daily routine of the villages we visit, the weather, and the progress of our church."

"Or the lack of progress," one of the men joked.

"We are simple men living simple lives. To us, the pope is the same man, no matter his name. He is the mediator for God."

Cencio was convinced Francis had no political agenda, or even an opinion on the Vatican or Pope Innocent. It was refreshing to see an authentic disciple of Jesus; there were so few left in Rome. But there were still issues to be discussed before he passed a final judgment on this unusual man.

"Francis, some in Assisi say you are a heretic. Others say you are insane. Heresy is a very grave charge that the pope takes seriously. Can you tell me why people say that, and what are your beliefs when you preach?"

"God would not allow me to be a heretic. If I were to say something wrong about the Lord, I would be struck dead by lightning. We only follow the teachings of our Lord Jesus Christ and walk in His footsteps to the best of our abilities. We are in no way critical of the church or the pope. When we are confronted with people that are, we correct their wrong thinking. It is our mission to spread the good news of Jesus to all those we come in contact with. To become disciples, we must become like the teacher and multiply His believers."

"I see a servant's heart in you, Francis. I see it in you and your men. I would like to recommend to Pope Innocent that we ordain you as a priest, help you finish this church, and send you on your way in this community. What would you say to this proposal, if called?"

"Brother Cencio, I am honored by your proposal, but the church that I wish to shepherd will have no need of walls. My brothers and I go to where the people are. We do not ask them to come to us. The church will be in them when we are present."

"There has to be a place to meet and worship, Francis. A church is at the very least visually symbolic of God's presence. Why else would God tell you to fix this broken church? No one is saying you can't go into the community as its priest, but there has to be a place to conduct worship."

"God put me in a place . . . this church, for instance. And from here I travel to the people, to spread the good news of Jesus Christ. This church is only a place where I lay my head at night and wake up in the morning. This building is not sacred. If it were sacred, would God allow it to fall into such disrepair? The cathedral in Assisi, or even the Vatican, is not sacred. God decides what is sacred, and the Gospels tell me my mission to bring people to Jesus is the only sacred action I take. Managing a building at the pleasure of the Vatican is not what God calls me to do."

"I thought you stated that the pope is the mediator between God and man?"

"I believe he is, brother Cencio, but God can always go straight to the source of His attention. In my case, He does not need the voice of the pope to speak to me."

Cencio looked at Francis, not sure what to make of him. As a Vatican official, many men claimed to him that they'd heard the voice of God. Most of them he dismissed, but this time he believed it. He knew Francis had a place in the church, but the function of static priest of a small village would not suit this man.

"Perhaps a more dynamic approach to a monastery would be a better calling for you, Francis. The Franciscan Order. You would become a ministry without walls. This role would allow you and your brothers to become an outreach for Christianity. You would go straight to the villages and take on the heretics in the places they live. You could become a voice for the church where the church has no voice. Do you think you can work within the parameters of an order?"

"I don't know, brother Cencio. Sit with us in this space. Eat and drink and tell me more. I sense God's presence is with us this day."

XXIX

The Wedding of Frederick and Constance

In the short time before the wedding, Frederick and Constance connected on many important levels. These were the first substantive conversations Frederick had had with a female since his mother.

Constance was exactly the person Frederick needed. She played many roles for Frederick, going beyond that of wife and queen.

At first, she was like the older sister Frederick never had. Constance listened intently, carefully to all of Frederick's stories. Seldom had he experienced such a welcoming and safe place. He quickly found himself telling her things he had never shared with anyone else. He smiled as he shared stories of his time with his mother, the games they played, and the books she read to him. She wanted to know more, eager to hear which were his favorites and why. Frederick laughed as he reminisced about those innocent days of childhood.

Married at a young age to a much older man, Constance had merely been a pawn in a political scheme. She had lost not only her father, but also a son at a very young age.

Finding herself in a desperate situation after the death of her husband, the king of Hungary, she was essentially a political prisoner.

Frederick and Constance shared stories no one else wanted to hear and expressed emotions others would never acknowledge. They were both pawns in the royal system as children and teenagers, and it seemed that only another in that situation would understand. In the midst of whispers and soft touches, they constructed a safe place, unblemished in a cruel world.

Constance and Frederick quickly, intently, and mutually agreed they would trust each other completely. They would not allow the other to be manipulated by anyone. They would only allow their very small circle of friends and advisers to get close to them. They became a small, close-knit family the day before their wedding.

—☶—

The sun burst through Frederick's window, awakening him with the immediate thought that today was his wedding day.

Something gnawed at him though, provoking him to a stressful state of mind.

What is the matter? he wondered. He couldn't identify the nature of his apprehension. His bond to Constance was certain. Never had he experienced such a complete trust in anyone since his mother, but something didn't feel right.

Maybe it was her age, or possibly the short time they had known each other. Once again, just as the moments before her arrival at Palermo, his mind raced, conflicted with the questions, answers and impatience. Something was bothering him. What was it? Why did it bother him so?

She was the most beautiful girl he had ever seen, and he was in no uncertain terms attracted to her. Any man would be fortunate to have her as his wife. So why was he hesitant? Why couldn't he mention this to Hector? The genesis of his discomfort continued to be elusive. He paced the room, searching his mind for an answer, but it wouldn't appear.

Later that morning, the wedding party assembled and organized to ride to the other side of Sicily for the ceremony. According to tradition and royal protocol, Frederick and Constance were expected to ride in the royal carriage.

"I'm riding my horse there," Frederick said to the servant who was waiting for him at the carriage.

"Wouldn't you rather arrive there fresh, my lord?"

"No, I want to ride. Get my horse."

"Very well, Your Majesty," he said, leaving for the stable.

Constance stepped onto the castle grounds in a beautiful white dress. . Once again, she mesmerized him; nevertheless, he was still unable to articulate his feelings concerning his soon-to-be wife.

"Is this our carriage?"

"Yes. Well, no it's yours . . . I mean, it's ours . . . mine . . . it's the royal carriage. But I'm going to ride to Messina on horseback. You will take the carriage."

She looked at Frederick. Detecting the young king's obvious nervousness, she smiled. "Maybe I would like to ride, too," she said, testing his motives.

"No, no . . . you'll get your wedding dress dirty."

"This isn't my wedding dress, Frederick. I won't wear that until the wedding."

"Well, you don't want to damage that beautiful dress. You can bring one of your maidens in the carriage for your entertainment."

He knew he sounded ridiculous, but the words just kept coming, as if he were unable to control them.

"All right, Frederick. I'll go in the carriage, and you ride your horse. Try and clear your head on the way."

She turned and stepped into the carriage.

Why am I acting so foolish? I'm more nervous about marriage than about going to war.

At about the halfway mark to Messina, Hector could take no more. He rode alongside Frederick, who was still occasionally muttering to himself.

"Exactly what is your problem?" Hector asked.

"Nothing," Frederick said defiantly.

"Then why are you not riding with your pretty wife?"

"She's not my wife yet."

Hector raised his eyebrows. "What is your apprehension to this marriage? Constance is the most beautiful girl anyone in Sicily has ever seen. You two get along as if you've known each other forever. What is making you so nervous?"

Frederick turned to look at Hector. He paused, looked away, and back again at him.

"I don't know. She's older than me. She's sophisticated. She's been married before to a king. I've never been with a girl before, and she has been with a king. I feel like she's my older sister. She will be my wife soon. She's—"

"Slow down, Frederick," Hector interrupted. "Get off that horse and ride with her the rest of the way. Tell her what you told me."

"But, Hector—"

"No, Frederick. Tell Constance what you are feeling. She's on your side, just like I am."

—◊◊—

Frederick sat silent in the carriage. Every imperfection in the road seemed to come through the wheels into the seat, jolting him to the very core of his being. Constance sat silent as well, not pushing him into any undeveloped thoughts.

"This road doesn't seem to be bothering you," he said as another bump radiated through his spine.

"I guess I'm used to it by now," she said.

He looked down, saying nothing for a long while. Constance crossed her legs and looked out the window. A dog barked in the distance while the carriage approached another small village.

"We could trade seats," he said, as if he had solved a great mystery. "Perhaps your side is more stable. Would you mind?"

"Perhaps we could both sit on this side," she replied, looking deep into his eyes. "I think this side does have more stability." Constance understood him already, knowing his needs as the king he was becoming, the husband he was about to be, and the insecure young man he still was.

Frederick paused for a moment, then in one motion got up and abruptly sat next to her. He glanced at her with a look of embarrassment.

"I'm sorry I'm acting so odd. It's difficult to understand the events as they transpire so rapidly. Three days ago, I didn't know you; now we're like brother and sister. I've never felt closer to a person in my life, not since my mother. Now we are about to be married. There isn't time to adjust. It all happens in an instant."

"You have all the time you need, Frederick."

"No, we don't. Soon we will be in Messina and—"

She put her hand on his thigh. "You have all the time you need."

"Somehow I cannot support the idea of being loved," Frederick said.

Constance smiled at him with warmth and understanding. "I have felt the same way at different times in my life. But know this . . . I love you."

A warm silence grew in the carriage. There was a fire visible through the window. Frederick put his arms around Constance. The bumpy road seemed to level off.

"Although I am young, I have been a sister, a mother, a wife, and a queen. I can be all of those roles for you too, Frederick. I will be whatever you need me to be."

"I will need them all, but at different times. Right now, I need my sister to talk to me about my wife. But soon I will be going to war, and I will need a queen to look over Sicily and not let the counts and barons take over again and ruin my kingdom."

"The carriage is beginning to fill up with all these women in your life," she said, laughing. "I will always know what role to play for you, my king. We will always work together for the good of this kingdom. I have been through as much as you."

"Is everything all right in there?" Hector asked, riding up next to the carriage.

"Everything is fine, Hector. It's my wedding day, and I'm marrying the most beautiful girl in all of Europe. I couldn't be happier."

He kissed Constance, and she smiled at Hector. Hector smiled back and rode past the carriage into town.

"I love you too, Constance," he said, looking into her dark eyes and smiling.

The royal wedding between King Frederick and Constance of Aragon went off without incident. Cencio presided in place of Pope Innocent; Frederick had insisted on the replacement.

Later that night, Constance and Frederick discussed Frederick's penchant for retreating into the forest-alone.

"You are a king, Frederick, and kings don't run off by themselves into the woods," Constance said. "What if you were to be killed all alone in the forest? How would anyone know? Who would be your successor? You have a kingdom to think about. You have a wife to think about. There are many factors to account for when you are a leader."

"But I need time to think. It's impossible when there are so many people around me. There are so many decisions to be made. I am able to think in the woods. This isn't about running off."

Constance got up from the table and walked over to the bed.

"Tomorrow, we shall take a company of knights across the Straits. You'll show me your childhood palace, and we will spend a day in the Royal Forest. Then when we establish a safe perimeter, you can go into the forest and contemplate your plans. How does that sound to you?"

Frederick thought about the proposal for a moment, and nodded in approval. "That sounds like a very good idea."

She smiled at him, lying down in the bed.

"Cencio was right," he said, watching her undress and throwing another log into the fireplace.

"Right about what?"

"I do miss my solitude."

"Tonight is our wedding night, my king. Did you wish to be alone?"

Frederick blew out the candle and walked toward her. The logs from the fireplace popped as the flames overtook them. He took off his shirt and sat next to her.

"Not tonight, my queen. This night, I wish to be alone . . . with you."

The next morning, Frederick and Constance crossed the Straits of Messina and rode the short distance to Frederick's old palace. The Aragon knights proceeded ahead, securing the grounds and setting the perimeter before the royal couple entered. Frederick walked inside and out, pondering in silence.

"This is where I lived my entire childhood."

"Didn't you also live at the Vatican as a child?" Constance asked.

"That's where my childhood ended," he said, pausing for a moment. "When I was here, my mother and I would visit the forest almost every day. There was a tribe of impala that would come around and . . ."

Frederick paused again, losing himself in thought.

"Come around and what, my lord?" Constance asked, trying to catch up on the mental sequence of his many moves.

". . . and then I was here again when Markward kidnapped me and invaded Sicily."

"The palace and the forest bring back many memories, don't they, Your Grace?"

"They flood my mind."

"Are they good ones?" she asked, putting her arms around him.

"Mostly," he said after another long, contemplative pause.

They walked into the forest together, Frederick showing her landmarks and remembrances of his past in the Royal Forest. Smiling, laughing, and pondering, they wandered to his old play space. Memories of his mother pervaded his thoughts and brought him back to the current matters of Sicily.

"I want you to be regent in my absence, Constance. I will be taking Hector and all of my staff with me, so this responsibility falls to you."

"I am honored to do so."

"Use the Saracens for security should anyone attempt invasion or violence. They will be there for you. Check in on the barons and counts often. Do not let them take advantage, and do not let them wreck our progress."

"I will do what is needed, and I will send messengers daily to keep you apprised."

"I know you will, my queen. I have total confidence in you. I trust your judgment as I do my own."

"Thank you, King Frederick. Would you like me to leave you alone now so you can consider these plans in solitude?"

"No. I am ready now. Let's go back to Palermo and start our life together."

XXX

A Dragon Comes to Sicily

Before they left for Messina, Hector brought Frederick to the docks to receive the first shipment of war supplies.

"My friends from the Teutonic Order in the Middle East wanted to help out," he said. "They are pleased to assist. No one likes Otto."

It was the first of many shipments to come from all across the world. Hector and Frederick watched while the vessel door opened and out trotted fifty of the most spectacular Arabian stallions Frederick had ever seen.

"They are the perfect warhorse," Hector said. "They are equipped to run all day in desert conditions. Running in Europe will be like a holiday for them."

The arrogance and confidence of these horses impressed Frederick. Each horse trotted off the boat with its tail high in the air, as if showing off. As they pranced off the gangplank, he noticed that not a single horse seemed rattled by the boat, the ride, or their new surroundings. Nothing spooked them.

"I can't believe how adaptable they are," Frederick said. "They just got off the ship, and they act as if they've been here their entire lives."

"They are crusader horses, or at least they fought against crusaders," noted Hector. "These horses have seen everything. They are survivors."

The last horse to depart was a black mare that towered above all the others. He walked slowly and in a very calm manner. When he reached the ground, he looked both ways, and then directly at Frederick. He snorted but kept his focus while Frederick walked toward him.

"His name is Dragon," Hector said.

Frederick brushed the horse's neck. Dragon kept his stance and stared straight ahead, as if transformed into a granite statue.

"He is for you, King Frederick," Hector said. "This is the horse you will take into battle."

Frederick looked at Hector, trying to fight off a boyish grin at his utter approval.

"Consider him your wedding gift."

"Thank you, Hector," Frederick said, still grooming Dragon with his hands. "He is a marvelous horse."

"Take care of him, King Frederick, and he will take care of you."

Over the next few weeks, Frederick's military training intensified. Hector knew this would be the most important education Frederick would receive. Frederick understood this, too, and threw himself into its theory, tactics, and swordplay.

Despite being a teenager, Frederick became a gifted student, and the more he learned, the more he questioned Pope Innocent's plan of knight organization and troop movement. He knew it was uninspired and predictable.

Otto was a seasoned veteran of combat; in fact, he was more warrior than emperor. He would anticipate this strategy before they ever reached Germany.

Because Hector was in the room and agreed to this strategy, Frederick assumed he had his support, but as the time drew closer to staging, Frederick could hold his tongue no longer.

On their morning ride, Frederick confronted Hector.

"What did you think of the pope's plan?" Frederick asked as Dragon slowly trotted. "Do you think we can expect knights to travel from the whole of Europe to Rome, only to turn around and go back to Europe to fight Otto?"

"I don't expect that would be our best plan."

Frederick sensed a slight opening and continued.

"Would it not cause undue strain on the knight and his horse to make that trip twice? That is foolish. It will take longer to stage in Rome, and then we travel on a straight path back to Germany. That defies good tactics, does it not? Otto's men will surely have intelligence on us all the way and can pick us off with mercenaries and militia until we are too weak to attack once we reach Germany . . . if we reach Germany."

Hector nodded in agreement. "That's the lesson we learned with Richard. He marched along the river toward Saladin's army, but along the way, the Saracens would flash attack with light cavalry, weakening us with every small assault."

"But King Richard's men were disciplined and a cohesive unit. There was no coverage, so there was time to prepare for sneak attacks, and the distance you traveled was shorter. We would take a collection of knights that had never fought together into a forest, and we will be unable to utilize our strengths, and blind to see an attack coming. There will be staging areas all along the way for ambush after ambush. Our force will be large and slow, the distance we travel much further. The chance of failure is far greater for us than for you and King Richard. We should consider an alternative plan."

"You want to change the pope's plan?" Hector smiled up at Frederick as if he knew he would arrive at this decision, yet equally impressed at his understanding of military tactics and history.

"Yes, I do," he said. "And your silence surprised me when we discussed this with Innocent."

"Well, young Frederick, if there is a secret strategy in the works, it's best to inform only those people that need to know. After all, we don't know who is for us or against us in the Vatican. It could be that Otto has friends inside those sacred walls. It's best not to let him know our true strategy."

Frederick smiled. "So you're thinking of alternatives already?"

"Did I ever tell you the story of Hannibal crossing the Alps?"

—ɯ—

"During the Punic Wars, the Carthaginian general Hannibal crossed the Alps in the dead of winter with elephants and an army of fifty thousand men. He surprised the Romans and won nearly every battle he fought for a decade. It was an audacious plan," Hector said, rolling out a map that charted northern Italy, southern Germany and a small part of the Mediterranean Sea. "But sometimes audacity is what's called for."

Frederick looked intently at the map while Hector continued.

"You cannot be seen as a figurehead boy king that Pope Innocent controls. If we stage this army in Rome, that's what it will appear to be, and that's what it will be."

Frederick continued studying the map.

"In order to gain the respect of the German princes and the German people, you must show them you are your own man. You must distance yourself from the pope as much as possible. There must be no appearance that they are fighting for the pope on your behalf. They must know that you came to Germany to fight for them. You aren't requesting knights to travel all the way to Rome only to turn back and march into Europe. Show them you are coming to them. Show them you are staging this campaign in Germany, and that Pope Innocent is a contributor, but not the catalyst of this war."

"And we shall cross the Alps to do so?" Frederick asked, his eyes glued to the map.

"Our plan will be the boldest the German princes have ever seen. When you arrive in Germany, they will know you are willing to risk everything for them. They will know you are their king."

"Will elephants be involved?" Frederick asked, looking up from the map with a dry grin. "Or may we just take the Aragon knights through the Alps to impress the German princes?"

"We can choose the latter. Although I have seen some spectacular, exotic animals in the forest since I've been here."

"Those were from King Roger, my grandfather. He had animals from all over the world. When he died, some of the animals escaped and were able to adapt to the environment."

"Perhaps we can do the same, King Frederick."

—⁂—

What Otto thought would be a relatively weak uprising in Germany proved to be difficult and time-consuming. His attempted attack of Sicily had served to create many more enemies than victories. It stirred up everyone in Europe, including the French, who pledged their full support to Pope Innocent. Soon the French declared war on Otto, and that brought the English—already in a territory dispute with France—as an ally to Otto. In addition, knights from all over the continent were answering the call of the pope to fight the excommunicated emperor.

Otto had miscalculated.

At the same time, Frederick was planning his arrival into Germany, determined to defeat this foe and accept the awaiting throne. Just months before, all evidence pointed to his dismal demise, and it seemed certain that Otto would either kill or capture the young king; today, he was a king, on the precipice of leading men into a continental war.

Times had changed. Fortunes were reversed. Legacies were emerging.

XXXI

Off to War

Palermo, Sicily

1212 AD

"The most important advice I can leave with you is to shut out feudalism from Sicily at all costs. Do not allow these feudal lords to split this kingdom up between themselves. Their reign of leadership almost destroyed Sicily. They wasted its resources. They allowed the docks to go to plunder and almost starved the peasant class to death. You have a basic sketch of how this kingdom should be run. Follow it, and do not take much help from the counts and barons. Let the knights oversee any dispute, and begin to create a government that can assist you in management."

Constance listened attentively while Frederick gave his instructions. Her husband had come so far in only a few months. The boy who was afraid to ride with her in a carriage was now a confident man able to wage war and run a kingdom.

"I understand what to do, my lord," she said. "I will manage this kingdom as a good queen. Then when our child is born, I can take my leave and rely on the staff I have created."

Frederick felt joy when she mentioned the baby but knew he had to put that news outside of his conscious thought. It would be tempting to get caught up in the excitement of his first child being born, but preparation for the war and the governing of Sicily had to come first for now.

"The bureaucracy Pope Innocent created at the Vatican is the only thing that impresses me about him," Frederick said. "We need that type of system in Sicily. It doubles our ability to govern and prosper."

"Yes, Frederick, I agree," she said, smiling and rubbing her stomach.

"It's been three months, and you're not even showing," he said. "I wish I could be here for the birth."

"You will be in spirit," she said warmly.

XXXII

Otto Struggles

Otto continued his siege in southern Germany against the princes that had nominated Frederick to displace him. He anticipated the assault on them would not be difficult; however, during the time he was away, the princes had fortified the greater castles to make their defenses as strong as possible. They abandoned lesser castles, and knights were sent elsewhere to aid in the upcoming war. They brought villagers of surrounding towns into the castles. This was not surrender, but a strategic move to prevent Otto's troops from pillaging food and supplies.

At each siege post, Otto's perspective gradually changed. Whereas he once saw an easy victory, he now feared a long campaign with a questionable result. Even his plan of returning to Sicily had become less promising. Frustration was beginning to set in to the equation. Instead of him leading the attack, he now saw the war coming to him. That was not his idea, and he would not sit and watch it happen.

"If we are to stay in Germany in order to put down these traitorous princes, then the war will be fought in Germany on the pope's terms," he said to his war council.

"Perhaps, Majesty, we should go south again and take down Sicily before it builds an army too great. Then we can return here and deal with the princes without the threat of other armies."

"No. We had our chance at Sicily—now we must fight here. Our troops cannot make that trip again, and if we leave, it is a certainty that France will ally with the princes and most assuredly keep us from returning on advantageous terms."

"Emperor, England will keep King Philip occupied—"

"King John will run home at the first sign of danger," Otto yelled. "Do not rely on England until General Longsword is in full command. King John has no stomach for conflict."

"Emperor, we are all in agreement that if the boy king were dead, Pope Innocent and the German princes would be forced to negotiate an outcome and keep you on the throne," a top strategist said. "Why not use the cities, militias, and mercenaries we paid tributes to on our way to Sicily to lay in wait for Frederick during his journey to Germany? Surely, the trail will not be hard to find."

Otto pondered this for a moment before speaking.

"This isn't something an emperor considers against a king. No, this would have to be done outside an emperor's knowledge; instead, this plan would have to be done by a strategist using back channels to organize militias and mercenaries along the trail. One would expect that not only the boy king would be a target, but also a plan to thin out the knight population along the way. Meanwhile, an emperor would continue the siege while this other activity was carried out."

XXXIII

A Change in Plans

F rederick, Hector, and the knights of Aragon left Palermo early one morning for Rome. There, they would connect with Pope Innocent and the knights he had recruited.

However, after arriving at Messina, the plan changed.

A fleet of ships captained by Henry of Malta met Frederick at the docks.

"King Frederick, the boy king of Jesi. You look just like Barbarossa," Henry said. "It's embarrassing that I cannot offer you a better transport than my modest fishing boats, but we will be honored to take you and your knights to any location you request."

"From what I've heard, your modest fleet of fishing boats could fill the Mediterranean Sea. Your fishing boats control the western seaboard of Italy."

"Oh, young king, you pay me a great tribute, but a tribute not earned. I am but a lowly fisherman. In fact, my friends call me 'Henry the Fisherman.'"

"We appreciate your generosity, Count Henry. It is a generosity that will not be forgotten."

"Generosity?" Hector said sarcastically. "You have no idea. The price this man charged King Richard to sail his troops to Sicily was staggering. I think Richard had to work on the docks just to pay him off."

"Richard wasn't on his way to save Italy, old friend. Besides, he had more gold than I had ever seen in my life. I had to take some of it by land or risk sinking my ships."

Frederick laughed, along with Hector and many of Henry's men.

"So have we decided on a destination, King Frederick?"

"It shall be given once we are at sea."

"I would love to see the look on Innocent's face when he realizes you have a new plan."

"We sent a messenger to the pope," Frederick said. "He will know what he needs to know soon enough."

"Very good, Your Grace," Henry said. "I love a good mystery."

The fleet landed at a secret port just outside the city of Genoa.

"We only used these docks in our privateering days when your father was king," Henry said.

"You mean your pirating days," Hector joked.

"When you do it on behalf of a king, it's privateering," said Henry.

Frederick spent several days on the outskirts of Genoa, organizing the evolving plan. He knew he could not be invisible the entire journey, but the idea to bypass Rome had cut the trek to Germany in half, and that was the half in which mercenaries or militias—either paid by or sympathetic to Otto—would have ambushed him.

There were many knights on their way to Rome who stopped in Genoa. Frederick was able to collect them and increase his troop size in the process. By the time he was ready to leave, the knights at his disposal had more than doubled.

While the move to cross the Alps was dynamic and unexpected, it was not without its own peril. The terrain was treacherous, and even in early summer the weather was inconsistent, rainy, sometimes cold and sometimes hot. And these changes could occur all within a few hours.

"At least we don't have war elephants and it isn't snowing," Hector said.

Frederick had no other option but to choose a zigzagging route through the mountains. Even in the Alps, there were towns known to favor Otto; so, Frederick had to keep his trail a secret for as long as possible.

The route was unknown from day to day, always temporary, reducing the opportunity for someone to track them. Even the knights were left in the dark. Each evening, Frederick and Hector drew a new map for the following day's march.

Essentially, they started on a conventional path, going northward until they reached the town of Asti, where Frederick split up his knights into two groups—the Aragon knights were one group, and the knights that met up with him in Genoa were the other. The first group was to go north for a day, then east. Frederick's group would go east for a day, and then north until the two met up again in the small town of Mantua.

The plan was risky, exposing Frederick with only half the knights at his disposal in case of attack. It also gave spies twice the chance to see Frederick or the other force.

However, Frederick also knew a large force would be slow and much easier to spot and attack than two smaller units. Dividing into two parts ensured a faster trip through the Alps, at least the most precarious part. And even if one or both groups were spotted, observers would misinterpret troop sizes and risk appearing inconsistent, reporting locations in different parts of the Alps. Confusing intelligence would be quickly discarded. By the time the deception was understood, they would be one united force, ready to attack.

The next day's march ended in the little town of Pavia. Frederick had been in the Alps now for several days without incident. By now, it was likely that most of Otto's Alpine allies were aware of Frederick's presence, just not his exact location.

"I hope our knights to the north are faring well," he said to Hector.

"Most of those knights are seasoned veterans of conflict," Hector said. "Don't worry about them. Stay in the moment here with us."

Frederick thought about that, but then he pushed back on Hector's assertion.

"But shouldn't a leader be concerned with more than just the moment he is in?"

"A leader has to be concerned with both, but at different times. When we are in the Alps with potential peril at every turn, you are a soldier, and a soldier has to stay in the moment or risk being killed. Tonight, when we are planning for the next day's march, you can concern yourself with the future."

XXXIV

The Battle of the Lambro River

On their way to Cremona, Frederick and his knights stopped by the banks of the Lambro River for a brief rest. Frederick tried not to show his fatigue to Hector or the other knights, but the march was exhausting to him. Silently, he wondered about the other group, but he did not want to seem unfocused. He dipped his wooden cup into the water for a drink.

Suddenly, an arrow flew over his head and stuck in the riverbed, then another, landing short in the water.

"Frederick, over here!" Hector yelled, pointing to a quickly formed rallying point for the surprised knights. Frederick struggled up the bank and made it to the knights, pulling his sword out of the saddle holster just as the Milanese soldiers approached.

Steel crashed into steel as the raiders rode into the camp before most of the knights could mount. Frederick watched for just a few seconds as his first battle began to unfold. The speed of this attack reminded him of the conflict he witnessed as a boy, then his mind moved back to the moment at hand.

Hector got on his horse and cut through an attacker's rusty chainmail with one swing of his sword. The horse fell near Dragon, who spooked and ran toward the river.

"Get on your horse, Frederick," Hector said, cutting into another rider's chest with a powerful blow.

Frederick chased Dragon toward the river and was able to mount just as a rider approached, his sword high above his head and poised to strike. Frederick was able to block the rider's blow with his sword; the contact radiated through his body. He rode past Frederick and attempted to turn back until an Aragon knight caught up to him and ran his sword through the Milanese soldier's chest. The rider fell to the ground beneath Frederick, who remained fixated on the dying man until Dragon galloped uncontrollably into the river.

After having gained control of Dragon, Frederick turned the horse to face the fight. He heard yelling from the other side of the river and heard men telling him to cross it; however, Frederick ignored them and rode out of the riverbed.

"Go across, Frederick!" Hector screamed. "They are militia from Cremona here to protect you."

Before Frederick could protest, Hector clashed swords with another rider.

"Go now!" he yelled.

Frederick rode down the riverbed and into the river, crossing the shallow waters to the other side. He turned to see the battle while he and the militia retreated toward town. He watched the battle as long as he could but was unable to determine if his men were winning or losing.

The militia brought Frederick into town and stayed with him at an inn. Typically, they had camped just outside of towns and villages, but there was no point in being covert. Everyone in Cremona knew what had happened.

"It doesn't look too bad," the surgeon said as he examined the small wound on Frederick's arm. "I'll just clean and bandage it."

"Just forget about it," Frederick said. "It's nothing."

"Let me just clean and bandage it, Your Grace," the surgeon urged. "Tell me about the ambush. How many attacked your knights?"

"I don't know. There were a lot of riders, but I could not estimate a count."

"Of course not. You were in the battle, and it was a sneak attack; no time to count troops. I just meant that in the broadest of terms—were you outnumbered?"

"The moment the arrows flew at me, my mind went into some sort of defensive perception. Nothing about it seemed real. I went through the motions, but it felt like I was acting out the battle instead of fighting in it. The only time it felt real was when my sword clashed with another rider's sword."

"Was this your first battle, King Frederick?"

"It was, and my first instinct was to ride off the battlefield."

"Sometimes that is the best move a king can make, my lord. You have experienced knights to fight battles. You are too valuable a target to remain in the fight."

—⁓—

Hours went by while Frederick waited for his knights to return. He knew it was wrong to leave the battle and wondered if he was ready to lead men after such a bad initial performance.

"Is there any news?" Frederick asked a militiaman who entered the inn.

"Nothing to report, my lord."

Frederick stared into his cup. The last glimpse he saw before riding away looked as if the knights had reorganized their center and mounted, but there wasn't enough information to know the outcome. There was no way to know the size of the militia that attacked. He was forced to wait in his guilt.

If this were Otto's army, the war would be over, he thought. *Maybe it is over. Maybe the militia destroyed my knights before we got out of Italy. Or perhaps they lost too much confidence in me this day and went back to their homes in Aragon and all over Europe. What would Constance think of me? What would my father have thought?*

It was the first time Frederick had recollected Henry in some time. He wished Henry, his mother, or Philip was still alive.

Before Frederick could ponder anything else, several horses were heard approaching the inn. Frederick bolted from his chair and through the door. Two knights dismounted, heading for Frederick.

"The battle is won, my lord," one of the knights said, blood saturating his uniform.

"Is everyone all right?" Frederick asked.

The second knight looked puzzled at Frederick's comment. He looked at the other knight before speaking.

"The enemy is destroyed, and the battlefield is ours."

Frederick knew that asking if everyone in the battle was all right sounded inexperienced. He wanted to amend his comment but could see the knights were struggling with their wounds. He let the matter pass.

"Where are Hector and the other knights?"

"They chased the retreating militia back toward Milan, Your Grace," said the first knight. "We could not keep their pace and instead rode here.

"Am I to wait longer for the outcome?"

"No, Majesty. The battle was won. The knights will return presently."

Neither Frederick nor the knights seemed to understand the other's meaning.

Frederick led the knights into the inn and had the physician tend to their wounds. Every hour or so, another small group of knights would return with little or no additional news. Finally, a larger force rode into town just as the sun began to rise, with Hector leading the way.

"What took you so long, Hector?" Frederick asked.

"We chased the militia halfway back to Milan before we caught them," Hector said, dismounting his horse.

"A real bed, boys!" he yelled at the knights. "No sleeping on the ground tonight."

The knights cheered and followed behind him. Frederick followed Hector inside the inn.

"The night is over. Why did you chase a retreating militia?"

"We chased 'em to teach 'em a lesson. You don't ambush knights and live to tell the tale."

The group of knights cheered Hector as he made his speech.

"You risk the knights to teach a Milanese militia a lesson? Our fight is not with Milan; it's with Otto. And if we lose knights in the Alps, we risk losing the war before we get to Germany."

"It was an insult to be attacked by a militia," said one of the knights. "An insult must not go unanswered."

Frederick looked angry, and the knights stopped cheering. Silence fell over the inn. Hector turned to face him.

"Walk with me, Frederick," said Hector. "Let's see about the horses."

They walked in silence back to the stable. Frederick began to speak, but Hector interrupted him; it was the first time in memory he had ever done that.

"The lesson was not for the Milanese; it was for the next militia or mercenaries that Otto pits against us. It was a warning to them that experienced knights are here to protect you, and if they attack, the price to pay will be extreme."

Frederick accepted Hector's appraisal.

"Why did you tell me to leave the battlefield? And why did I comply so easily? Was I scared? Did you sense fear in me?"

"'Twas prudent you leave. The militia's only goal was to kill you. Once you crossed the river, they had already failed."

"But I was all too willing to cross. I should be there to lead my knights on the battlefield. It was wrong to leave."

"That was no battlefield. That was an ambush, an attempted assassination. You saved knights' lives by crossing."

"It felt more like I was saving my own life."

Hector reviewed each horse in the stable while the two of them spoke. He arrived at Dragon's paddock and stopped.

"You did not put this horse away wet, did you?"

"No, I washed and dried him before they put him in the stall," Frederick said, puzzled at the question.

"Well, I think the river washed him pretty well, don't you think? I did not know Dragon could swim. That's quite a talented horse you got there, King Frederick."

Frederick smiled. "How many men did we lose?"

"Several were injured, but none died."

"I'm glad to hear that."

"It won't always be that way. We will lose men on this journey, and in the coming war. But these men know that. You should start working on getting into a place in your mind where you can accept this. You will lead men into battle, and some will die."

Frederick looked up at him. "I know, Hector."

"Your instincts were good today. You will lead your men on the battlefield one day soon, Frederick."

"You mean yesterday, Hector. You and your knights rode all night."

"So we did," Hector said, looking up at the sun as it began to rise over the tree line. "Today, we rest. Tomorrow, we will meet the other knights in Mantua."

Instead of sleeping, Frederick took this time in Cambria to write Constance. His thoughts were never far from her . . .

My Dearest Constance,

We are now in the middle of the Alps journey. I cannot disclose where we are going, but I can say that we reached Cambria safely, despite an ambush at the Lambro River by a Milanese militia.

I did not respond well to the fighting. Hector told me to cross the river during the ambush, and I gladly went across. It concerns me that I left the fighting, but Hector said it was for the best. Still, a leader shouldn't leave the fighting. There will be more skirmishes, battles, and ambushes. I pray that I react better in the future.

Please write me soon, my darling, with stories of your pregnancy, Sicily, and any trouble you are having with the aristocracy of our kingdom. I miss you greatly.

With sincere love,
Frederick

"You're late!" one of the knights yelled at Hector as they approached the town. "We've been waiting here for almost a day."

"The mighty Milanese militia detained us for a wee bit o' time on the Lambro River," Hector said.

"Yes, we heard. The news made it all the way to Mantua. It's all they're talking about in the town square and taverns. We, on the other hand, ran a disciplined march and saw no action whatsoever. I think your rout of the Milanese ruined it for us."

"Sorry to steal the glory," Hector said.

"The glory of beating a ragtag bunch of Milanese militia? You may have that glory, Hector."

"I would have gladly traded it for a good night's sleep."

A messenger rode to where Frederick and Hector were mounted.

"We are certain Emperor Otto has gotten word of our movement and has concentrated all of his forces in Merano, my lord. It's a small town a day's march up the road from here."

"That town favors Otto," Frederick said.

"Yes, and now it favors him all the more," Hector said.

"We should confront them now that we're at full strength," Frederick said.

Hector said nothing. The knights cheered at the prospect of a battle.

Halfway down the road, Frederick was growing indecisive. His instinct was to go head first into this town and prove his leadership in a full-blown battle. But was this a wise decision?

Hector was unusually quiet the entire morning, choosing to ride further down in the ranks. At about the third-quarter mark of the journey, he emerged next to Frederick.

"Today's a good day for a battle, isn't it?"

"I suppose it is, Hector."

"Is something on your mind, King Frederick?"

"I question the merits of this action. Is this another lesson to teach the militias?"

"No, it's not. We know they wait for us. It's an honorable conflict; no lesson to be given. It's just an army in the way of another army's progress."

"But our progress involves making it to Germany, not defeating a collective army of northern Italians."

"I have no rebuttal to that."

They rode together a little further and slowed to a walk from a trot.

"Then what do you recommend?"

"I suggest you offer up an alternative plan before we reach Merano."

Frederick slowed the walk until Dragon impatiently stopped, side-stepping in a circle until Frederick gained control.

"We can go west into the Engadin region. Surely, we would meet no resistance on that trail."

Another knight moving up caught wind of Frederick's comment.

"The Engadin is brutal," he said. I took it on the way down and swore I would never take that cursed trail again."

"Whatever they have planned for us in Merano cannot be as bad as that trail," said another knight.

"We will prevail, King Frederick," said a third knight, and then several others agreed and cheered their approval.

"I have no doubt we would prevail," Frederick said, confidently and with authority. "But our fight is not there. Our fight is with Otto, and he is not at the end of this road. Only a costly, time-consuming distraction awaits us there."

As the murmurs and groans grew, Frederick turned to look at the group.

"When I risk my knights in a battle, it will be against Otto and his knights, not against a collection of militias in a town we don't need. Our fight is in Germany, not Merano."

The knights seemed to understand this logic. The groans and complaints died down.

XXXV

The Engadin Region

The Engadin Region was indeed a treacherous path through the most difficult part of the Alps. No wonder many armies were willing to engage in battle before traveling this route. The roads were rocky and treacherous, intermittently ending and dropping hundreds of feet with little notice. Dismounting and remounting, riders walked the many stretches where horses could not be ridden. The weather compounded the problem. Winter was impassable, but even in the summer it was unpredictable. One moment the temperatures soared, draining the remaining power from the travelers; then the heat turned to frigid cold in a matter of hours, aided by gale-force winds, torrential downpours, or constant rain. Any traveler taking this path must battle multiple foes of terrain, climate, and fatigue.

One afternoon, the rain was constant, turning the meager soil between the rocks to mud. The knights struggled with their footing, slipping on the rocks and through the waterlogged dirt. They were too strong-willed to complain aloud, but Frederick could see the discontent on their faces. He knew of their desire to fight a human foe far before this natural one; instead, they sidestepped the battle waiting for them. He knew with each slippery step that they probably wondered if this was the right choice. Knights were there to fight, not climb mountains.

For long stretches, Frederick's army trudged up and down the slopes in silence. They wove single file until the road widened, then they walked in pairs. During one short respite, the knight who had warned of this treacherous path stood beside Frederick.

"The road is worse than I have ever seen it."

"Yes, it is a challenge far beyond what we anticipated, but it is nothing we cannot conquer."

"I am ready to wage war on any foe, Your Grace, but it has been days and we have several yet to go."

With that short interchange, Frederick understood his next challenge. This was an unknown battlefield for most of these knights. But here, he would resurrect his leadership one slippery step at a time. He silently pondered the task at hand, turning this collection of soldiers into one cohesive army. He had taken this path to avoid a danger but soon found it was the better path to their success, albeit on worse footing.

At the next wide part of the path, raising his voice, he commanded, "Stop. We will take a rest." The men all sat together, falling to the ground in near exhaustion and exasperation.

"We have been traveling this road for days. We have done well, despite the weather and terrain. However, rough road is ahead. The road is wide enough in parts. Walk side by side, in pairs, and lean on each other. Helping each other will double our strength."

Hector watched in silence, knowing this road was more than a diversionary tactic from the militia; it was also an opportunity for Frederick to gain credibility in the minds of the knights. They needed to see him as the leader.

After a much-needed rest, the party moved on, pleased that the rain had momentarily stopped. Struggling to balance, one knight reached out, oblivious to whom was at his right. "Lean on me," Frederick commanded. Together they plowed ahead, inching up and down the slopes, gaining speed in their teams. Little by little, over the course of the next few days, the army leaned on one another, literally and figuratively. One knight would slip, and another would stabilize him. One knight would fall to his knees, and another would help him up. Amidst them was their king, helping and encouraging.

For many grueling days, Frederick and the knights persisted, determined to succeed in this battle against the elements. They entered the Engadin region as a group of independent knights, but the rigors of this road had melded them in their mission. They left the Alps as a cohesive unit ready to fight together in war.

XXXVI

A Brother

With the memory of the Engadin region now behind them, Frederick and his knights crossed the final foothills of the Alps into Switzerland. He called for a day of rest before they continued toward the German city of Constance.

As the day progressed, the Swiss abbey monks began spreading the word of his arrival. By nightfall, three hundred knights had been added to Frederick's group.

"The bishop of Chur begs a meeting with you this evening before your departure, King Frederick," said a messenger riding into camp.

"Tell the bishop it is granted."

"'Tis quite a colorful fella, the bishop," Hector said with a reflective smile. "I look forward to his arrival."

"How do you know him?"

"He aided us in our crusade. We traveled through this region on our way to Sicily, and he was there with additional knights. No one ever spoke to King Richard in the way he did. He treated him like an old friend and rarely called him 'king,' that usually drove Richard to violence, but he seemed to welcome the drop in title when it was the bishop. I look forward to seeing him again. The warrior monk!"

Later that night, a shadow-like group of people emerged from out of the mist, as if from nowhere. They were not knights or militia looking to join the cause; their cause was just beginning, and their journey was in the opposite direction.

At first, the knights on the camp's perimeter discouraged the group from staying; however, their leader, a young man named Nicholas, was able to persuade them to seek permission from King Frederick to stay the night before their journey into the Alps. Nicholas confidently advanced along with the knights to meet King Frederick. Frederick looked up at the tattered, dirty, skinny young man. He reminded him of what he looked like not so long ago. He stood up from the campfire to greet the boy.

"My lord, I request my crusaders be allowed to stay in your camp this night before our journey into the Alps."

"Crusaders?" Frederick said, puzzled.

"Yes, my lord. We are a group of children, common men, and women who have heard the call from God to retake Jerusalem. We answer that call."

Several of the knights laughed at the prospect. Frederick looked over at Hector and stood up.

"Let's go see your crusaders. Where are they now?"

"They are at the front of your camp."

The two walked together through the camp, with knights alongside.

"What is your name?"

"Nicholas, my lord."

"And I am King Frederick."

Nicholas walked along, saying nothing for a moment, and then looked Frederick in the eye. "What are you king of?"

"Sicily," Frederick said, smiling at Nicholas's innocence. "But soon I will be king of the Germans."

"You're the boy king—"

"I'm not a boy anymore."

"No, my lord, I meant no disrespect, but that is what you are called in Cologne, where I am from."

"What is happening in Cologne? Do they favor the princes, or do they favor Otto?"

"Cologne is split. Some stand with the princes, and some stand with Otto. The knights that favor Otto left to march south with him before we started our crusade on the Rhine River."

"Otto is moving south?" Frederick asked.

"That was the word the knights received, my lord," said one if the knights nearby.

"And how is it you know of the knights' military movement, Nicholas?"

"My lord, they had a parade when they left town to fight alongside Emperor Otto. Everyone in Cologne was aware of their plans."

"I guess they didn't expect anyone in Cologne to reach you sooner than they did, King Frederick," said one of the knights.

"Can you go and tell Hector of this news?" Frederick asked of the knight.

"Yes, King Frederick."

"I will be back presently," he said to the knight, then turned to Nicholas. "Now let's see your people, Nicholas."

"Yes, my lord."

Frederick followed Nicholas into the midst of his group. All of them looked frail, unwashed, and hungry. He saw no security threat from them, despite his doubt that they were truly on crusade.

"How did you get here from Cologne?"

"We took boats down the Rhine, collecting new crusaders along the way. We fished for food until we started walking toward the Alps. We haven't eaten since we got off the boat."

"You may enter this camp, Nicholas—all of you are our guests tonight."

"Thank you, my lord."

"I should like to talk with you again later. Would that be possible?"

"It would be possible, my lord."

"One last question, Nicholas: you said Cologne was a split town as far as allegiance goes. Whose side were you on?"

"I am on God's side, my lord."

Frederick smiled at his honest, yet spectacular answer. His guess was that the peasant class had no favorites in such matters.

"Help yourself to any food or drink you see," Frederick said. "We will talk again soon."

—⚉—

The bishop of Chur was a round man with bright red cheeks and a bowl haircut that was the fashion of the stylish medieval monk. He rode a small donkey into Frederick's camp that looked as if its little legs might be forced into the ground by the weight of the rider.

"What did that donkey do that you punish it so, bishop!" Hector joked to his old friend.

"Careful, Hector, or I will ride you back to Chur."

The two men embraced and briefly caught up on old times.

"Is this the boy king I have heard so much about?" he asked Hector, looking at Frederick.

"Yes, bishop, may I present King Frederick of Sicily."

Frederick extended his hand, but the bishop moved past it and hugged Frederick as though he meant to push the air out of his lungs.

"I knew your dad and granddad, Frederick. You are already like family to this poor priest."

"A poor priest who owns half the land and most of the horses in the Chur region," Hector said.

"Hector, when you are a priest, they call it stewardship. I don't own anything," he said, looking back at Frederick. "I am a penniless priest ready for God to take me home."

"Well, not just yet, Bishop. I believe you have something for us."

"Yes, I do."

He walked back to his donkey and took out a large parchment from the saddlebag and returned to Frederick.

"This is a bull of excommunication, my son. Hopefully you'll never see another, but this one will help you. It will be your key to the town of Constance."

Frederick looked at Hector for clarification. Hector turned and looked at the bishop. Frederick did the same.

"This document is from Pope Innocent. It's his official excommunication of Emperor Otto from the church. This document deems Otto an outlaw of anyone associated with the church. Present this bull of excommunication at the gates of Constance, and they will let you in."

"They wouldn't allow me entry otherwise?"

"And that's the second reason I'm here. At this moment, Emperor Otto is marching an army south to Constance in expectation of your arrival there. You would do well to muster this army tomorrow morning and beat Otto to Constance. Show them this document, and they should favor you over Otto."

"I thought southern Germany favored the princes? Is my entry into Constance in doubt?"

"It shouldn't be if you show the bull to the bishop of Constance, and, of course, if you get there before Otto."

"Nicholas was right about the knights of Cologne," Frederick said.

"Who is Nicholas?" asked the bishop.

"He's a young man about Frederick's age who has led a band of destitute men, women, and children from the Rhine River area on a crusade. They camp with us now," Hector said.

The bishop shrugged. "That's how bad conditions have become since Otto was crowned emperor. Now if a priest preaches crusade, the peasant class and children are persuaded because the prospects of staying in their villages is so grim, they prefer a doomed journey and a falsely promised entry into heaven than the current life they lead. This is why your campaign is so important, Frederick. Not just for the princes of Germany, but for the peasants and children of Germany, too."

"So you are familiar with this crusading phenomenon, Bishop?" Frederick asked.

"Yes, I am. What you have in your camp is called the Children's Crusade. Nicholas is not alone in this call. A French shepherd named Stephen has started a crusade as well composed of all children and peasants. You must turn these poor people back. Their mission is doomed to failure and will likely result in death for all of them."

"I will be speaking to Nicholas later this evening. Pray that I might convince him to turn back, as I, too, agree with you, Bishop."

"I will pray for you, my son, and I will pray for your mission as well. Now, I must take my leave."

"Thank you for your visit, and for your counsel," Frederick said.

"You are welcome, my son. I have one more thing for you in my saddlebag. It's a letter from your beautiful wife Constance."

He reached into the bag and handed the letter to Frederick.

Hector and the bishop embraced and slapped each other on the back. Neither said a word, but all was understood. The bishop mounted the overmatched donkey and rode off.

Frederick returned to the quiet solitude of his tent where he read Constance's letter.

My dearest Frederick,

I hope this letter finds you in good health and through the Alps and into friendly lands. I sent this letter to the Bishop of Chur. He is a family friend from years ago. I hope you get to meet him. You will like him.

All is well in Sicily. The nobles wait to hear word of your progress before they take any actions for or against the crown. They have not posed a problem for me to effectively act as regent.

I love pregnancy, Frederick. I wish you could be here for the birth, but all is going along well. I pray for your safety and hope to hear from you soon.

My sincere love,
Constance

—ɯ—

Frederick returned to the middle of his camp to find a few of the "crusaders" at each of the campfires. The knights had taken in the children and peasants for the evening; Nicholas, however, was harder to locate.

"He was here earlier, Your Grace," said one of the knights. "He was the one who set us up with this bunch."

Frederick focused on the ragtag group at the fire, the target of the knight's humor. Together, the knights and these poor souls bonded quickly. Campfire after campfire, Frederick found the same result.

Nicholas had been there first, depositing a few of his followers with knights. All the knights welcomed them gladly and with charity and warmth. No wonder the two groups were getting along so well. The knights were splendid hosts with their unexpected guests. This surprised Frederick. He had never seen his knights like this. This was a group of men on a violent mission taking time to show kindness to strangers in their camp. Could Nicholas be the reason?

Frederick finally caught up to Nicholas at the very last tent. He was mending the injured foot of a peasant old enough to be his grandfather, and an Aragon knight assisted Nicholas with the first aid. Frederick watched in awe.

"A word, Nicholas," Frederick said.

"Yes, my lord," Nicholas said without looking up. "I will be there presently."

"Very well, Nicholas," Frederick said. "I shall await you in my tent."

Another knight walked up to Frederick, watching Nicholas bandage the old man.

"I see why they follow him, even on such a fool's errand. He is the most caring, charismatic leader I have ever seen." He looked at Frederick and quickly revised his observation. "Well, except for you, my lord."

Frederick laughed. "No need for clarification. I see what you see."

The knight continued. "He warms the hearts of men, women, children, and even knights. His eyes see no class structure—to him, all are royalty. He is a natural leader because he sincerely cares for all in his custody."

Frederick paused, astonished at his appraisal of Nicholas. "Is it possible that he is more than just an impressionable, young peasant fleeing the desperation of Cologne?" he asked rhetorically.

"Ready, my lord," Nicholas said as he stepped next to Frederick.

Together, they walked into Frederick's royal tent. He watched as Nicholas looked inside with awe. For a royal tent, it was not very ornate, but Nicholas had never seen furniture, carpeting, bedding, and linens in a tent before.

"The tent makers say they are descendants of the Apostle Paul's family in the Middle East. I'm not sure that's true, but they do make a quality tent unlike any you can find in Europe."

"It is amazing, Your Grace."

"You seem to have brought our two groups together," Frederick said. "What is your secret?"

Nicholas paused, still in awe of everything within his view.

"There is no secret, my lord. The knights have taken a vow to help and protect those in need, and as you can quickly see, my flock is good people in need. It was only natural the knights would want to help them."

"Would you like a drink, Nicholas?" Frederick asked, reaching for a flask of wine.

"Water, my lord, if I may trouble you for a cup."

Frederick called for his servant, directing him to fetch a wooden pitcher of water. He nonchalantly set aside the goblet of wine he had poured.

"They are your flock?"

"Yes, my lord. Each and every one who chooses to follow me on this crusade for God is a part of my flock, and it's my responsibility to look after them. I am their shepherd."

"I hear there is a shepherd from France named Stephen that is crusading in the same way as you."

"Yes, my lord. I pray for him every night. I pray that we will one day meet and he will join in our crusade for God. I pray it with all of my heart."

"You call this a crusade for God, but is this truly God's will, or is this the will of your priest in Cologne? I hear he is adamant in his sermons for crusade."

"God speaks through the priest, my lord."

"Nicholas, sometimes the priests speak on behalf of the pope, and sometimes the pope has more political messages to send than a message from God."

"I don't follow, my lord."

"The priests are preaching crusade for the knights. They want the knights, who fight for Otto, to fight against the Saracens in the Middle East. It is a diversionary tactic to remove knights from Otto's army. The message was not meant for peasants and children. No, this is a political message, not a holy one. It is merely delivered by your priest, Nicholas, but it comes directly from Pope Innocent."

Nicholas paused at the firm words, pondering the implications, hesitating before speaking. After a moment, he sipped from the cup, looked straight at Frederick, and spoke.

"I do not doubt that matters go on in this world that I do not understand. I do not dispute that a priest may have spoken to an audience that did not hear. But there was another audience, my lord that heard God's words in that sermon. I heard God's message. Children heard His call. There is no doubt in my mind that the priest was God's messenger on that day. He was a messenger for the outcast of Cologne and the Rhine River Valley. We were starving and dying. We are looked at as a waste of resources. We do no good there, my lord. Useless, overlooked, and even despised. But now we are on a crusade for God, and we are doing His will. We have meaning, and we have a heavenly purpose. There is no doubt in my mind this is God's message, sent to me. I am to lead this flock to the end of this journey. God has willed this of me."

His clear sense of purpose impressed Frederick. His complete confidence in what God had intended him to do was exactly how Francis would have behaved if put in this situation. No matter how misguided it seemed to rational men of the world, his rationale didn't seem to come from this world.

Frederick also knew, however, that Nicholas was a young, inexperienced leader with peasants and children following him. He had no advisers and no protection. He had no supply lines and no real expectation to feed his flock with any consistency. Frederick knew he had to stop this crusade before they went any further. This was not Francis building a church, but a misguided band of peasants and children headed for their demise. He could not allow that.

"Nicholas, you have to trust me. I know the land you are about to cross. There isn't enough food or water for your flock to make it into a town, and it's unlikely the town would welcome you if you did. You will surely perish in these mountains."

Nicholas began to speak, but Frederick continued.

"And if by some miracle you survive the Alps, no one will take you to the Middle East without payment. You have no way to pay for passage."

"God will provide for us, my lord," Nicholas argued, refusing to accept the words of Frederick. "Look at how far we have come already. And look how many have chosen to follow us from other towns as we went down the Rhine—and just as it seemed certain we would starve, your camp appeared out of the mist, as if by miracle. No, my lord, God will provide for those strong of faith."

Frederick shrugged his shoulders, grabbed the pitcher, and filled Nicholas's with water.

"And if you were to make it to Jerusalem, what is your plan against the Saracens?" Frederick asked.

"We shall preach the word of God to them, my lord, and convince them of the strength of our God."

"The Saracens will massacre you and your flock if you try to convert them to Christianity. It is a crime to do so in the Middle East."

"It won't be me converting them; it will be God, my lord. I will only convince them of His greatness."

Frederick could see that worldly logic was pointless; this was a crusade of faith for Nicholas.

"I pray that your journey is not as perilous as what I foresee. But I fear you and your followers are doomed."

"They are not my followers, Your Grace. They are followers of Jesus, and many wise men in Cologne believe that your journey is just as perilous and just as doomed, but this has not stopped you either."

"The circumstances are very different, Nicholas."

"My lord, you have your journey in this life, and I have mine. I do not understand the politics of this land. I only know which direction God is leading me. God points me to the Alps and beyond; He points you at an emperor in his homeland and tells you to defeat him. Despite the peril, here you are in Germany obeying His will. You, too, are doing God's will. You have no idea how badly the people of Germany need you to fulfill this mission. I will pray for you, too, King Frederick, with all of my heart."

"Did your parents try to talk you out of this crusade, Nicholas?"

"I am an orphan, my lord. My parents died when I was very young."

"Mine too."

"But God was with us both, my lord. How else would we have made it this far?"

Frederick and Nicholas talked the rest of the night, and Frederick eventually stopped his attempt to convince the steadfast Nicholas to stop his crusade. In the morning, he gave Nicholas a letter before their mutual departure.

"If you reach Genoa, ask for Henry the fisherman. He isn't really a fisherman; he is the count of Malta, and he commands many ships departing Genoa and all of the ports of northern Italy. He is our friend. Give him this letter, and he will secure you safe passage to Sicily. Once you are in Sicily, my wife, Queen Constance, can take care of your people until you find a way to Jerusalem. Or perhaps you will find Sicily to your liking."

Nicholas looked at the letter of introduction written by Frederick. "You are married, my lord?"

"Yes, and by the time you reach Sicily, I will likely be a father."

"It will be an honor to meet your wife and child when I reach Sicily. My flock and I thank you and the knights for all of your kindness and hospitality."

"Good-bye, Nicholas. God be with you."

Frederick watched while the crusaders gathered their things and took their leave into the Alps, chanting a German prayer in unison.

"Time to go, King Frederick," Hector said. "We have a long ride ahead, and we must make it at cantering speed."

"Call the men to horses, Hector. I will be ready to ride presently."

"You couldn't talk him out of it?"

"No," Frederick said, mounting Dragon.

"But you did become close to him, didn't you?"

Frederick pulled the reins, and Dragon turned to face Hector.

"He is my brother."

XXXVII

The Race to Constance

"The word from Milan is that King Frederick has cut an inconsistent path through the Alps toward Switzerland, Emperor Otto," a messenger from Italy reported.

"It was smart for him to bypass the main roads," Otto said. He cut off a chunk of his apple with a knife much too large for the task. "But there are dangers in crossing the Alps, too."

Otto sat back down with the dispatch, looking at his top military advisor.

"How many knights do we have in camp?"

"There are over two thousand knights and one thousand infantry, Emperor."

Otto looked at the messenger. "And how many knights does the boy king bring with him?"

"The dispatch does not say, Emperor."

"I know what the dispatch says. I'm asking what you saw."

"I was not at the battle," he said meekly.

"Milan sent me a dispatch from a messenger boy who wasn't even a witness? Where were you, boy, when the men of Milan were fighting my enemy?"

Before the messenger could speak, the advisor interrupted in order to answer Otto's original question.

"His knights total —two hundred fifty to one thousand."

"Why such a wide range of troop size? Are the reports guessing at his numbers?"

"We cannot account for losses at the Lambro River attack, and there may or may not be an additional collection of knights riding independently of Frederick."

Otto laughed with contempt at the report.

"This is quite an operation our Italian allies are running. First, we have an infant messenger who was not a combatant, or even a witness of the news he dispatches. Now you receive intelligence of a phantom band of knights riding all over the Alps. At this moment, after several reports, we know nothing. I wonder sometimes whom these Italian Lombards truly favor—themselves, I suspect."

"We know King Frederick is avoiding our mercenaries by going through the Alps, and we know that will take longer," the advisor said.

"So what? So, they will get here a little later, but they will get here unscathed."

"Perhaps there is an opportunity if Frederick struggles in the Alps."

Otto looked up from the dispatch. "What are you saying? Are you suggesting we go with what we have in camp? Meet the boy king somewhere in southern Germany?"

"All reports indicate we would have the superior numbers, the better knights, and the element of surprise if we ride swiftly. We also choose the ground we fight them on."

The messenger, clearly uncomfortable, shifted his stance, which alerted Otto.

"Get this boy out of my sight!" Otto screamed, and the messenger quickly left the room. "Get on your horse and ride back to Italy, you coward!" he screamed out the window while the messenger ran for his mount.

Otto turned his attention back to his advisor. "I don't care about ground. I don't care about numbers. We will fight the boy king and his tutor where we see them. If we find them in open land, we will slaughter them where they stand, but it's more important not to allow them entry into a walled town. The only way that pitiful army can survive is if they gain protection and hide behind walls. Is there one near their exit region from the Alps?"

"The town of Constance," the advisor said, looking at a map.

Otto slammed the tip of his knife into Constance on the map.

"Then we shall ride to Constance and end this war before it begins. After that, we will deal with these treasonous princes in the south."

—ᴍ—

While both armies rode hard toward Constance, it became clear that the entire outcome depended on this race, at least for Frederick. No dispatches, intelligence, or sneak attacks would make any difference.

Otto's men were experienced warriors, but somewhat undisciplined riders. Their long and narrow lines of cavalry slowed their progress. They made better time than Frederick did, but they had more ground to make up and had to avoid territories and towns that favored the princes that might be lying in wait. Their infantry also slowed their progress.

Frederick's knights rode in a slower, but more disciplined and concentrated group, oftentimes splitting a cantering speed for a trot to save the stamina of the horses. They also had the advantage of no infantry to hold them back. The race would prove to be a virtual tie.

Frederick arrived at the gates of Constance to find the banners of Emperor Otto already flying on the town walls.

"If Otto is here, my lord, we must bypass and go to another walled town," an Aragon knight said.

"But our horses have no ride left in them, and the next town is a day's ride away," another knight said.

Frederick looked at Hector for counsel. It seemed there was no good option available.

"We must ride to the gate and demand entry," he said confidently. "Those banners do not mean Otto and his knights are here. I think we have beaten their main force to Constance."

"Then what do those lion banners represent?" Frederick asked.

"I believe that is the emperor's servants, supply lines, and advance staff. His knights have not arrived. Otto is notorious for his long lines of knights riding single file and coming in at sporadic times to battle. This is his early advance servants preparing the town for his arrival."

"If you are wrong, we are riding into an ambush," said the Aragon knight. "Our defeat would be self-inflicted."

"I'm not wrong," Hector said, commanding his horse to canter toward the gate. "I know he's not there."

Frederick followed Hector to the gates of Constance, with his knights behind. There was nothing to do but hope Hector was right.

—ɯ—

"What business do you have here?" asked the sergeant-at-arms. He looked down at Frederick and his knights from atop his perch at the gates.

"We request an audience with the bishop of Constance. I am King Frederick of Sicily, emperor elect by the princes of Germany."

"I know who you are," the sergeant screamed in a strong, gravelly voice. "You are the boy king from Sicily who challenges for the German crown. We have accepted Emperor Otto into Constance. You must yield this town to Otto and move on."

"You accept an excommunicate into Constance?" Frederick yelled. "Is there to be an interdiction on this town? Are you willingly defying the pope and church and God to provide aid and comfort for the excommunicate Otto? Is this town heretic?"

"What do you mean Emperor Otto is excommunicated?" the sergeant asked hesitantly.

"We request an audience with your bishop. Go and get him."

The sergeant looked down at Frederick for a moment, and then disappeared from the tower.

"It sounds like Otto is already here," Frederick whispered to Hector.

"He's not here. His servants and the like are here. 'Twas a nice speech you gave there. Scared the hell out of the old sergeant-at-arms."

Frederick smiled, and they waited.

After a few minutes, the gates of Constance opened and an old man dressed in red-and-white garb walked outside alone, the gates closing behind him.

"I am the bishop of Constance," he said, looking up at Frederick. "Prove your claim, or move away from this town. We do not wish to be a part of this conflict."

"By sheltering the excommunicated Emperor Otto, you have made yourself part of this conflict, Bishop," Frederick said while Dragon began to stir restlessly.

"We make a safe haven for no one," the bishop said, backing away from Dragon. "We have only his cooks behind this wall. No military presence of the emperor is in this town current. Now either dismount that wild Arabian animal and produce proof of your claim, or ride on to another town. Your aggressive rhetoric is wasted on me, young man."

Frederick got down from Dragon, opened his saddlebag, and took out three letters: one from the pope, one from the bishop of Chur, and one from the Papal legate of the region, the archbishop of Bari. He handed them to the bishop.

The bishop said nothing as he studied each letter. After several minutes, he rolled the letters into the cylinders and handed them back to Frederick.

"I do not like being put in this position," the bishop said, "and I do not like you or Otto bringing bloodshed or siege to this town. Your two families have done enough damage to Germany. This is a political disagreement that has escalated to military conflict. It should not involve the town of Constance. And the church should not make decisions like this."

"Do you doubt Pope Innocent's authority on this matter, Bishop? Do you doubt he has a claim to excommunicate Otto?"

"A priest from a small town should not affect the course of destiny between two kings fighting over a crown. My decision could easily see Constance burned to the ground, or bring with it the wrath of the king I side against. I pray you will ride to another town for sanctuary that already favors you and the princes. There are many in the south of Germany, as you know. Pope Innocent has made it clear that he wishes to play a role in European politics. I do not."

"I regret it cannot be done," Frederick said, putting his hand on the bishop's shoulder. "But if you allow us time to organize, I promise to defend this town in a way that would frustrate Otto from attempting a siege. It is not our intent to start this war here, but rather stage our defenses and fight him in the north."

"I pray this does not mark the end of our town. I pray that Pope Innocent sees the wisdom in the future to stay out of political matters between kings who aspire to power and control of lands. These matters should not involve the church."

Frederick silently agreed with the wise bishop.

"I will pray alongside you," he said to the bishop.

"Make ready your defenses, King Frederick," the bishop finally said. "You may pass through our gates." He looked up at the sergeant-at-arms. "Open the gates! Make way for Emperor-elect Frederick!" he yelled.

And the gates slowly opened.

—ɯ—

"We should secure these knights inside the walls, my lord," one of the Aragon knights said. "It would allow us to wait for the princes of Germany to assist us without losing our army before we are at full strength."

"It would also allow Otto to lay siege without us defending as honorable knights," said another knight. "How do we know if the princes will ever get here in time?"

"I made a promise to the bishop to defend against a siege," Frederick said.

"But this will be riskier for the knights. This is sending them into a battle where they will likely be outnumbered," Hector said. "But isn't this exactly what we were saving these knights for?"

"Yes, it is, Hector. Our battle will be here, if God wills it. We will not hide behind these walls. Make ready our defenses."

Hector set his forces along the north side of the wall facing Lake Constance and fortifying the bridge that crossed the Rhine. In order for Otto to stage an assault, he would have to cross that bridge, or ride east the length of the lake and attack from the flank. Any rearguard tactic would take additional days, which would allow too many other forces to make it to Constance and further disrupt Otto's plans. The likelihood was that Otto would fight from the bridge with greater numbers and attempt to overwhelm the Aragon knights defending.

Hector prepared the defenses outside the walls, while Frederick spoke to the citizens and militia still inside.

"People of Constance!" he yelled while a crowd gathered around him. "Hear me good people of Constance," he said even louder as men on the walls turned to listen, militiamen came out of their barracks, and people walked out of their homes to hear the boy king speak. After a moment, the crowd murmurs ended and total silence grew inside Constance.

"People of Constance, I am Frederick, king of Sicily. I am emperor-elect, nominated by your princes to be king of the Germans. I am the rightful heir to the throne through my father, Henry VI, and his father, Frederick of Barbarossa."

"Long live King Barbarossa!" someone shouted.

"My family has established many castles and towns in this area. German blood courses through my veins."

He let Dragon walk a bit forward before pulling the reins tight.

"I come here at the request of your princes to contest the excommunicated Emperor Otto the Welf. He rides toward Constance as we speak for one lone reason: to kill me and destroy my knights. He has no claim or grievance against Constance, save you granting me sanctuary; however, by granting me this help, your town is now as invested in this conflict as I.

"Your bishop has informed me of your neutrality in this battle, and I respect your position. Otto has been of northern Germany, and I am an unknown king from a faraway land. There would be no reason for your allegiance toward either. Constance is a town known for its fine garments, merchants, and fishermen. It is outside of such political matters, or so it was.

"Good people of Constance, I promise you that Europe is about to be plunged into a war involving every kingdom, every country, and every town within its borders. England, France, Sicily, Italy, Aragon—and most of all Germany—will feel the effects of this war, and every town will be called upon to choose their side.

"Your bishop allowed me entry into Constance because I showed him proof of Otto the Welf's excommunication from the church. Before he allowed me inside, he prayed I would take my knights away from this town and meet Otto elsewhere. Your bishop is a good man and only allowed me entry because he has to accept the pope's wishes, even above his own best judgment. I now see it isn't a just decision to force a town into conflict because of a Papal document.

"If you do not commit to my cause, I will honor your bishop's prayer and march my knights across the Rhine Bridge and take Otto on there. It will put my knights at a great disadvantage having the river at our backs, but I will not wage this campaign by forcing a town against its will to aid me.

"I pray you will see the wisdom of committing this town to the purpose your princes have called upon me to do. I promise you, as emperor, I will bring Constance and Sicily together as allies in trade, not as territories of conquest. I will be an emperor of goodwill, and Constance will again flourish once Otto the Welf has been defeated.

"But the hour of truth fast approaches. My knights now defend the lake region of your border. They have well-fortified the Rhine Bridge, the likely advance point Otto will use. To enhance our positions, we ask for your help. We request your militia fortify the walls and visibly reserve my knights so that Otto sees the total defenses and the reinforcement potential backing my knights.

"I ask that you commit to my leadership as emperor-elect and help me now. What say you, Constance? Will you help me?"

XXXVIII

Otto Approaches

The rumble of galloping stallions shook the ground of every town and village Otto and his knights rode through. The long, single-file line of riders seemed endless to the observers who dared to wander outside and see the spectacle.

Finally, the Rhine Bridge crossing to Constance could be seen, but it was a sight that stopped them in their tracks. Within moments, Otto caught up to the lead riders.

"Why have you stopped?" he asked.

One of his knights pointed to the other side of the bridge. "They have fortified the bridge, Emperor," he said, "and it looks as though his numbers now match ours."

As Otto looked across the river from his vantage point at the top of the hill, rage poured out of him, and he roared a groan equaling that of a large bear.

"I will take that town apart brick by brick! I will burn it to the ground and salt the earth beneath it so no one again will ever dare inhabit this place! I will kill every person behind that wall!" he screamed, punching a tree. "They think because they lay on the border of Germany that they are not a part of my empire? This is treason! I will punish them beyond any comprehension of the word, and I will have Frederick's head on a stick!"

"Is it your intent to attack the fortifications of the bridge, Your Grace?" asked his military advisor.

Without facing him, Otto let his response explode out of his throat, as if angered by the question.

"We cannot let this act go unpunished! We cannot retreat back to Brunswick and allow this movement to gain strength!" he said, punching the tree again. "The enemy is in front of me. We must attack!"

The analyst went to where Otto stood, then looked Otto in the eyes, grabbed his shoulders, and turned him in the direction of the bridge. Otto pushed him away, saying nothing.

"Look past the bridge, Emperor. They have a battalion posted at the lake, and another in reserve near the walls. Another battalion stands on the wall. If we attack the bridge, the walled battalion may be archers. They would rain down arrows on us until we are destroyed. If not, it would deplete our forces by half. We would go into a siege with only half the knights we came with."

Otto was irate. "If we cross that bridge with even half the knights we have now, we will force that town into surrender," he said, now staring intently at the bridge. "Constance does not have the stomach for a siege, not after what we will do to cross it. They would be more likely to flood out of the back gates than resist."

"Emperor, we have no idea what lies in reserve behind those walls. Every prince in southern Germany may lie in wait there. Our advance staff is in there, and without a word of their observations, we know nothing. If they fortify outside the walls with this many knights, there is no telling the amount inside."

"Or maybe the boy king has stuck his entire force outside the walls to frustrate our advance," Otto said hesitantly. "And there is no one inside the walls except women and children, the liabilities of Constance . . . perhaps all of his assets are visible."

"We cannot risk it, Emperor. We could be attacking a town that out-numbers us dramatically. And once we capture the bridge and lay siege, our exit strategy would be hampered by the very same narrow bridge if it turns out they are hiding knights inside."

Otto turned away from the bridge in disgust. Several knights made their way toward him, wondering what their plan would be now.

"We can't go north either," he said, somewhat calm. "We took no effort to hide our intent. Every prince in Germany knows where we are. To ride north would be to ride into certain battles—not to mention, I have no account for the French."

"Philip is fighting in Normandy, my lord," said another advisor. "He poses us no threat. His focus is on King John's invasion from England."

"He will certainly split his force in half and have his son Louis lead them. He knows half of his knights can scare John into retreat and the other half can aid this uprising."

"Perhaps it would be wise for us to be seen retreating north, Emperor, then slowly flank east around the lake and observe Constance for a few days from the south entry. If we are in need of an exit procedure, we can utilize the wilderness to the west of the Rhine and regroup in Aachen."

"That would be a trip I would dread," said Otto. "Nothing is worse than slinking through the wilderness in retreat. We must do everything we can to avoid that outcome."

"Yes, Emperor," said the advisor.

Otto led his knights down the hill and toward the bridge, turning east before reaching the river. After spotting Hector and the knights defending the bridge, he turned north again, down the most likely trail to take in order to go back to northern Germany.

Hector's knights roared their approval in seeing Otto's retreat. Soon, the men in the towers gave word to the town inside the walls.

"King Frederick!" yelled a militiaman from the tower. "Otto has begun his retreat. The town is safe."

Frederick smiled and rode off to meet Hector and his knights.

That evening Frederick had found some time to write Constance.

Love of my life,

We have reached the beautiful town of Constance. We beat Otto's army here by four hours! We were able to display a show of strength that caused him to retreat back to Germany.

It is the third Constance now that has been a guardian angel to me. My mother, the town, and you my dearest. I love you so much.

I cannot get into specifics of our mission in Constance, but we will spend time here building an army. The people of this town showed great bravery in allowing us safe passage. I hope to one day repay their bravery.

I was relieved to hear there were no complications with the nobles and particularly with your pregnancy. I pray every day for you to be safe and for our baby to be born with great health. I pray that God wills it.

I must end this letter, my dear Constance. I hope that we will be together soon.

With all my love,
Frederick

XXXIX

Building an Alliance

Over the next few days, Frederick met with an assembly of German princes and nobles. All of them swore allegiance to Frederick and contributed knights for the war against Otto.

The princes had formed the equivalent of a feudal system of government once Otto made clear his intent to value the conquest of lands over the well-being of Germany. But unlike the barons and counts of Sicily, these nobles had the best interests of their lands and the people in them in mind. Despite their best efforts, Germany struggled desperately because of Otto spending large sums of imperial taxes on his war efforts and conquests.

Frederick saw the potential of Germany and its princes. If given a peaceful and commerce-friendly environment, he believed it would thrive. His thoughts of an economic revolution had to be for another time; for now, he knew he had to keep the focus on the war. Without a victory over Otto, no other plans would matter.

While Frederick met with the German leaders flocking to Constance, Hector began incorporating the incoming knights into the existing force. In his opinion, this transition was of vital importance.

"It would be too risky to pile up large numbers of knights, then point them in a direction," Hector said. "It has proven ineffective too many times in battles, and even crusades where a smaller force outmaneuvered and defeated a larger one."

Hector's plan was to keep each of the noble's knights together and form battalions of one hundred to two hundred soldiers. If the nobles stayed to fight, he became the battalion commander; if not, the leader would be chosen within the battalion. Frederick and Hector would organize the battalion leaders, directing their movements and orchestrating the larger-scale plan.

Communication and movement would flow through the battalion leaders, then back to Frederick and Hector. Each day, battalion leaders would meet with them to discuss strategy and tactics. Runners would dispatch messages to and from the battalions. Hector discussed this strategy with the princes who stayed in the camp. He also trained techniques, jousting, and war games to get an idea of the talent and experience level of the incoming knights.

—m—

Most of this was done outside the walls, and unbeknownst to Frederick, observed by Otto. He had set up his base camp in the mountains and was now well established.

"He builds an army before our eyes, and we sit and watch," Otto said to his advisor. "It goes against everything I believe."

"Word has probably reached our favored princes and towns by now, Emperor. They have been instructed to send reserve forces of knights, who will ride here soon. They have to travel through the wilderness because the roads are filled with knights still coming to Constance. When our reinforcements arrive, we will have the advantage. And when they march out from behind the gates, we will destroy them."

Otto paced while the advisor laid out his plan of patience.

"And if the French come, what advantages have we then? The enemy is before us every day, playing games. I cannot bear to watch it," Otto said. "If those knights are not here by tomorrow, we attack."

—m—

The warning bells of Constance rang loud from the tower. "Riders fast approaching!" the sergeant-at-arms bellowed.

The threat of siege woke the town prematurely, despite the unusual amount of knights. Frederick arose abruptly and met Hector outside his room in the town square.

"Is it possible Otto would attack us under such conditions?" he asked.

"It would be a surprise, at a minimum," Hector said. "But walls have never proven a hindrance to Otto."

"An army of knights approaches fast with banners I cannot discern, my lord!" the sergeant yelled from the tower. "It looks like hundreds of riders coming from the south . . . maybe thousands."

"Let me get a look," Hector said, climbing the stairs to the tower. "Ready the defenses."

The militia immediately went to their posts on the walls while knights quickly mounted their horses, awaiting the front and back gates to open. Frederick jumped on Dragon's back and rode to the tower where Hector had positioned himself.

"Is it Otto?" he asked, looking up into the sunlight.

"No."

"Who is it?"

Hector watched for a moment, then turned to answer Frederick.

"Make way for Prince Louis!" a French officer said to a soldier in the tower. "He wishes a word with King Frederick of Sicily."

"Yes, bring me to the boy king," Louis joked, not much older than Frederick.

"Opening the gate for Prince Louis, future king of France!" the sergeant yelled down to the gatekeeper.

"Now there will be two kings in Constance," one citizen said. "There has never been a time like this in the history of our town."

Prince Louis entered Constance with his small advance guard, his huge army beginning to appear through the forest in a larger context. The initial estimate of hundreds of knights proved pleasantly wrong; it was much larger.

"I think he brought the entire French army!" the sergeant yelled.

"We brought half my father's knights," Prince Louis said. "We number somewhere around five thousand. I hope that will be an appropriate amount."

Most of the nearby militia laughed at the prince's jest.

"We appreciate France's generous contribution to Germany's cause," Frederick said, smiling as he rode toward Prince Louis. "Welcome to Constance."

"You must be King Frederick, the boy king of Sicily."

"And future king of the Germans!" someone yelled.

"And Holy Roman emperor once we beat Otto!" yelled another.

"If childhood is measured only in years on this Earth, then I may well still be a boy," Frederick said, riding next to Louis. "But if life experience at all plays a role, I feel as if I'm an old man."

"So I've been told," said Louis, now laughing. "You may call me Louie. All of my elderly friends do."

"And you may call me King Frederick," he said in laughter.

"Where is the messenger from Aachen?" Otto asked. "Why have we no word for a day now?"

"No word yet, Emperor," said the advisor. "We have sent a search party into the wilderness to collect him."

"We have waited long enough . . . too long. Today we go down the hill and finish off this weakling."

"The risk is still high, Emperor, but we have a plan in place to ambush the knights outside the walls, and the ones who come out to perform their training exercises. If King Frederick sees his assets being destroyed outside the walls, he will likely dispatch all of his knights into the battle in order to conserve those outside. With our reserves then joining us from an opposite position, we could rout him and render Constance without defense and Germany without rival to your crown."

Otto watched the walls of Constance. He waited for the gates to open and knights to come out for their daily exercises.

"Ready our knights. Send the reserves to the extreme flank with word to attack when the second wave of knights leaves Constance."

Otto and his generals began unfolding their plan. They moved reserves through the coverage of trees to the opposite flank, but before they made the call to attack, a stunning sight changed everything. Out of the tree line far from their base camp, riders appeared in large numbers with blue banners and flags.

"Is that a French brigade approaching Constance?" Otto asked sarcastically.

"No, Emperor," said the advisor, as the massive force thundered toward the town's gate. "It looks more like King Philip's entire army."

"I thought you said they would be fighting John in Normandy?"

"It seems they split the army in half, Emperor. Half to fight John—"

"And half to aid the boy king, just as I said," Otto interrupted. "Now what do we do with half our knights riding to the other flank? We cannot attack, and we cannot retreat until we get those knights back."

Otto's blood boiled. He turned to the general and punched him in the face.

"You were the one who said that Philip would be occupied in Normandy, weren't you? My instincts were to attack this town days ago; instead, I listened to generals and advisors and waited. Now the town is not within our attacking ability, and my reserve knights ride away from our exit strategy. Never again will I go against my instincts. All advisors, walk away from my sight."

Otto hovered over the general he'd punched. The man held his cheek and struggled to get up; his chainmail weighing him down.

"Get up and send a unit of knights to stop our reserves from flanking this town. Bring them back to the base camp so we can regroup and go back to Aachen. Do not tell me you don't have the strength to arise from under your chainmail. Are you a German warrior, or are you a child? I will leave you here for them."

As he turned to watch the French, another advisor walked over and stood next to him.

"Do not speak to me. Walk away from my sight, or risk being beaten to the ground and left here for the French."

The advisor walked off, and Otto grabbed the young squire tending to his horse.

"Is that Prince Louis leading the French?" he asked, grasping the squire's face and whipping it in the direction of the gate. "Philip has sent his son to fight me? The boy king and the prince will lead this army against me? No matter the numbers, if they pursue me on my journey back to Aachen, I will attack them."

The squire cowered under the gaze of the raging emperor. Otto shoved him away and stormed off.

—◊◊◊—

The contrast between the two young monarchs was striking. Louis was tall and thin, had a muscular build, and his blond hair spilled out from under his crown. He looked every bit like the prince he was.

On the other hand, Frederick looked like a merchant's son. He was short and ragged, with long, unruly red hair, and tattered clothing that looked as if he wore it all the way through the Alps. Although the king of Sicily had a crown, Frederick rarely wore it.

The people of Constance saw him as a young Frederick Barbarossa and endeared themselves to him, no matter his choice of clothing or lack of a crown.

Their worldview was at odds as well. Frederick was a deep-thinking, skeptic of everything, including religion. He had tutors off and on during his education, but their teaching had to make sense to him or facts be proven for him to acknowledge them. He was an intellectual for his age, and a critical thinker.

Louis was also intelligent, but more traditionally educated. He believed what teachers, parents, and clergy told him without much question. He did not doubt any of his authority figures; he had no reason to. This had shaped him into a trusting and accepting person. Louis expected to be treated as a prince, while Frederick anticipated earning his title because of his childhood experiences.

"My father sent me here to assess your talents and your support among the German princes," said Louis. "I will write to him that you are a talented leader with the full support of Germany and that France should stand ready as an ally, if requested."

"It is requested," Frederick said.

"And it is given," said Louis.

The two young men shook hands and formed the alliance of France, Sicily, Aragon, and southern Germany.

"How have you structured your knights for combat and communication?" asked Louis.

"We have them in battalions organized as they came to us," Frederick said. "Each noble is a battalion commander of his given knights. They report to Hector with any battlefield decisions."

"Hector is your military advisor?"

"Yes. Hector is my military advisor, tutor, mentor, and much more."

"It's good you have someone like that. Send for him," Louis said. "We have much to discuss, and Hector should be a part of this, as will my advisors."

"On our journey to Constance, we captured a German rider in the wilderness," said the top French advisor to the group now assembled. "He did not have much information, save to say he was on his way to Otto and that he would be relieved by another rider somewhere between Aachen and Constance. They told him to ride through the wilderness away from all towns until he reached the relief rider. It is our belief that Otto is or was in the wilderness to the south and west of Constance for some time and may still observe the town from a secret base camp in that location."

The news stunned Hector, the German princes, and Frederick most of all.

"We watched him retreat northward," Frederick said. "We trained on the south lawn almost every day. Why wouldn't he attack us?"

"It does go against every tendency Otto has ever exhibited in warfare," Hector said. "Are you sure he has been sittin' up there waitin'?"

"We believe he was there and that his numbers must have been inferior to your own," said the French advisor. "Otherwise, he would have attacked."

"No doubt half the French army showing up has sent him in retreat toward Aachen," Hector said.

"My advisors and I concur on that as well," Louis said. "No doubt he will take the wilderness back to northern Germany. The missed opportunity is unfortunate."

"Was it the intent of King Philip and France to engage Otto before regrouping with the other half of your knights?" Hector asked.

"King Philip's instructions were comprehensive. He left very little room for the unknown," the advisor said. "However, Otto and his imperial army, hiding in the forest next to Constance, has found the scenario that King Philip did not cover."

"The spirit of my father's instructions was to appraise the strengths of Frederick and the princes," Louis said. "If we found them of value as an ally, we were to attack Otto from the eastern flank of Germany. Given this unexpected event, I believe the spirit of the order would be to attack Otto as soon as we are upon him."

"It would not be advisable to deploy a wilderness campaign, Prince Louis," said the advisor.

"Why do you think Otto's smaller force would fare better in the forest than us?" Frederick asked.

"It would be difficult to catch them. Even if we did, our superior numbers would not be advantageous in the wilderness."

"And Otto's knights have been with him for months. They are a cohesive unit," said Louis, deferring to his advisor's thoughts. "You and I have just met today. Our knights have never fought together. If we make a mistake in such complex warfare, we could destroy both of our armies."

"It will be best to ignore Otto now and confront him in northern Germany on the eastern flank, as King Philip has ordered," said the advisor.

Frederick stood up, walked to where Hector was sitting, and put his hand on his shoulder.

"Do you remember how the Romans dealt with Hannibal in Italy?" he asked quietly.

"Yes," Hector said.

"Do you think it would work in this instance?"

Hector looked up at Frederick for a moment, then nodded in the affirmative.

"My friends and allies, Prince Louis . . . please indulge us for a moment," Frederick said. "Hector is going to tell you a story from Roman history. At first it will seem to make no sense to our current situation; that is because my former tutor is long-winded. But when he is finished, I think we may have the basis for the plan we should employ against Otto."

XL

On the Trail of Otto

Within a few days, the allied knights of Frederick and Prince Louis had not only closed the gap on Otto, but also gotten ahead of him on his way north. Despite a lead of one day and significantly fewer knights, a trek through the wilderness proved difficult for the emperor.

Frederick and the French army made up the ground easily by taking the friendly roads of southern Germany. At about the halfway mark between Constance and Aachen, they crossed the Rhine River and cut Otto off from his destination.

Along the way, more knights joined Frederick, until their contribution was nearly the size of the French army. By the time they crossed the Rhine, they more than doubled Otto's force.

With the advantage in knights, the attrition strategy they had all agreed to implement would need to be reconsidered. Word had been sent to King Philip, but no reply had been received. The debate to attack Otto head-on began to surface among Frederick and Louis's generals and battalion leaders.

"We have a much larger force, and we have the high ground," one of the French generals said. "What would stop us from attacking when we have such an advantage? We could destroy his knights and end this war."

"We should remain patient," said another.

"Look what patience did for Otto."

"We are ill-equipped for a wilderness campaign," Hector said. "Nothing has changed since we left Constance. There, we all agreed to a strategy of attrition until we hear from King Philip. This will conserve our knights from a battle style with which they are unfamiliar. Without more archers, we could potentially take heavy losses, as our knights are a heavier, slower-moving force and prefer an open battlefield to a forest. Unless Otto chooses to attack our advantageous position, it would be a mistake to give away our good ground."

"The spirit of the order given by King Philip was clear," said another French general. "Attack Otto if the attack is available. When will it ever be more accessible than now? We cut him off from where he is staging his entire force."

"And what if that force got word that Otto has encountered us and is riding to his aid right now?" Hector asked rhetorically. "We would be surrounded on both sides. That is another part of this campaign that is unknown. 'Tis best to be grateful for our good high ground and await word of King Philip's movement and his orders."

"We shall hold this ground and force Otto further west, away from Aachen," Louis said sternly to his over-aggressive generals. "We shall await orders from my father on our current strategy and his current progress. This plan has been implemented and has not failed us at present. We shall not abandon a plan that thrives."

There was an uncomfortable silence in the tent until Frederick spoke.

"We should be getting word soon from our raiding battalions that followed Otto northward, attacking his rear guard, supply lines, and hunters. They are likely the reason we now hold this high ground ahead of Otto. His communication and food supply has been severely limited by those battalions already reporting the past few days. This has been no holiday ride for him in the forest, and it will be no better for him, as we have closed off all direct routes to Germany. He will either have to attack us or travel even further west to avoid us—delaying his arrival in Aachen and further starving his troops."

"And this is the strategy the Romans used against Hannibal?" a French general asked.

"Yes," Frederick replied. "It's called the Fabian Strategy. Instead of directly attacking your enemy, you plague him with smaller attacks on supply lines or ambush his hunters or messengers. Would you like Hector to go over its origin again, General?"

"Oh no, no, no," the general said, shaking his hands. "We well remember Hector's lecture on the subject. It was comprehensive."

"That's funny. When Hector was my tutor, I vividly remember a similar reaction to yours. Why do you suppose you have that effect on your listeners, Hector?"

The group laughed as Hector shrugged his broad shoulders and looked away.

"You were a bad student, Frederick. 'Tis all the explanation you will get."

—⁓—

"When was the last dispatch received from Aachen?" Otto asked as he rode alongside one of his generals.

"Two days, Emperor. Only one dispatch has arrived since we left for Aachen."

"It should be two per day. Something is amiss ahead of us. It's not just these rear guard sneak-attacking raiders we're dealing with here. They are from a larger force in front of us."

"The scouts have seen nothing, Your Majesty, except for forest."

"Beyond the scout's eyes there lies an army—a militia, mercenaries, or assassins. I sense it. I don't know its exact location or size, but it waits for us. It hampers our communications, and it is linked to these raiders to the rear who attack our supply lines and hunters. I can only hope it's something we can eventually attack—something that will soon stand and show itself and fight us face to face. I tire of tactics, patience, and retreat, which my advisors assured me, was prudent. That prudence now has us in the dark and trudging through the mud of the wilderness. I yearn to see an army ahead we can attack."

—⁓—

The next day, scouts arrived back at Otto's camp and described in great detail the army sitting on a hill in the wilderness just a day's ride away. He rode to within view and saw they were too large to attack, and that they blocked his way back to Aachen. His rage finally boiled over.

"By God, I swear it. There will come a day when this army faces me on a proper battlefield—a day when deception and tactics are absent from the outcome. I vow it before God and all, on that day I will kill every knight, militiaman, infantryman, prince, and king in that army. I will spare none. I will take no prisoners for ransom. I will wipe this army's existence from the annals of history—save the head of the boy king that will rot on the end of a spear! No army will ever again force me into maneuvers. I will not die in the forest like a peasant, the victim of bad tactics."

He glared at his generals and advisors and continued his rant.

"Get this army back to northern Germany with any plan you wish. Get us past this army on the hill. Atone for your mistakes. Get me back to Aachen to fight another day on a wide-open battlefield."

His advisors silently looked at one another as Otto rode away toward the middle of his camp.

"Before this campaign is over, I fear that our heads will be the ones lost," one general said.

"Do not fear," an advisor said. "These two boys will make a mistake along the way. They will not run a flawless campaign in the woods. They have superior numbers of knights. That is all. We must advise the emperor to remain patient and wait for our chance. It will come. Until then, we stay in the forest and ride as far west as we have to, and as far north as we can go. We will get this army back to Aachen, and Emperor Otto will have his day with this enemy."

The attrition strategy continued to push Otto further and further west near France. His army couldn't turn north into northern Germany, but they were able to keep their troops mostly intact.

The strategy had also kept Otto from contacting his reinforcements and allies in Aachen. His knights were frustrated, tired, and hungry. Each day, Frederick's rear-guard-raiding party would ambush the extreme flanks of Otto's army, and then disappear as if out of nowhere. It was exactly like the Saracen attacks Hector had witnessed in the Middle East crusade with Richard. Otto had no answer.

There were skirmishes between the frontlines, but nothing that ever escalated. Otto would test Frederick and Louis's resolve, but the alliance remained strong. Otto knew the numbers were just too overwhelming to risk an all-out attack.

Frederick and Louis would often ponder more aggressive offensive maneuvers on Otto, but with too many unknown events in France and Aachen, they always decided to hold an advantageous position until word arrived from King Philip. The two young men had gained some battlefield experience in the skirmishes, as well as in leading the army through the forests between Germany and France. But they both knew that soon this facet of the war would have to end.

The next day, the dispatch from King Philip finally arrived.

"King John and England have retreated from Normandy and are back in the British Isles. The French army has suffered minimal casualties and will soon be prepared to take on Otto and the German alliance. Bring your armies to Paris." Louis looked up from the letter. "He wants us to cut Otto loose and march our knights to Paris."

"It feels wrong to just leave Otto," Frederick said. "We have the assets to destroy him, and he is right in front of us."

"He fears we will make an overly aggressive move and destroy the advantage we may have once at full force. I respect his wisdom in warfare. My father has seen everything there is to see. But I, too, want to send our knights down the hill to win this war. Our knights deserve that glory."

"We can't go against your father's directives. He sees a bigger picture than we do on the frontlines. I respect his authority in this matter, but we should announce his order and our intent before we change our minds."

—ↄↄↄ—

The camp began the business of preparing for their journey to Paris. Some of the knights sat in front of various campfires and celebrated the coming war. Frederick and Louis stayed in the royal tent and talked about the future . . . and the past.

"When I am emperor and you are king of France, we shall crusade together and take back Jerusalem from the Saracens," Frederick mused.

"You have Saracens in Sicily, don't you?"

"Yes. They are a brave and rebellious people living in the western mountains."

"Will you rid Sicily of them upon your return?"

The comment gave Frederick pause. Never had he made the connection between the Saracens of the Middle East and the Saracens of Sicily. To Frederick, the Saracens in his kingdom were as Sicilian as any other group.

"I don't know, Louie. I called upon them to help defend Sicily against Otto. They have earned a stake in the kingdom."

"But that was a desperate situation that called for you to implement every possible asset. You owe the Saracens nothing, Frederick. They are your sworn enemy for eternity. Surely, when you return as Holy Roman emperor, you will purge them from your kingdom."

"Most of those Saracens have lived in Sicily for generations. They were in the mountains when my grandfather Roger ruled Sicily. They are not a part of the Saracens who occupy Jerusalem. I see a distinction between them."

"Both are of Islam, Frederick. Both are pagans, and their very presence in Sicily is heresy."

"There are Jews living in almost every kingdom in Europe. Is that not an equal smear on a Christian kingdom?"

"Jews live among us under very rigid regulation, and in very limited circumstances; there are no such standards put upon Saracens to live among us. The pope has made no such edict for their residence."

Frederick stopped the discussion for a moment, filled their cups with wine, and set the cask back on the table. He cleared his throat and continued.

"The pope has been my guardian for most of my life. He was protectorate of Sicily even longer. In that time, I was kidnapped and left for dead, given to irresponsible foster parents to be raised and nearly killed by his Holy Roman emperor. As for Sicily, the protectorate was unable to defend her against invasions too numerous to list. Even city-states in Italy found it easy to invade and plunder, with no answer from its protectorate. He allowed Sicily to fall into utter ruin. The docks are decrepit, and the feudal system was the only true governance—only it did nothing except oppress its peasant class into starvation. They thought nothing of Sicily, but rather of their own personal wealth. No, Louie, do not talk to me of Papal edicts that act as our bellwethers of conduct. Pope Innocent's term as guardian and protectorate has expired. I will rule the kingdom of Sicily within the parameters of my own code."

Louis could see the rage in Frederick when he spoke of Pope Innocent. He filled their cups again with wine, surprised they could be so far apart on what he considered to be a fundamental truth. At the same time, he was pleased they could have such heated words while maintaining their friendship and mutual respect. They had bonded beyond issues and opinions. It wasn't important if they agreed or disagreed; they were partners in the cause.

"Pope Innocent is the most important man on Earth. He is the mediator between God and man, between God and king. We must obey his laws, for they are of God."

"You should try living with him," Frederick said, downing the cup of wine in one breath. "Then you would not consider him such a divine force."

"I have heard how strict he was with you as a child. I know your experiences are vastly different from mine. But we must consider our stations in life. We will be kings and emperors one day. We know our roles and must allow the pope to be above us in lineage to God. We must not disobey, as God Himself wills it."

"God wills us to be kings, Louie, and we are kings. God has no need for mediators to see His will done. Pope Innocent did nothing to see me rightfully made king of Sicily; in fact, he went to great measures to see it not so until I could be of use to him. Despite him, I am now rightful king of Sicily. God willed it. God needs no arbiter. He births kings to do His will on Earth."

Before the discussion could advance any further, a messenger arrived for Frederick outside the royal tent. Frederick exited and returned with a message all the way from Sicily.

Frederick read the dispatch and looked up, stunned.

"I am a father," he said. "I have a son!" he said, louder this time, smiling at Louie. "I am a father!" he yelled.

"That is great news, Frederick," Louis said with a smile. He hugged his friend. "What will your son's name be?"

"Henry. He will be named after my father," he declared while opening up the tent, and calling out, "Hector, where are you? I have a son!"

Hector quickly approached the royal tent. "'Tis a good way to end this campaign," he beamed.

> Dearest Frederick,
>
> Congratulations, my dear. We are the proud parents of the next king of Sicily! His name is Henry as you requested, in honor of your father. Words cannot appropriately express my happiness at the birth of this beautiful baby.
>
> I pray for your continued safety on the battlefield and for your return soon to Sicily.
>
> Love always,
> Constance

—◊◊—

The march to Paris was perhaps the best days of the campaign for Frederick. He had time to talk with Hector and Louie about impending fatherhood and all the events of the day. It would soon be time to focus on the war, and these few days were a needed respite.

Each French town the army marched past brought with it the celebrations of a conquering force. They showered Prince Louis with praise and flowers. He had always been the people's favorite monarch in France, while his father was more comfortable with governance, policy, and warfare. Philip kept a low profile, and Louis filled that void.

They stayed the night in the French town of Champagne and lingered the next day to visit the enormous fairs of the region. Prince Louis strategically met with the count of Champagne, intent to gain his loyalty for the coming battle against Otto. Frederick mingled with the merchants at the fair, surprising them with his many questions. They didn't expect his sincere interest in their businesses and displayed exceptional knowledge of economic issues. For such a young king, he had command of a number of subjects, especially merchandising and distribution. They would never have suspected that Champagne was the largest town Frederick had ever seen, except Rome.

That evening, Hector met a girl at a local inn and found himself intrigued with her. She captured his attentions and affections. He returned to the fair the next morning, appearing at her booth dressed in full knight's uniform, less the chainmail and armor. Meanwhile, Frederick was drifting throughout the fair when he noticed Hector.

Approaching him, he commented, "I would very much like to return here after the war."

"I would like that, too," Hector replied, preoccupied with the girl.

"Why do you have your uniform on? We don't leave for Paris until tomorrow."

Hector began to respond, but Frederick interrupted.

"Hector, did you bathe? I don't think you've bathed since Italy."

"Is there a service that you require from me, King Frederick?" he asked in a frustrated Scottish brogue.

Frederick laughed, finally understanding the circumstance with more clarity. "No, sorry to interrupt."

"No interruption, King Frederick. May I present to you my friend, Sophia of Champagne?"

Sophia was a beautiful French girl with long blonde hair and blue eyes. She curtseyed to Frederick. "It's an honor to meet you, King Frederick."

"The honor is all mine, Sophia," he said in French.

"We shall pray for your success in Germany, and your safe return to Champagne one day," she said to Frederick, but looking at Hector.

"Hector and I pray for the very same thing."

—∿—

The trip into Paris had the appearance of a Roman tribute. King Philip Augustus and his knights stood poised at the very end of the route. Frederick understood this celebration was primarily for Prince Louis and the French army, but he enjoyed being included.

"Louie," King Philip said, rising from his throne on a stage in the town square. "You are safe."

He looked the part of a regal, wise warrior king. His gray hair and tan features showed his age. He wore his eye patch as a badge of honor from battles of the past.

"It is good to find you well, Father," Louis said as he climbed onto the stage and hugged King Philip. The crowd erupted in applause. Turning to face them, Louis pronounced, "It's great to be back in France."

On cue, the crowd cheered wildly, as did the knights. All enjoyed being included in the moment.

"He will make a great king one day," one knight said.

The crowd roared its approval at the splendor of the royal family gathered together in the town square. It was a rarity to see them all in one public venue. Adding to the splendor, the entire French army assembled alongside the knights from all across the continent.

It was a regal sight indeed.

King Philip looked down at Frederick, who was still atop Dragon.

"We are very pleased to have you here, King Frederick. Please, join us."

Frederick dismounted and walked to the stage, and Philip put his arm around him.

"Collect your generals and meet us in the palace. We have much to discuss."

"Yes, King Philip," Frederick said quietly to the great king.

He looked down at the huge crowd gathered, noting the knights surrounding the throne. He also took in the spectacle of the present moment, mindful of his past, concerned for the future. Memories flashed of days long ago, sneaking out of the Vatican, later escaping from assigned "parents," and sleeping under the tattered docks of Palermo. He smiled and walked into the palace.

XLI

The End Game

Paris, France

1214 AD

"First, let it be stated that we are all grateful you boys didn't march my troops into the Rhine and drown them all," King Philip said, and the room erupted into laughter. "With the help of wise advisors, both French and from other lands, you boys were pragmatic in your use of the knights and dealt Otto a blow he may not even understand. The attrition strategy was the perfect plan for what you faced. Today, Otto's men are tired and without morale. He is just now organizing his entire force. Your success gave us time to organize ahead of him and scout possible battlefields for our inevitable fight with him. It is clear that this entire war will be won or lost in one decisive battle. I believe he will throw everything he has at us in an all-or-nothing campaign. He is not a patient man, and you have frustrated him beyond the point of any logical campaign of the war. We have him where we want him."

While he spoke, generals spoke up with chants of approval for Louis and Frederick.

"A toast to Prince Louis and King Frederick," one of the generals cheered. "They prosecuted the early stages of this war as well as any leader could be called upon to do."

"Here, here!" was the outcry of all

"Now on to the matter at hand," Philip resumed. "It has been reported that Otto has arrived in Aachen but is still in a state of disorganization. The loss of communications for those many days kept most of his knights in the dark, and they are spread all over northern Germany, rallying to him in Aachen but not yet a cohesive force as we are. Because of this, we no longer feel the need to defend Paris. We have the time to march this great army north and meet the emperor on a battleground of our choosing."

"King Philip, if we do march north and wait at a battlefield for Otto, what would our recourse be if he did, in fact, bypass us and march toward Paris?" one of his generals asked. "Would the advantage not be back in his favor?"

Without hesitation, another general chimed in, "Can you imagine attempting to defend Paris and prosecute an offensive campaign against Otto? To protect Paris, we must leave it. Otto is only interested in destroying an army, not a city."

The back-and-forth dialogue in the presence of kings was surprising to Frederick, but Philip insisted they speak openly. Matters of warfare were too important for ceremony.

"It is our opinion and the opinion of those near Otto that his battle plan has shifted from a territorial strategy of occupying French cities to that of a search-and-destroy mission. He will seek this army wherever it is. His intent is to destroy us, then take the lands, titles, and spoils he wants afterward."

―∽―

Aachen, Germany
July 26, 1214 AD

"Our force is now at seventy-five hundred men, Emperor," Otto's general said. "And fifteen hundred of them are knights."

"And what word of the French?"

"They have moved their army from Paris, heading north."

"They are marching toward us?"

"It would appear so, Emperor. Paris, it seems, is left undefended."

"What makes you think that?"

"They have approximately fifty-three to sixty-three hundred men in route, with thirteen hundred knights."

"So they are all in one place? Philip, Louis, the boy king, and the German princes all allied in one force?"

"With that large a force, Paris must be defenseless," another general observed.

"Paris is irrelevant!" screamed Otto. "Why do my generals always quack and quack about tactics and timing? Enough about plans and defenseless towns full of peasants. It was tactics and patience that almost got us killed in the wilderness! We nearly starved to death because of cowardly planning. Never again! This is the time to seize our victory, to end this war.

"Look, our enemy is in front of us. They are smaller than us, and we are superior warriors. It is Philip who has sworn an oath to tactics this time and will now pay for it. Their spies probably assumed that all of the British had left with John the coward. They have been fooled, unaware that Longsword and his battalions have stayed on to fight with us. This child who aspires to be emperor thinks he marches toward a smaller, unorganized force. He doesn't know the greatest general in the British army, Longsword, stands by my side. He underestimates us. We are larger and poised to attack. We shall waste no further time. We march on our enemy tomorrow. We hit them wherever they are. Kings will die this morrow. I swear it to God before you all."

With history unfolding before them, King Phillip and Frederick boldly left the crown jewel of Paris undefended. They were confident their combined forces would prevail against Otto and his allies.

King Philip and Frederick led their allied forces to the town of Tourneau, where they would hold their final war council. They entered knowing that Tourneau was in the region of Flanders where Count

Ferdinand had fled from to fight alongside Otto, but the town had remained loyal to King Philip.

"Count Ferdinand will no doubt command a large group of knights for Otto, but he was unable to convince this town to remain loyal to him. He knows there is no turning back from this decision. I expect him to fight with an all-or-nothing style. Keep this in mind if you are the commander going up against him."

During the council, Philip displayed his bold leadership, stunning even his generals. "In this battle of destiny, it is fitting that Frederick will lead the left column, while Louis will lead the right."

Surprised and somewhat stunned, the generals initially praised their potential, but raised concerns as to the lack of significant battle experience the two of them possessed.

"We have seen their leadership and agree that they have the makings of excellent leaders; however, Your Excellency, we have to question their ability to lead in such a critical battle. The fate of France, Germany, and all of Europe rests on the outcome of this battle. Otto has vast experience. We must not give any edge to the enemy. Do we not have trusted leaders with extensive experience?"

"They have proven themselves as able, patient commanders under battle conditions," Philip said. "And they have more at stake than anyone else, except for me."

"Some things can be reversed, even when King Philip makes the suggestion," one of the generals whispered to an advisor from Aragon. "This isn't one of those things though."

The French scouts burst into the council, their message greatly anticipated. Suitable ground was located for the battle, just as Philip required, lying just ten miles north in a small farming village called Bouvines. The terrain was favorable. As if on cue, Otto was arriving and was last spotted about fifteen miles south of Bouvines in Germany. The conflict between the two great armies was now imminent.

"Bouvines, it will be," Philip said. "Make ready the army. We march at the next day's light."

—⚬—

My Love,

By the time you read this, the war will probably be over. Otto and King Philip have moved their armies near the French and German borders, and one final battle seems imminent. Our final war council met today and it was determined that I should lead the left column. It is a great honor and with it brings great responsibility. I hope that I am capable of this great challenge.

I pray for your well being and for Henry. My love for you and my son knows no boundaries. Please say a prayer for me. Our fate should be known by the day's end tomorrow.

Yours in eternal love,
Frederick

—⟋⟍—

King Philip crossed the bridge over the River Marcq, just outside Bouvines. He gazed down the road built by the Roman legions centuries ago and motioned for Frederick and Louis to cross with him.

"The scouts did well," Philip said to them. "This is perfect ground for this battle."

Louis looked perplexed. "Father, I see no obvious benefits to this ground. I do not understand what we gain by staging the conflict on this land. The grass underfoot is wet. The terrain is flat in all directions. The river and marsh cut off any exiting strategy. What do you see on this cow pasture that strategically advances our cause?"

"Come with me, boys," he said, riding onto the battlefield. "You are right, Louis. There are no obvious advantages on this battlefield. But look closer: the advantages are subtle, but significant. Yes, the ground is wet, particularly near the marsh and river. But as we ride away from the wetlands, observe how dry it becomes."

They rode a little further.

Philip continued. "The ground we stage our columns on will start here. The ground Otto's army will occupy will be back there in the mud, if he chooses to engage us. And that mud will only get worse after we ride over it with our troops."

Frederick smiled at Louis. "And from a distance, Emperor Otto won't recognize the difference in terrain. He will only see an army on level ground."

"Not that Otto will likely ponder those thoughts for long," Philip said. "But if he does, he will see an army with seemingly no significant advantage. And he will surge that army over the bridge without further analysis."

Louis had ridden a little further down the field and yelled back to his father, "I see we do have a retreating exit, if needed. The marsh and river do not intersect as they appear to from the slightly lower elevation of the bridge."

"It gives us a way off the battlefield, but not Otto," Philip said. "Not that Otto will even consider a retreating option before a fight."

"And the sun will be behind us," Frederick said. "Right in Emperor Otto's eyes."

"You boys have learned warfare and tactics quickly. And you have learned through experience as well. But your experience level is about to increase tenfold or more."

"We are ready, Father. We have fought this enemy every day for months in Germany. We know what—"

"This is a different enemy, Louis," Philip declared. "This isn't a smaller enemy pinned down in the wilderness. This is a very large army on a wide-open battlefield. This will not be the small skirmishes you had with him in the woods; this will be all-out warfare. It will come at you much faster than you can imagine."

"We understand the distinctions, King Philip," Frederick said. "We will govern our actions accordingly."

"Command your columns from the rear. Dispatch your generals to convey battlefield tactics. Stay behind your knights if at all possible."

Philip's horse circled, as if sensing his apprehension. He steered the reins and calmed his mount.

"There is no way for you to prepare yourselves for this except to experience it. Lead your columns from the rear. Listen to your generals and make confident, crisp orders. Stay out of the conflict if possible. You are far too valuable to your men than to risk death in pursuit of honor."

Both Louis and Frederick nodded in agreement.

"We are ready, Father."

Philip's horse reared into the air, then settled, spun around, and faced the other way. Philip gained control and said, "Ready your knights. Dispatch your generals to stage our columns. Do this swiftly. Otto will not be far behind."

XLII

The Battle of Bouvines

July 27, 1214 AD

The horn blasts started the action on the battlefield.

"Call to arms!" a battalion leader yelled. "Everyone to your weapons!"

The disciplined French army worked in unison, assembling their weaponry and moving toward their staging grounds. Frederick's column worked quickly, efficiently, and effectively as well, but not to the precision of the French.

A second horn blast pierced the air.

"Call to horses!" a general said to the French knights. "All knights mount and follow your generals!"

King Philip led the way, and his column followed to their place on the Bouvines battlefield. Once positioned, he returned to orchestrate the other columns' positions.

"It's like watching a master move chess pieces on a board," Frederick said to Hector.

"Aye, he is a master tactician. But you keep attention on your flank. These men will depend on your sound decisions today."

Frederick nodded and rode into his position on a very small foothill just behind his column. He watched while Louis did the same on the opposite flank. Philip and his generals took up positions behind his center division, parallel to Frederick and Louis.

The complexity of Philip's plan was surprising, given the experience of his division leaders. Three columns of infantry and cavalry knights working as independent divisions required accuracy and coordination usually found in seasoned veterans. But to also act as reserve for the adjoining division, if needed, seemed unheard of for untested commanders. Despite this gallant approach, Phillip was confident. Cavalry would lead the flanks, while infantry led the center.

Understanding Otto's mindset, they anticipated his notorious infantry opening a hole for a knight surge up the middle. Philip countered by placing his infantry as a buffer, slowing the progress of the German knights, and providing time for the French knights to stage their surge. This strategy potentially linked all three columns while allowing them to operate independently if the battle broke in that manner.

The contrast between Philip and Otto was striking. Philip was a pragmatist. He left as little to chance as possible. Observe, maneuver, execute. King Phillip's tactics extended beyond the battlefield, to also understanding his opponent. He knew Otto, his history and personality, his strengths and weaknesses. King Phillip planned accordingly.

Otto, on the other hand, was Philip's antithesis. He treated the battlefield as if it was on fire.

The emperor relied on speed and power. He called upon a superior number of knights and infantry to create overwhelming violence in the middle of the battlefield. His unwavering battle philosophy rested in the belief that if he dominated the center of the field, all other columns, divisions, and flanks would crumble. Nothing could withstand the center thrust, which would be his lone plan in every battle. Predictably, at any cost, he would seek to cut the opponent's center columns and divisions to pieces. This lone strategy, executed perfectly, was why he led with the most-feared infantry in all of Europe. It was why his best knights always followed immediately behind, ready for the surge. Emperor Otto was a fierce but predictable warrior. To defeat him, you had to neutralize his center attack.

One last piece was yet to be set on this particular battlefield. It arrived from the distant St. Denis Cathedral in Paris. While Otto might be unimpressed and unmoved, French troops reacted jubilantly, cheering wildly as the Oriflamme was placed behind the French division. This sacred silk standard of France was reserved only for battles when France faced heretics or rebels. Its presence noted a defiled foe, a pestilence to be removed, and an enemy of God that must be vanquished. With Otto under excommunication, the banner was hoisted and proudly flown behind Philip's center division.

"God is with the French this day," a French soldier said upon seeing the Oriflamme's approach. "God wills this victory."

"The Oriflamme has always inspired more ferocious and heroic attacks among the French," King Philip said to a nearby general. "We pray it does this for us today."

—⦙⦙⦙—

Otto approached the Marcq River Bridge, confident in his strategy, determined in his mission. To his pleasure, he saw an army of equal or smaller strength, staged on level ground with infantry regulars leading the center column.

"This is what I have envisioned," he said to his general. "We have them in our nets. We will destroy this army, on this field, on this day."

His general began to attempt the organization of the columns that were across the river.

"Ferdinand's division is mostly present," the general said. "And most of yours is here, as well . . . all of your infantry. We can begin as soon as Longsword's division is present."

"No!" Otto said. "No more waiting. Our enemy is before us. Put Ferdinand on the left flank. His knights are present. I will wait for my infantry to cross after he is staged. My knights will follow behind them. Longsword can take the right flank behind me. They are formed in three divisions. We shall fight them as the same."

"Is it wise to put our army on the battlefield with an entire division missing, Emperor?"

"This battle will be won in the center. We will surge through the French and kill Philip. That will end this fight. I do not need Longsword to be here to rout their center. My infantry is superior to theirs. They will cut a hole for me and my knights to ride through. Once that happens, all else is insignificant . . . save one small matter."

He rode to a small unit of archers dressed in black leather outfits. The archers wore no armor, and their horses were lightly packed.

"Do you see that small assemblage of trees on the other side of the river near the left flank of Philip?"

"Yes, Emperor," the unit leader said.

"Take your men there. Train your arrows on the boy king. Do you see him there, hiding behind his knights?"

"Yes, Emperor."

"Is the distance too far for accuracy?"

"It is a long shot, Emperor. But with a volley of arrows from the entire unit, we should be successful."

"I want him just as dead as his uncle Philip. Do you understand?"

"Yes, Emperor. The result will be the same."

Otto led his horse away.

The German call-to-battle soon drowned out the French horns. The Flemish knights began assembling as Count Ferdinand saluted Otto.

"Get those knights on the field, Count. My infantry will follow you, and my knights will be behind them."

"Do we wait on Longsword before engaging, Emperor?" Ferdinand asked.

"No. We hit them as soon as we are staged."

—⁓—

By the time the two armies were on the battlefield, the midday sun was high in the cloudless blue sky. A light breeze blew across the pasture and lifted the many banners of emperor, king, and nobleman alike. The knights' armor glistened in the sun.

"This is a perfect day for a fight," Otto said.

From across the battlefield, Philip agreed. "Conditions could not be better."

It was clear to all involved that this battle would settle the outcome of the war and determine the events of Europe for years to come. History would be made, whoever prevailed.

Count Ferdinand wasted no time getting his knights in position, as Otto had instructed. He struck Louis quickly, the first wave carrying jousting poles. Louis sent his knights to counter also carrying poles, and a violent crash was heard when the initial collision took place.

"It looks like that joust favored Louie," Frederick said.

"It didn't hurt that they began their charge from the mud," Hector said.

Ferdinand immediately sent a second wave of knights into the fray, which included him. He was strong and able as a leader and warrior, fearless in fight. He saw no future aside from winning, as he, a French defector, knew his fate was sealed anywhere in Europe; it was either victory or death.

Louis saw Ferdinand's second wave riding into the battle and answered with another wave of French knights. He also decided it would be prudent for him to lead the second wave once he saw Ferdinand out in front. Word quickly reached Philip that his son was now a combatant and not just leading the flank from the rear.

"Should we send a reserve unit to defend the prince, King Philip?" an advisor asked.

"The right flank is in no peril," he said sternly. "It is in no need of reserve. Louis has made his choice."

Philip knew war was a game of strategy, not emotion. He had to remain patient and let the plan unfold. Although this was an early, unexpected turn of events, it in no way changed his plan or troop movement. No man's safety—even his own son—could alter what had been put into motion. Philip anticipated that Louis might ride into battle if he saw Ferdinand do so. He would have to trust his son and let the battle commence.

Phillip turned his focus on Otto's developing center and the slow trickle of knights and infantry crossing the bridge. Then he looked across the river and saw a banner he was not expecting to see, a banner that could change the outcome of the entire battle.

"Send word to King Frederick that William Longsword's division rides onto the field," King Philip said to a runner. "This should not change our strategy in any way. Longsword will no doubt lead his men from the front. This is not a good reason for him to follow suit. Do not wait for reply."

The French knights absorbed the impact of both waves of knights and made significant headway onto Ferdinand's side of the field. Infantry on both sides was now participating in the fight. These warriors were brutal in comparison to the knights. They fought with swords and spears on foot. They fought hand-to-hand with their adversaries. The shrieks and screams usually came from the pain inflicted by the infantry. It was never a good outcome if a knight dismounted and fell into the infantry's fight. Several nobles and knights were dismounted by the French infantry. Banners lay on the ground. Some knights turned to retreat, but the French infantry clogged the battlefield and confusion led the way. Several French infantrymen forced Ferdinand off his horse, then beat and stabbed him before taking him prisoner, spelling the end of the flank being of any service to Otto.

Louis continued the rout, calling for troop movement while he fought bravely in the center of the field. The French had won this part of the fight impressively, taking many prisoners in the interim.

"Louis is routing them, Hector," Frederick said. "He fights like a king."

"Keep your attention on your flank," Hector said. "That is Longsword's banner flying against you. You will need to be at your best."

"Who is Longsword?" Frederick asked.

"He is England's greatest general, maybe the best in the world. He fought with Richard years ago and with King John in Normandy. I knew him well. He is a friend and an honorable man."

"Then why is he leading a division for Otto?"

"He is Otto's uncle, John's half-brother. They are all related some-how. He is actually King Henry II's son."

"So he fights on behalf of his family?"

"Yes, I am surprised he didn't go back to England after the disaster in Normandy. But I suppose this is their last chance to change the outcome of what happened there."

"If they win here, they can reclaim what they lost," Frederick said.

"That must be their thinking. This battle has ramifications for so many in Europe. So stay focused on leading this division."

"I will, Hector."

Before the fight between Louis and Ferdinand had finished, Otto and his division had crossed the narrow bridge and set up in the middle of the field directly across from King Philip. He saw the struggle Ferdinand and his flank was encountering but chose to concentrate his assets in the middle. A runner arrived from the Flanders' flank, requesting reserves to save the division.

"We cannot do it," Otto said. "Ferdinand's division is on its own."

"Emperor, we cannot let the left flank be destroyed," a general said. "We have reserves to send. We outnumber this army."

"No! I need those reserves to overrun the center. The king's division wins battles among kings. My infantry and reserves will clear the way for me to ride all the way to Philip. We will win this day on that strategy alone. I will not be diverted from this attack because of complications on my flanks."

"Philip is the person he came to fight," said one of his generals to another. "He doesn't care what happens to Ferdinand or Longsword. He is here to fight and kill Philip. He is an assassin with Imperial credentials."

Otto sent first his infantry to soften the center for his knight surge. The German infantry were the strongest foot soldiers in all of Europe. They stormed the battlefield with axes, long poles, hooks, and lances. They looked like ancient Vikings, and they terrified most infantries they faced.

The French infantry met them gallantly but could not stand up to the onslaught. After an hour, the middle of the battlefield was filled with blood, dead bodies, and injured infantry on both sides, but particularly French casualties. It was a horrific sight, but Otto saw an opening leading directly to King Philip.

Soon, Otto and his knights rode through the hole. Philip also saw the gaping hole from the hill overlooking the center and sent French knights to fill it. The German surge spilled past the knights and nearly made it all the way to Philip.

Frederick also saw Otto's progress and sent waiting reserves to the middle to hold off his advance. With the exception of an errant arrow occasionally flying over his head, he had seen no action; however, Frederick's reserve movement possibly saved the center division. Not far behind, Louis also sent a reserve unit into the center, which created a stalemate in the middle of the battlefield and kept Otto and his knights from reaching Philip.

Now with time to reorganize, Louis sent the majority of his knights into his father's battle in the center, and the French began to turn the tide. Despite having a larger army, Otto was now outnumbered in his own battle in the middle of the conflict.

While the battle raged in the center and concluded on the French right, Longsword marched his division fully onto the battlefield. He saw the distress in the center and the disaster of the Ferdinand division. His first impression was to help Otto, but it was too haphazard to venture any plan. It would be difficult to stage reserve help not knowing what Otto's plan might be. But he would send reserves nonetheless in an attempt to save him.

"Always a pleasure to fight with an impulsive, emotional leader such as Otto," Longsword said sarcastically. "This will probably go down as the most important battle of the decade, and Otto has advanced into a hornet's nest, and destroyed an entire division before one-third of his force has even arrived."

He looked to his right and saw the Sicilian banners unfamiliar to him leading a division of uniforms he had never seen before.

"Is that Henry's boy leading a division?"

"Yes, my lord," said a unit commander. "It's King Frederick of Sicily leading knights from Sicily, Italy, Aragon, and Germany."

Longsword pondered that for a moment while his division staged itself against Frederick's flank, and reserves began to organize for their assistance of Otto in the middle.

"How old is Frederick?"

"Don't know, my lord, but he is surely still in his teen years."

"Hold the reserves."

"Hold, my lord? Emperor Otto is in peril."

"If we throw all our assets at Frederick's division, we can overwhelm them. If we completely rout that flank, we can hit Philip from his rear and surround the center. Louis seems occupied with taking prisoners. If we swiftly destroy the other flank and suddenly engage Philip from his rear, Louis may not realize what is happening before it's too late to aid his father."

"Are you calling for our reserve force to be combined with our knights and infantry, my lord?"

"That is precisely what I'm calling for, General. We will outnumber Frederick's division dramatically . . . and it appears he has sent his reserves into the center. He cannot draw upon them now. Our assets will be best served in routing that flank swiftly, then turning and pinning King Philip right in the middle of it all. Combine the reserve and infantry to begin the attack."

—◊◊◊—

"That looks like a very large infantry," Frederick said to Hector. "Do you think ours can hold?"

"'Tis not just infantry. That's his reserves filing in next to his infantry in the lead. Longsword is one of the best generals in the world. We will have our hands full holding him."

There was a long pause while they watched Longsword staging his columns, infantry, and reserves in front of his British knights.

"Can our infantry hold?" Frederick inquired.

"I don't know."

"If they can't hold, we will be routed. Our knights will not even get a chance to fight Longsword. They will be bottled up in a mass of infantry."

Hector thought for a moment. "It may be necessary to send our knights in a flanking tactic around the infantry skirmish and into Longsword's knights before they rush the center of the columns."

"But if we time that wrong, Longsword's knights and infantry will have a wide-open field to our rear. He would surround King Philip in the center, and our knights would be cut off to help."

"Aye . . . 'tis why we must not time it wrong."

Frederick looked at Hector for a moment, and looked down the hill at Longsword and his magnificent knights. He knew this could potentially decide the entire battle.

"Okay, Hector. I leave it to you to time this right."

Hector smiled and pulled the reins to turn his horse toward the knights. Once he reached them, he yelled, "We flank the infantry and surprise attack the English at first contact."

The knights roared their approval at this bold maneuver.

"Ride as near to the infantry as you can. We don't want the English to see our surge until we are upon them."

Hector aligned the knights along the left side of the column. He left a unit of knights to protect Frederick, and to defend the rear of the division in case Longsword did break through the surge. Arrows flew in from an odd trajectory but did not injure any of the knights before they began their secret surge down the left flank.

The contact point between the two infantries was at a narrow dirt road that casually crossed the battlefield. The English hit with ferocity, knowing they had to break through rapidly to allow Longsword's knights to ride through the hole. Frederick's infantry held on, but the superior English numbers were taking a toll. Several times Frederick saw holes open in his line, only to be closed before advantage could be taken.

Suddenly, from the extreme left came Hector's knight surge, hitting the British with force and surprise. Several knights were knocked off their horses and landed hard into the mud. The sounds of jousting poles crashing into shields filled the air. Horses fell to the ground, and infantrymen quickly approached. It was confusing and bloody for the British knights, but the vast majority was able to survive the unexpected surge.

Longsword was able to regroup his cavalry in time not to be routed, but Hector was able to cut them off from his infantry, thus forcing them to fight in close quarters without a surge and nowhere near Philip's rear.

The two battles on Frederick's flank essentially stalemated for hours. His reserve force was able to be reclaimed from the center and had stabilized the fight against Longsword's infantry and reserve. Philip's center strategy had broken Otto's breathtaking surge. Many of the German knights had fled the field, while others were just arriving. Despite an occasional knight showing up to aid Otto, his division was defeated.

Hector and his knights had almost fought their way to Longsword. The British knights were surrounded, and Hector thought they would break soon. Longsword and his knights fought valiantly, though, and did not break.

Frederick watched from the foothill while his knights fought tirelessly for him. The Aragon knights had escorted him all the way from Palermo. The German princes had started with him in Constance and quickly believed in his abilities. The Italian knights had crossed the Alps with him—all had stayed until this conclusive, bloody battle. It was hard for Frederick to focus on strategy and tactics amid the bloody violence he was witnessing. Philip was right; this was nothing like the wilderness campaigns he and Louis waged against Otto. This bloody battle was killing and maiming people he knew.

Time and time again, the knights would hit Longsword with great force, and Longsword took the blows and continued fighting. Longsword was an incredible leader in the eyes of Frederick. He not only fought a smart campaign under duress, but led his men in battle. Frederick wished he had gone down the hill with his knights. The only battle he saw was still the occasional stray volley of arrows from archers unknown or unseen.

Otto also fought alongside his fractured cavalry; he fought fiercely, even in the knowledge of near certain defeat. He turned to see Philip still directing what seemed now to be a successful campaign.

There were brave leaders in the middle of the clash leading from the front. They were to be commended for their bravery. But the victorious leader was behind his men—still very much engaged in its twists and turns and very much focused on which moves to make to assure victory.

Frederick looked down the hill again to see Hector's progress. Just then, another arrow flew over his head from an odd angle away from the battlefield, then another from the center division. Frederick looked in the direction where the arrow had come from and saw Otto pointing at him to a small unit of archers on the battlefield. The archers let off another volley that flew over Frederick's head.

"It's a difficult shot up the hill," Frederick said to his knights.

The small unit of knights said nothing but surrounded Frederick to protect him from the archers.

"Can you imagine an emperor attempting the assassination of a king on the battlefield?" one knight said.

"It shows his lack of character," another knight responded.

From the forest on the other side of the river, Frederick heard a hissing sound, and then felt an intense, sharp pain. An arrow pierced his shoulder. He screamed in agony and shock. The knights rode to him, seeing the archer unit riding into the forest. More arrows volleyed in from down the hill, missing long. Frederick fled the hill, and the pain intensified when Dragon began his canter. Another stray arrow hit one knight during the retreat. Frederick could not handle the intensified pain of riding, so he stopped Dragon and looked down the hill.

He saw Otto in the center of a chaotic battlefield, looking back at him. It was as if Otto pondered riding up the hill to kill Frederick. With the chaos of retreating knights and the French taking injured prisoners, Otto was invisible in plain sight of all—except for Frederick.

The stabbing pain of the arrow began to dismiss all reason from his thoughts. His rational battlefield logic had disappeared. He could only focus on the pain and his rage.

And his rage was trained solely on Otto.

He knew what Otto intended. It was completely against the rules of engagement for a king to assassinate a king. But Otto did not see Frederick as a king . . . or he didn't care. Any respect Frederick had felt for Otto had vanished, replaced by foolishness, pain, and anger.

He looked down the hill again. The slightest movement caused pain to radiate up his arm and shoulder. There was Otto on his black stallion, the man who had killed his uncle, the man who tried to kill him in Sicily, and again today on this battlefield in such a contemptuous manner. But it wasn't just Otto down there. In Frederick's mind, it was Otto, Pope Innocent, the death of his parents, the treatment of him by his foster parents, and most recently the death of a knight defending him from a cowardly archer attack in the woods. All of his life's injustices sat on the black stallion in the center of the battlefield down the hill. His rage quickly boiled over.

Finally, Otto seemed to discount the idea of killing Frederick as reckless. He turned his horse away and slowly rode away, following the retreat off the field. Frederick's fury intensified. He could not allow Otto free passage, even in defeat. His wrath for the symbol Otto had become would not allow it.

He screamed in agony as he pulled the arrow out of his shoulder and threw it aside; the pain nearly caused him to lose consciousness. Then he started down the hill with Dragon in full gallop.

"Otto!" he screamed upon approach. "Otto!" he yelled again and again.

Otto turned from his retreat to see Frederick riding at him.

"Look at this," Otto said to no one in particular. "This is too good to be true. He's riding right to me with a hole in his shoulder. I will put another hole right through his heart."

If he could kill Frederick, his army's loss in the battle might not cost him his imperial crown. With his contender dead, he could retreat back to northern Germany and negotiate an agreement with Pope Innocent. As Otto kicked his horse and headed straight for Frederick in the middle of the abandoned battlefield, Frederick drew his sword and charged.

Otto held tight to his shield, but the impact of Frederick's sword broke it in half. The concussion of the blow threw Frederick off Dragon. He lay still, face down on the ground. Otto tried desperately to stay on his mount but finally fell off several yards away from Frederick. His horse stayed close to him, and he drew his sword and approached the motionless Frederick.

Louis saw what had happened and yelled in Frederick's direction. "Frederick, get up! Get up!"

He rode toward Frederick from the other flank. Hector also came fast from the opposite flank, and even King Philip from atop the hill.

All three knew they would not reach him in time.

—✀—

Frederick tried to sit up, but could not. He looked down the battlefield, but his vision was blurry. Time seemed to stand still. Then he heard a voice and looked up and saw his father standing in front of him.

"Surround yourself with Italians, and you wind up face down in the mud."

"What?"

"You heard me, boy. You can't fight a battle this epic with Italians as your soldiers."

"I have half of Europe behind me. I have France, Aragon, and Germany."

"Not enough Germans; but none of it matters."

"What does matter, Father?"

"You have to kill Otto. He is hell bent on killing you."

"I understand."

"If he does, all is lost. Our bloodline will end. The Welfs will rule Germany for generations. All will be lost."

"I have a son now, Father."

"If you are killed on this battlefield, Otto will return to Sicily and kill your son and your wife. I'm sorry to be so hard on you, son. I'm sorry I wasn't there to train you for this moment. Your mother spoiled you. You need to be a German warrior now. There is no time for anything else. You must get up from the mud and end this Welf's life. Everything depends on it."

"I know, Father."

—✀—

Otto closed the gap quickly, knowing he must kill Frederick and immediately flee; any hesitation would cause him either to be captured or killed. Once in striking distance, he raised his massive sword above his head.

Just then, Frederick rolled over and ran his sword through Otto's stomach, then stood and pushed it deeper into him. Otto grasped the blade and looked at Frederick in disbelief. He screamed at a volume that alerted the entire battlefield. Frederick wildly stared at Otto, his eyes filled with wrath. Otto moaned in an inaudible groan and held his bleeding torso. Frederick fell to the ground unconscious, his shoulder bleeding fluidly through his armor.

XLIII

The Aftermath

K nights and generals all rushed to Frederick's aid, and to King Philip's protection. Louis and Hector also rapidly approached.

The battle now won, French knights continued to take prisoners. From the British right flank, Longsword looked fixated on Frederick, seemingly unconcerned with becoming a prisoner.

"Did you see that?" he said to a British general. "Henry's boy ran Otto through."

"We must retreat, my lord. The battle is lost."

"I wonder if he is all right."

Longsword began the retreat, but not before seeing Frederick sit up. He seemed to smile in his direction before leading his knights off the battlefield in retreat.

"The battle is over, nobles," he said to a small group of knights only now arriving at the battlefield. "Turn around and ride away from here. There is no glory left. King Frederick has all that is left to acquire."

Somehow in all the chaos, Otto was rescued by a retreating German knight, or his body recovered; that was not to be known on this day.

Finally, King Philip, Hector, and Louis had reached Frederick and were by his side. Physicians attended to him and quickly determined that his injuries were serious but not life-threatening.

"In time, he will recover fully," the French physician said.

"Congratulations, King Frederick," Philip said. "You have earned the right to be called king of the Germans."

"I cannot believe you came down that hill," Hector said. "What were you thinking?"

Frederick groaned and weakly smiled but said nothing.

"This was a great day for us all!" Louis said jubilantly. "A great day indeed, and my brother Frederick is here to share it with us—alive to share in the glory!"

XLIV

The King of the Germans

"We have good news, Frederick," Philip said as he entered the hospital room with Louis and Hector. "We have found the eagle scepter."

"This is one of the relics you must possess to be the king of the Germans," Hector said.

"We found it on the battlefield," Louis said. "Otto must have left it in his haste to retreat."

"I didn't know I needed relics to be a king," Frederick said.

"There are others you must gain as well," Hector said. "There is the German crown, and—"

"Can't I just have my own crown made? I would prefer to—"

"No!" Philip snapped. "These relics, the crown and scepter, must be in place for you to ascend."

"All right, King Philip. I won't have a new crown made," Frederick relented. "I hear the French kingdom has increased after Bouvines. Did I fight on the side that took lands away from my empire?"

"Well, your empire is a little smaller than it was. But don't blame me for that . . . you can blame your predecessor."

"That's all right, King Philip. Those lands spoke French all along."

"As did Normandy," Louis said. "Where John experienced his greatest loss."

"The Battle of Bouvines will change the political landscape of Europe for decades to come," Philip said.

"King John lost all claim to Normandy and was forced to pay ransoms for the return of many of his nobles. I've never seen so many prisoners taken in such a massive, face-to-face battle."

"The defensive armor outdistanced the killing weapons," Hector said, "which was why there were more prisoners than casualties among the nobility."

"Not so among the infantry," said Frederick.

"For the infantry it was a bloody ordeal on both sides," said Hector.

"So what will happen to John?" Louis asked.

"The defeat and premature retreat angered the British landowners," Philip said. "They lost their estates in Normandy, and their confidence in John. He will be forced to sign something called the Magna Carta, which will limit his power as king of England. They were talking about doing this to him even before his humiliating loss in Normandy. Now he will be unable to resist their pressure."

"It's unthinkable," Louis said. "John will go down as the worst king in European history."

"The Holy Roman Empire lost a little land, but gained a great alliance," Hector said to Philip. He turned toward Louis and continued. "An alliance that will last for generations."

Hector paused for a moment.

"It was an honor to again fight with the French and their great king," Hector told Philip, referring to their alliance in the Third Crusade.

"The honor was ours, Hector. King Richard was a bastard, but a great warrior. He would have been proud of this one going down the hill to battle Otto," he said, pointing at Frederick.

"I believe you are right, King Philip," Hector said. "Richard would have loved to see Frederick knock Otto on his ass."

"Otto will have to surrender the German crown and other relics to you soon, Frederick," Louis said. "All German kings abide by that, right Father?"

"Otto lost everything. His excommunication will never be lifted, and his titles of king of the Germans and Holy Roman emperor will be stripped from him. He has probably retreated to a German cave and will never again be a factor in German politics. But he will relinquish the crown and scepter. He may have been more of a warlord than an emperor, but he won't tarnish the honor of Germany or the Welf family name. You will have your crown before coronation."

"Coronation," Frederick said, looking at Hector. "It had not occurred to me what victory meant . . . until now. We should leave for Germany soon. I want to meet with each prince in their own regions to thank them and gain their support and ideas in bringing prosperity back to Germany before I return to Sicily."

"We will leave when you are able to travel," Hector said. "When you are fully healed, we shall meet with the princes."

"Will you go to northern Germany, or just the friendly regions?" Louis asked. "Not all of Germany is pleased with the outcome of Bouvines."

"Whether they like me or not, I am king of all Germans, Louie. The north will have to make terms with me, and I with them. I need all of Germany to come together, not just the part that favors my family; otherwise, the war was for nothing, and civil war will start again as soon as I leave."

"He speaks like an emperor already, Hector," Philip said. "You have trained him well."

"I cannot take credit for his talents, Your Majesty. God gave him his abilities because he was destined to be a king, just as you and Louis are."

"Without Hector, I would not be here today. I would still be living on the streets of Palermo, or worse. If it is God's will that I am a king, then God sent Hector to me. I will continue to lean on him as counsel. I know the German princes still see me as a young foreign king that is more the pope's choice than their own. I pray that all three of you continue steering me in a wise direction."

"Let me tell you something, Frederick," Philip said sternly. "All of us will provide you with counsel if asked. But I, too, became king at a young age and had these same thoughts. Here is what I learned, your first piece of advice from me: every decision you make falls on you, and no one else. Seek good counsel on whatever matters you need. Gather as much intelligence and wisdom as you can, then make the decision that is best for you and your empire. Remember that you are emperor and that if you follow Hector's counsel or mine, ultimately it is your choice—good decision or bad. All glory or shame lies in your hands and on your head. All credit begins and ends with you."

"I will remember, King Philip."

———⟶

"So you have finally recovered," Louis said to Frederick. "I guess fragile Italian bones take longer to heal."

"His wounds healed at a very rapid pace, Prince Louis," said the physician, not understanding the humor.

He stretched out Frederick's arm and had him make a circling motion to prove his point.

"See? Perfectly healed. No pain in the shoulder, and full range of the arm restored."

"Thank you, Doctor," Frederick said. "You have done a tremendous job on me. Your hospital is the finest in all of Europe. I can only hope one day to have as fine a facility as this in Germany and Sicily."

The physician smiled approvingly.

Frederick and Louis left the hospital and rode back to Philip's castle. There, all of Frederick's knights assembled for the anticipated journey to Germany.

"When will you be going?" asked Louis.

"As soon as Hector returns from Champagne," Frederick said. "He has acquired quite a fondness for that region. It has been a month since I first sent him to establish our trade relations. What I thought would be a simple trip has evidently grown much more complicated. This is his fifth time there."

"Maybe something is there that is more interesting than trade relations," Louis said. "Perhaps Hector is building trade relations with one of the maidens of Champagne."

Frederick laughed. "You know, he did introduce me to a girl when we were there. Her name escapes me."

"Don't worry, I'm sure he will refresh your memory when he returns. When is his anticipated arrival?"

"Tonight. If he's on schedule, we shall ride for Aachen tomorrow."

"Are you sure Aachen is a wise start to your journey?" Louis asked. "It is, after all, where Otto staged his army. He could be in hiding there. Its loyalty is at best undecided."

"I have to reach out to northern Germany; otherwise, I am king of half the kingdom, and a rival will no doubt challenge me in a few years, or when I leave Germany." His eyes lit up. "Sophia . . . that is the name of the girl Hector introduced me to."

Louis smiled. "Your mind never stops working on a problem until you have it resolved, no matter how trivial."

They walked through the castle door into the corridor to the great room to a roar of applause. Frederick turned to Louis in confusion at the sight of servants and a gathering of knights.

"This is a victory celebration we have waited to start until your brittle bones healed."

The Aragon knights all cheered and surrounded Frederick, carrying him on their shoulders into the center of the grand ballroom.

"We delivered his wife to him in Sicily," one of the Aragon knights said to a French general. "We followed him through the Alps and fought with him in the wilderness, and at Bouvines. We watched him go from boy king to warrior . . . now soon to be emperor."

"We would follow him to the gates of hell."

They planned the march to Germany for the next morning, but on this night, the wine flowed. The knights joined with Frederick in celebrating the fruits of their respective hard-fought victories, appreciating the results of their labors. In the same room, the knights from Aragon declared war on the French while the Italian knights were poised to fight the German knights. The battle of the grand ballroom was about to commence.

Hector returned later that evening.

"This is usually how these celebrations go," Philip said. "Best for the royalty to retire and yield the room to our gallant knights."

Frederick and Louis laughed and walked into an adjoining room, with a cask of wine under each arm. Hector followed them closely.

"No matter the knights' condition, we leave at first light."

"Or maybe we should make another stop in Champagne," Frederick said mockingly.

Hector looked at him, puzzled.

"Yes, I'm not sure you spent enough time there," added Louis.

"What are you two talking about?"

"What was that girl's name you introduced me to in Champagne?"

"Her name is Sophia."

"Is?" Louis asked. "You said that in present tense, Hector. Is she still present tense?"

Hector shrugged his shoulders, and turned to walk into the grand ballroom. Suddenly, a chair flew across the room toward the door. He sidestepped out of the way.

"I'll let you lads gossip among yourselves like two school girls. We will be ready to ride at first light." He disappeared from the room.

"He's not one to open up," Philip said.

"No. It has never been his strong suit," Frederick said. "But I will be glad to have him in northern Germany."

"How long will you stay ithere?" asked Louis.

"I don't know," said Frederick. "I want to meet with every prince. I don't like the feudal system that exists in Sicily, but most of these princes risked their lives and livelihoods to change things for the better. That is not the type of feudal lords I am accustomed to. In contrast, the nobles of Sicily fled the island the moment they heard Otto was on his way. I will have to observe this country and its leaders before I decide what to do or how long to stay."

XLV

Peace and Prosperity in Germany

The northwest trail to Aachen was a little more crowded than Frederick expected. He wanted to bring only the princes of Germany and their knights on the trip, but the knights of Aragon would not hear of it.

Neither would Hector.

"The king does not travel adversarial roads without a large force of knights. Northern Germany is still unknown, and we must consider that the Aragon knights will not leave your side unless we kill them, so they are going with us."

Frederick waved to a crowd of people in Reims, a small town on the border of France and the province of Champagne. It astonished him the amount of attention being paid to him.

"I accept your advice, Hector. I do not want to be unsafe. On the other hand, I do not wish to appear as occupiers in my own kingdom, or that I rule through intimidation; instead, I want the princes out front with me once we reach Aachen."

"I understand your intent, and your desired appearance for Aachen and all of northern Germany to see. I promise you we will build that image. We will not appear as an aggressor."

Hector looked down the road at the crowd. It was already as far as the eye could see, and swelling. But Frederick appeared nearly oblivious to it all, lost in his own thoughts and focused on his ultimate goal of peace and prosperity for Germany.

Hector smiled and rode alongside Frederick.

—ɯ—

The large city of Aachen sat in the northwest corner of Germany. It was an important part of trade, military, and religion to the kingdom. Under Otto, it was reduced into little more than a fortress for his knights.

All industry withered, except for that which served the military. Religion was essentially forgotten and quickly faded into irrelevance. With Otto unseated, Aachen itself was a ghost town—a city that time forgot. Any concern for an insurgency seemed misplaced.

"This town does not have an appetite for revolt," Hector said to Frederick. "It isn't in them to attack a German king, no matter his residence."

"Aachen is an historic town," Frederick said. "I can see the potential to make this the gateway to European commerce."

Frederick turned to count Palatine of the Rhine, an electing prince of Germany who rode with him from Constance to Bouvines.

"Can you direct us to the cathedral, Count Palatine?"

"I will, King Frederick. It is very near the tomb of Charlemagne."

"Very good. I want to see that as well. Charlemagne is important to my plans here."

"Not much fanfare for the arrival of a new king," Hector said, turning around to speak to the knights behind him. "Keep a close eye out for assassins or mercenaries."

"Here is the cathedral, my lord," said Count Palatine.

The Aachen Cathedral stood at the end of the road. Its grand design and size dominated the landscape and brought forth Aachen as the ancient seat of the Western Roman Empire it once was. The tomb of Charlemagne fronted the cathedral but had fallen into significant disrepair. The cathedral had fallen apart as well.

"This would make a great project for Francis," Hector said to Frederick. "I wonder how he is doing?"

"I pray he is safe," Frederick said. "I pray we see him again soon."

Frederick entered the cathedral to meet the archbishops of Mainz, Cologne, and Trier. Along with Count Palatine, they made up four of the seven electing princes of Germany.

It was of importance that a majority of electors be present in Aachen, as Frederick had chosen this time to be coronated king of the Germans. It was traditional for this ceremony to take place here, dating back to the latter stages of the Roman Empire.

Frederick knew he should keep this tradition. The people must connect him with the glory of this city, and the lineage to this great emperor.

"We are pleased to see you here safe, my lord," said the archbishop of Mainz.

"Your coronation will be tomorrow," said the archbishop of Cologne. "We are honored you have followed the history of German kings and chosen Aachen, despite its allegiance to the previous king."

"The war is over, Archbishop. We go forward as one united Germany."

—⁓—

The following morning, Frederick presented himself to the archbishop for coronation. He arose early, careful to focus his thoughts on his mission of unifying Germany. There was a part of him that couldn't embrace the high ceremony; inside, he was still conscious of that street child, fleeing from the brutal tyranny of one such as he who was not taking the throne. It was an unsettling notion, but one he accepted as divine, heaven-sent, and beyond earthly revocation.

The details blurred in his mind, hearing the words, accepting the charge, making the pledge; instead, images of his precious Constance and newborn son distracted him. This was merely his duty, a requirement for the religious hierarchy, a ritual to build credibility for peasant and prince alike.

He already knew his place, and he was anxious to move on.

—⁓—

Frederick was crowned king of the Germans before the electing princes, and a small stoic crowd inside and in front of the cathedral. After the ceremony, Frederick left the cathedral and delivered remarks near the tomb of Charlemagne.

"Citizens of Aachen, citizens of Germany . . . I begin my journey through this kingdom in this historic town not to establish myself as ruler or victor, but to restore the splendor that was once Aachen. Before the tomb of Charlemagne, I make a vow. I will rebuild and repair what time and war have eroded. I speak not only of structures and roads, but commerce, trade, and goodwill.

"Emperor Charlemagne saw fit to give favorable trade agreements and lower taxes to stimulate the Aachen economy. With war taxes of the past decade stifling this town, I see you have suffered. But your suffering is at an end. On this day, I declare that the trade agreements and taxes be restored to the levels you enjoyed under Charlemagne's reign."

Up to this point in his speech, the Aachen crowd had been respectful. But with the mention of lower taxes, they viewed the young emperor in a new light and began to cheer.

"Aachen will again be the trade center of northern Europe. Germany will again trade with France, Italy, and Sicily. Your goods will again be sold at the fairs of Champagne, and your town will flourish again as it once did . . . as it never has before."

A singular voice arose from the silence, "Long live King Frederick!" Another echoed this remark, until the swell of approval became a wave of applause and a chant of confirmation.

"Tomorrow begins the rebuilding of this proud city. Improvements to this great cathedral and many other buildings will renew Aachen as the beautiful city on the mountain. But the first improvement made will be to move emperor Charlemagne into a golden tomb. That project will commence this very day, and I will personally oversee it to completion."

The Aragon knights stood amazed, looking at each other in amazement.

"I had no idea he had a speech like this in him," one knight said to another.

Frederick, continuing amidst the growing sentiment, was now yelling to be heard over the raucous crowd. But the crowd was satisfied with what they had already heard and was now more intent on shouting their approval than being able to listen further. The commotion of coronation could not have been any more pleasing.

"He is full of surprises," another knight said. "He has come a long way on this journey."

"From a boy to man," Hector said, watching Frederick with pride.

The crowd, catching their breath, quieted enough to hear the young emperor's next words.

"My countrymen, it is my intention to make this one united empire, one Germany. No longer will we be northern and southern Germany in constant civil war. This empire will stand together as one. It will be a partner in continental prosperity with our neighbors to the west and to the south. The days of division in Germany have hereby ended."

With his final words, the crowd erupted into a deafening roar, shouting and cheering, applauding, and making noise in whatever way they could.

The people of Aachen had never heard such a speech. Any passion delivered by a king was in regards to an upcoming war. Never had a king spoke of their town's interests.

That afternoon, Frederick not only officiated over the interment of Charlemagne's new tomb, he also took a shovel and broke ground beside the workers. By the time their efforts concluded, Charlemagne had a shining golden tomb and Aachen had a beloved new king.

When Frederick left the next morning, the streets were filled with well-wishers, cheering him and his knights. It was a successful first leg of the journey. The next town, however, would be Cologne—the city where Otto was rumored to be hiding.

—⚏—

Frederick crossed the Rhine River into Cologne, Germany. Count Palatine of the Rhine and the archbishop of Cologne accompanied him.

Cologne was a middle-sized town that sat directly on the Rhine. Much like Aachen, it had been an important trade route before Otto's war. It had since been taxed into depression, though, and its trade routes evaporated during the conflict.

"When we arrive, let me lead the discussion in the beginning, Your Grace," the archbishop said. "I have known Duke Albert for some time."

"Tell me about him," Frederick said.

"The duke favored Otto, as had Cologne and all of Saxony," said the count. "It is rumored the duke is aiding Otto."

"I know that, Count. But what do you know about the man?"

"The duke is a broad-shouldered man with long black hair and a beard cropped close to his face," the archbishop claimed. "He is untrusting of anyone or anything that is not German."

"He sounds like my father," Frederick said.

"But unlike your father, he rarely leaves Saxony," said the count. "Even this trip to Cologne was further than he usually goes to meet people—kings included. But he happens to have a small estate here."

"Why did he favor Otto, considering the condition in which Otto left Saxony?" Frederick asked.

"He favored Otto and the Welfs in political issues because they were of the north," the archbishop said. "His primary concern has always been Saxony, not of larger issues to do with country or empire. Otto's loss at Bouvines was of little importance to him, except his concern that you might attempt to rule Germany instead of allowing the princes to rule their own regions. Even though Otto was no friend to Saxony, he did leave the duke to govern as he pleased."

"Despite his narrow worldview, the duke is an effective leader," Hector said.

"That is the only qualification I require for the duke to govern Saxony," Frederick said.

—⁂—

Frederick, Hector, and the archbishop entered Duke Albert's small castle and walked up the stairway. The duke was standing over a large wooden table with a map of Saxony spread out and discussing orders with his staff.

"Come in. I will be with you momentarily," he said dismissively.

Frederick looked at Hector, who looked back at him and said nothing, and then at the archbishop, who looked forward so as not to make eye contact. Frederick chose to let the duke's insolence pass.

"I have word from Aachen that your lofty promises were well received, Your Grace," said the duke. "Congratulations, King Frederick. It is always good for a new king to set platitudes of great height for his subjects."

"This young king has laid the groundwork for a new Aachen," said the archbishop. "We hope he will do the same for Cologne. He seems able to end the divisions in Germany. He has my full support."

The duke stood steadfast in his reticence. "That is an important endorsement, Archbishop," the duke said cautiously. "Is he promising improvements and autonomy for the church here?"

"No more than any other establishment."

The duke turned to Frederick. "How do you plan on restoring Aachen and Cologne, King Frederick?"

"Aachen, Cologne, and all of Saxony should be the primary trade center for northern Europe. This region should tie into the fair at Champagne and ship its goods all the way to Sicily. In order to get this region up to those standards, upgrades must be made. This plan has already begun in Aachen. Cologne and Saxony, I pray, will be next."

"With due respect, King Frederick, that is the why; I asked *how* you will achieve this. I, too, want Saxony to flourish as a region and trade with the entire world. But the markets and tradesmen do not exist for this dream. The reality is, Saxony is structured to survive, not craft goods and ship them to Champagne. With our taxes higher than we can already afford, those dreams are just that. Saxony cannot afford to dream."

Frederick chose to again ignore the disrespect and focus on the duke's substance. He looked at Hector, who seemed to be deferring to him. It surprised him that Hector had not corrected the duke to use proper protocol when speaking to the king.

"You and I are partners in the improvement of Saxony, my lord. I, too, want what is best for the people of your region. But my idea is for the good of the empire, as well as Saxony. How I plan to accomplish this is to use the taxes once used for war to rebuild this land and re-establish these ancient trade lines between Germany, France, Italy, and Sicily."

"High taxes have crippled Saxony," said the duke. "We cannot—"

Frederick interrupted, "No, Duke, high taxes and the civil war crippled Saxony, and the entire empire. I have seen its effects as far south as Constance. I have seen its toll even in Sicily. I am lowering taxes to a pre-Charlemagne rate, but all of the revenue will stay here. None of it will go to the crown for two years. And even then more treasure will stay with your people. It will stay in Saxony, to rebuild and improve it. A commercial dock will be constructed to send your goods down the Rhine to the entire world, and goods will be sent to you. New trade partners will pour wealth here. Meanwhile, war will no longer drain German resources. You will soon find a time of enlightened enterprise that will pull Saxony out of its depression."

"These riches you speak of will flow from northern Germany south to Champagne, then to your kingdom of Sicily," the duke responded. "These riches will originate in Germany and come home to Sicily. Saxony does not need to contribute its labor and work product to the rest of Europe. Saxony will be self-sufficient, as it always is. We will survive and flourish as a region without the help or disturbance of the rest of Europe."

"You see only half the picture, Duke. The riches will flow from Sicily and France to Saxony, then back to Sicily, France, and Saxony again. It's called circulation, and the only way it can succeed is if the riches flow both ways to everyone involved."

The duke shrugged his shoulders and groaned, then stood up from the table and walked over to the window.

"What is it you want from me, King Frederick? I see no place for myself in your plan."

"I have four requirements of you, Duke."

"Name them, please," he said, turning to face Frederick.

"I want you to remain as the duke of Saxony and manage the improvements and day-to-day business of the area. I do not like the feudal system that exists in Sicily, but in your case, I see you have the best interest of Saxony in mind. Collect the lowered taxes and put them into improvements."

The duke stepped closer to Frederick. "I agree to the first . . . and the next requirement?"

"I want your allegiance."

"You are king of the Germans," the duke said, laughing. "You have a majority of electors without me. Of course you have my allegiance. There is no question of it."

"But what I am asking for goes beyond the blind acceptance of the election and victory on a battlefield. That hollow allegiance is why Germany has been at war with itself for decades. What I seek is agreement with my vision for Saxony and a leader that is behind me. Once I leave here, it will be years before I return. It is essential I know you are a partner in this plan. Because once I leave, you are Germany to these people. Now, under those conditions, do I have your loyalty?"

The duke looked at Frederick for a moment. The room remained silent. Then a hint of a slight grin adorned his face.

"You have it."

There was another pause in the room until the duke spoke again.

"That sounded like a final term, King Frederick. I thought you had four?"

"I do. The third term is that you accept the changes that are coming. You cannot oversee these projects from your castle. You may have to travel more than you are accustomed."

"I am no friend to change."

"Change isn't looking for friends, Duke Albert. Change is like the wind; it blows into our lives, and we either open our sails to it, or it blows us into pieces."

The duke walked off again, only this time Frederick stood and pursued him, putting his hand on the duke's broad shoulder.

"But with the change comes opportunity. Change will translate into success. Cologne and all of Saxony will flourish under these changes."

The duke turned and smiled at Frederick, slapping his back and walking back to the group.

"And your final term?"

"I want you to locate Otto and collect the royal crown, robes, and scepter. In order to be crowned Holy Roman emperor, I need the royal relics to be recognized as king of the Germans."

"What makes you think I know of Otto's whereabouts?" asked the duke. "Aiding a fallen excommunicated enemy of the king would be treason."

"The bloody business between me and Otto ended on the Bouvines battlefield. I have no punitive message to send to Otto, or to anyone providing him comfort or a place to hide. Otto isn't a fugitive or enemy to me. He just happens to have relics that I need when I get to Rome. Secure those for me, and you will have my thanks."

"You would allow your rival to recover from his wounds and rebuild an army to fight you?"

"You are the duke of Saxony, and you have pledged your loyalty to me. There will always be Welfs in this region that have rebellious aspirations. I expect you to discourage those attempts. And as Saxony begins to rebuild and flourish, I doubt many will wish to return to the dark days of civil war. So you see, Duke, I have no rival worth the energy of destroying. My energies will instead go to economic prosperity. I only want from Otto what is owed me."

The duke stared at Frederick in disbelief. Then he looked at the others in the room, as if looking for confirmation that this was unprecedented.

"I told you he was impressive," said the archbishop.

The duke nodded but said nothing.

"We shall locate Otto and the German relics, King Frederick," said the archbishop, with the duke nodding in the affirmative. "You have my word on it."

Hector looked on in amazement at Frederick's ability to deal with the duke. He held his tongue throughout the negotiations, letting Frederick take the lead. Hector knew Frederick was a sharp student but had not seen this aptitude for negotiation and diplomacy. He wondered quietly when or how Frederick had become so adept and seasoned.

He began to see what Frederick's mother saw in him so many years ago.

Harsburg Castle
Lower Saxony, Germany

Duke Albert of Saxony walked the lonely hallways of the castle that was once the imperial castle to the Holy Roman Empire. He turned into the quiet room that Otto was now hiding in. Otto was injured and struggling to sit up in bed.

"Are you all right, Otto?"

"They say my wounds are critical, yet I have hung on for weeks. The physicians do not know what they speak of."

"I am here for the relics."

"If the boy king wants his crown, have him come here himself."

"He sent me, Otto. You have nothing to gain by keeping them."

"They were lost on the battlefield."

"We both know that is not the case."

"Why are you taking the side of a Staufer? We are of the north. The Welfs will take back the throne just as we did before."

"No, Otto. This time it's finished. It's time to rebuild Germany . . . all of Germany."

"Since when do you care about all of Germany, Albert? We are men of Saxony. Men of the north."

"Otto, we are men of the north, and I have fought alongside you, but that time is over. You were a king and an emperor, but you are dying. This king from Italy has a plan for Germany, which includes his leaving and allowing the princes to govern. It is best for the Welfs to comply. Think of your family, Otto. The Welf name will not survive another rebellion."

"The British have fled, and I'm sure the French are in pursuit of the Welfs. They want to rid Europe of us all. So does the boy king I am sure."

"No, Otto. No one is in pursuit of the Welfs. Philip is in France. Frederick is heading south as soon as you turn over the relics. Do what is right for your family. Do what is right for Germany."

"Enough," Otto said weakly. "The crown is in the treasury room along with all of the other relics. Take them, but do not turn them over until I am dead. I want to die as king of the Germans."

———✦———

Frederick and his knights rode into Brandenburg, Germany, to meet Albert II. Albert was the Brandenburg margrave and a prince of Germany. Frederick noticed bear banners all over the town square in anticipation of his arrival.

"What do these banners symbolize?"

"Albert the Bear was the most famous of all the Brandenburg margraves," answered Hector. "He was very nearly king of the Germans. The people revered him and his son, also a great margrave. Unfortunately, Albert II has lived in their shadows."

"Do you know why he favored Otto over me in the civil war?"

"It is somewhat of a mystery. The margraves had a history of supporting your family as late as Frederick Barbarossa. Albert was an ally to your uncle Philip's campaign, so his backing of Otto was a surprise. I suspect it was a shaky truce between them."

Albert welcomed Frederick and Hector into his castle. Unlike other princes and European leaders, he was not a man of ceremony or small talk. He started in as quickly as they could sit down.

"Let me first state for the record," he said, looking at his scribe, who was writing down the words of the meeting. "It is my sincere regret to have taken the side of Otto. With no real presence of knights, and no walls to secure this region, and so close to Otto's northern troops, I felt no choice but to unwillingly ally myself with the Welfs. I have always been an ally of your family and hope to be again now and in the future. With that said, I fully accept any penalty, punishment, or taxation you feel necessary to implement upon me."

"I fully understand your decision to stay loyal to Otto," Frederick said. "There was no army to protect you once the princes elected me, and Brandenburg has always been peaceful, with no need for knights. There was no way for you to resist Otto. The matter is concluded in my eyes. I have no will to impose any penalty on you or Brandenburg, Lord Albert."

"I am appreciative of your generosity, King Frederick. I'm not sure I could remain as margrave if you were punitive to Brandenburg."

"Why is that, Lord Albert?"

"I am not Albert the Bear, my lord. I am not even as popular as my father was. If this region was to be punished because of my decisions, I doubt I would survive."

"I understand your situation here," Frederick said. "I, too, had a popular father and grandfather. To this day, as I ride through certain towns and villages of Germany, they think I am the second coming of Frederick Barbarossa."

Albert laughed and sat up in his chair.

"No one thinks I am the second coming of Albert the Bear, Your Grace, but I take your meaning. I have done nothing noteworthy as margrave."

"Then we shall have to help one another become the noteworthy leaders we are destined to be."

"What do you propose, King Frederick?

"I want you to become an important part of the reconstruction of Germany. In fact, I want you to be a leader in this movement toward peace and prosperity over the militaristic endeavors of previous German kings. I want Brandenburg to be a model for all of Germany. I want to give you autonomous rights to the Brandenburg lands and treasure to rebuild and expand this land. Is this something you can find glory in, Lord Albert?

"I, too, want all of these grand accomplishments. But you must remember: I am a man of far less stature or promise than you assume."

"Lord Albert, you have more than you are acknowledging. I would not be here offering you this pledge if I felt you unworthy. No, you are the very man to bring this place peace and prosperity. I am not looking for a strong military leader like the lords who have come before you. We have the powers for our time but can only lead within the opportunities we have. We cannot live the legacies of another. That would be foolish."

"You speak with wisdom far beyond your years, Your Grace. We need peace. We want prosperity. I have always been a peaceful man and feared the contention of wars. You can see it was my fear that drove me to support Otto."

"That is your wisdom, not your weakness. Some may have thought it bold to stand against Otto, but you cared for your people and in your actions protected Brandenburg. It is that wisdom and strength that I desire. That is the leadership we need to unify Germany. You stand above the rest. Will you stand with me? Will you lead Brandenburg in this epic quest?"

"I would very much like that, King Frederick. I believe it is within me to make Brandenburg into your vision for the future; however, I must ask, with all due respect, my lord: what is it you want in return?"

"I expect your loyalty, and I expect Brandenburg to pay taxes to the Crown after we have rebuilt this region. I will not be in Germany for years to come; therefore, I need its princes to oversee Germany in its best interests. I trust you to do that for Brandenburg, Lord Albert."

"I will abide by those terms, King Frederick."

—⁂—

The Kingdom of Bohemia

"Tell me about King Ottokar of Bohemia," Frederick said.

"Throughout the years, Ottokar has been a supporter of both Welf and Staufer kings," said Count Palatine.

"He has also rebelled against them," Hector said.

"Ottokar was one of the five electors to vote for you, King Frederick," Count Palatine said. "He took a great risk and was instrumental in beginning the end of Otto's reign."

"Hector and I do not sit in judgment of him, Count. I merely wish to better understand the man I am coming to meet."

"He was one of the first to pledge support to Frederick in Constance," Hector said. "He was there before the French. He was with us in the wilderness and Bouvines. His loyalty is not in question."

"His large contribution of knights may well have turned the tides in the early stages of the war," Frederick said.

"He keeps an ample supply of knights in Bohemia at all times, in fear a rival family will overthrow his shaky claim to the Bohemian kingdom. Because of this, he is not afraid to fight."

"He just likes to make sure he is on the winning side," Hector said.

"Why is his claim on Bohemia on shifting sands, Count Palatine?" Frederick asked.

"Generations ago—maybe a century ago, I'm not certain—but an ancestor of Ottokar overthrew another family for the Crown. Since those days, this tiny country's throne has seemingly been in play. Ottokar has twice now had to declare himself king and add to his reserve of knights to hold the peace against the warring rival families."

"It sounds all too familiar," Frederick said, smiling at Hector. "We shall have to remedy this situation for King Ottokar before we go."

—ɯ—

Upon Frederick's arrival at Bohemia, King Ottokar organized a reception for him, which was attended by the entire town. Before Ottokar could deliver his speech, Frederick asked to make an announcement to the town. He opened a large scroll and began to speak.

"For his courage and loyalty, I grant the golden bull of Sicily to King Ottokar of Bohemia, which makes him and his heirs king of Bohemia in perpetuity. Let it be known to all that to attack this great king or the kingdom of Bohemia is to attack the King of the Germans, the King of Sicily or the lands of those kingdoms. Long live King Ottokar. Your bravery will never be forgotten!"

The crowd cheered its approval, and Frederick hugged King Ottokar and returned to sit next to Hector while Ottokar began his speech.

"What exactly is a golden bull of Sicily?" Hector asked.

"Something we need to invent, I suppose."

"So what was that scroll you opened up in front of the town?"

"Otto's bull of excommunication."

Hector looked at Frederick, stupefied by his quick thinking. "It's been on Dragon this whole time?"

"I just never had any reason to remove it since Constance."

"Well, I guess we should have a scribe craft a golden bull of Sicily pretty soon. I expect King Ottokar might want to post it in his throne room."

Frederick smiled. "Now that he is officially recognized as sovereign king by the King of the Germans, his main concern is settled. He is free to pay his taxes to the empire, remain loyal, offer military assistance when needed, and provide an escort of three hundred knights for my journey to Rome for the coronation, or if I return to Germany. And with us going through the Lombard region of Italy to get to Rome, we could use another three hundred knights, don't you think?"

Hector stood by in silence.

XLVI

So Long to a Trusted Friend

The German tour had been successful. Frederick met with each prince and gave him control of his territory in exchange for loyalty to the Holy Roman Empire and himself as emperor.

Initially, both Frederick and the princes had been distrustful of one another. Frederick had been skeptical of the princes due to his dealings with nobility in Sicily, and the princes had thought Frederick was a foreign teenager with no substance. Now they stood unified, and confident in one another.

Frederick was pleased to find that these seven nobles were more focused on their region's success than their own. They did not mistreat their peasant class, and they acted fair and just on matters, whether it was in their own best interest or not. As a whole, their diversity of talents and their love of Germany impressed Frederick. He would have no concerns leaving these men in charge.

The princes were equally impressed with Frederick's ideas for Germany and happy with his intent to reside in Sicily. His advanced vision of the prosperity and potential was simply astonishing to them, given his short time there. But the fact that he was leaving so much money with them made it all the more convincing. He clearly cared about their well-being more than Otto ever did.

There was only one person more impressed with Frederick than the princes—Hector. He had trained Frederick to be a king. In battle, Frederick had proven to be brave and a quick learner. He displayed a wisdom and willingness to listen to counsel. He also knew when it was time to act. His penchant for strategy impressed Hector, especially his diplomacy in building alliances with the princes. He flourished in everything put before him, both in Germany and Bouvines. Frederick was no longer a student; he was a leader, possibly a leader for the ages at such a young age. Hector could not have been prouder. He had come a long way from the boy he'd met in Palermo.

While they rode to meet Louis in Champagne, Hector found quiet moments on the trail to begin preparing Frederick for the next step.

"You did well in Germany," Hector said. "The princes were impressed with your plans. For the first time in years, I think this kingdom has a real chance to be united. The last time was when your grandfather Barbarossa took Germany into crusade. But to unite in war is one matter; to unify in peacetime another. The latter is much more difficult."

"Thank you, Hector, but I fear Sicily will be a greater challenge. In Sicily, I will not be giving the barons and counts what they want, and I will be staying, not leaving them to rule. I fear we have our work cut out for us."

"You will do fine in Sicily. You have saved the empire, and you saved Sicily. Constance has already laid the groundwork for your kingdom while you were away, and the nobility knows what is coming. Word of your accomplishments has reached them and, I suspect, impressed them. You will be a great king in Sicily."

"I will be in need of your help. You are a valuable counselor and teacher."

"You are no longer in need of a tutor. You have demonstrated your ability to lead. Your valor at Bouvines proves you are a great warrior. Your performance in Germany proved your ability to rule. Your words in Constance and Aachen proved your wisdom to build the kingdom. You have exceeded what I can teach you."

Frederick turned to look at Hector, sensing where this conversation was headed.

"All that I have accomplished was because you were behind me. None of it would have happened without your counsel, guidance, and direct interaction. Your job with me is not over."

"All I can do for you now is hold you back."

"How do you foresee holding me back? You have in every way enhanced my learning and understanding."

Hector paused for a moment and rode closer to Frederick so none of the knights could hear their conversation.

"It's not me directly. It's the perception that you are still in need of a tutor. At your age, you will have to fight those perceptions for many years to come."

Frederick attempted to interrupt, but Hector continued.

"All of Germany was convinced you were the pope's pawn. They expected you to do his bidding and nothing more. To them you were the boy king who was raised by Innocent. Those who have met you now know that is not the case. Even the archbishops know it to be false. You didn't mention Pope Innocent in Germany, and neither did the princes.

"But to keep your tutor alongside you would only keep the perception that you are a child and I am your regent. It was why I remained silent in Germany; I wanted them to see your thoughts were your own, that the business of this empire went through you, not a team of advisers—or me."

The two rode in silence a while, then Frederick spoke.

"Are you saying you aren't returning with me to Sicily?"

"I will be staying in Champagne."

"What would make you choose Champagne, of all places?" he asked, somewhat mystified, but then answered his own question. "Is this related to the girl you met there?"

"Her name is Sophia."

"Yes; Sophia . . . well, take all the time you need in Champagne—with Sophia, I mean—but after that, return to Sicily as my advisor."

"The relationship with Sophia is of more importance than that. I am a chivalric knight. Sophia is the woman I am dedicating the rest of my life to."

A knight from a following rank rode next to Hector.

"Give me a moment," Hector said to the knight before he could speak.

Hector increased his horse's speed a bit to get out in front of the knights. Frederick followed him.

"I didn't realize things were so serious with her," Frederick said. "You have never mentioned her before. I guess all of those trips to Champagne should have served as evidence. Do you plan on marrying her, Hector?"

"The relationship between a chivalric knight and his lady is stronger than the bond of marriage. I do intend to marry Sophia, but in doing so, it is because I dedicate my life to her happiness, and marriage will make Sophia happy. Do you understand the difference?"

"I understand the distinction that you see, but I also remember the conduct of knights toward women in Sicily. You are a rare breed, Hector. Most knights have long since abandoned the chivalric code for matters of warfare and riches."

"No true knight will abandon the chivalric code. Those men you speak of in Sicily were not knights. They were dishonorable men with enough money to buy a horse, armor, and weaponry. The men who rode with us from Aragon, Germany, and France—those were knights. These men behind us are knights, and to a man they live by the chivalric code."

"It's not the same with kings and queens. My father married my mother without knowing her. I married Constance in the same manner. Our marriages are more political and strategic than chivalrous or romantic. I wish kings also lived by the code of a knight."

"You do. You are called upon to protect the weak and helpless, just as a knight. And I fully expect you to devote your life to the happiness of Queen Constance once you return to Sicily. She did, after all, give birth to your heir and keep your kingdom running while you were away."

Before Frederick could reply, a rider approached and handed him a letter.

"Louie awaits us in Champagne," Frederick said after reading the letter.

"It should be quite a reunion."

"Indeed."

They increased their horse's speed to canter, followed by their knights. "We will never hear the end of him beating us," Frederick said.

—⟋⟍—

Frederick spent the extra days in Champagne finalizing the trade routes he had arranged. His empire was poised to become a major supplier to the fairs.

"Goods will flow from Sicily and Germany and be sold here," he said to the count of Champagne. "We look forward to this partnership for years to come, my lord."

"This trading will also extend to merchants wishing to send goods from Champagne into Germany, Sicily, and beyond," said the count. "It is a grand plan, Your Grace. I am honored to call the emperor a partner."

"I will provide shipping to sell these goods throughout the Mediterranean, and even into the Middle East and the Orient. Once my Palermo dock is repaired and modernized, it will be of great use in opening new markets all over the world."

"It is a partnership we eagerly anticipate, Your Grace. Never before has an emperor been more conscious of Europe as a whole, rather than his own lands."

"It is my intent to keep the peace in Europe through prosperity. The peasant class will no longer starve to death if they have a bad crop. This economy will flourish for all—from the top to the bottom of the economic scale—and no one will wage war because they will be too prosperous and busy to risk such a venture."

When Frederick returned from the Champagne Fairs to his tent, there was a letter waiting for him.

My dearest Frederick,

Congratulations, Emperor! You are a king, a father, and an emperor all in the same year. God's will shines down on you, my king. And it is my honor to be your queen regent and wife.

I heard you fought valiantly at Bouvines. All of Sicily is excited with your conquest! The kingdom goes well in your absence, but Henry and I anticipate your return with great eagerness.

Give Hector and Sophia my love and blessings. We pray for a happy union between them.

My love always,
Constance

—〰—

The wedding of Hector and Sophia was supposed to be a simple ceremony, but with Philip and the French taking charge, it ended up being quite a royal affair. Two kings, a prince, and every noble in the region attended. King Philip gave the bride away, and Frederick was the best man.

Frederick was happy for Hector, but he knew he would be on his own from now on.

—〰—

The journey to Rome was a time of reflection and melancholy. Frederick was returning as a victorious king about to become an emperor. This should have been a momentous occasion for him, a time of celebration, recognition, and vindication; instead, he dreaded the very thought of coronation.

He was going to a place that triggered tortured childhood memories. This was the place they brought him as a child in need of care, grieving the loss of his parents. The man who was supposed to nurture him had abused him; now that man, draped in holy attire, would be placing a crown on his head. A man he questioned, a man he knew and detested. Again he would be alone with this man, with no family present, at this man's home. Memories flooded his mind, blurring the moment. He approached his coronation, but it seemed more like returning to his troubled childhood.

Once the knights entered the gates of the storied city, they erupted in ecstasy, proclaiming his arrival loudly, igniting the celebration, but Frederick was unmoved. He did not share their enthusiasm.

"Rome is the largest city I have ever seen," an Aragon knight said.

"Paris, and some of the German cities, are larger," another knight said.

"Maybe in population, but there's no city like this. This is still the center of the universe in the hearts and minds of most Europeans."

"The Vatican is in Rome," another knight said. "That's why it's so important."

Frederick stayed out of the conversation with his knights, not wishing to speak of the mystery and splendor of Rome, and particularly not of the Vatican. He better remembered his secret explorations, sneaking out of the Vatican grounds to investigate the forbidden surroundings. He smiled at the thought, reliving his curiosity satisfied. Eventually, those memories returned, bringing him back to his troubled and traumatic time with Innocent. Abruptly, he interrupted the conversation.

"Find an inn where we can eat and sleep for the evening. I meet with Pope Innocent tomorrow and need rest."

"My lord, you must eat," an Aragon knight said. "Are you not feeling well?"

"I'm fine," Frederick said, downing his third cup of wine. "I'm just not hungry. I'm going to bed now."

"He's just nervous about meeting with the pope," another knight said.

"Who wouldn't be nervous?" the Aragon knight mused. "Even kings are nervous to meet the pope."

Frederick was nervous to meet Pope Innocent, but it went much deeper. Frederick had conquered Otto on a battlefield and successfully negotiated with the German princes, but in his mind Innocent was a much more difficult challenge.

He was about to face the demons of his childhood. There, on that holy ground of the Vatican, he would do battle with another ruler who had sought to destroy him. His fear for Otto paled in comparison. Somehow, he could not draw upon his negotiation with Innocent in Assisi because Hector was there and did the majority of the speaking. This time it would be only the pope and Frederick in the Vatican.

Just as it was in his childhood.

He fell asleep feeling as alone as he did the first time he'd first slept in Rome.

—m—

Frederick walked down a stone path with his mother in a hazy forest in silence. They approached a shimmering palace coming into view as they neared.

"What troubles you, Frederick?" she asked, looking down at him as though he were a child.

"I'm going back to the Vatican, the place I was sent when you died. I have to spend time with the pope. I will have to negotiate with him, and I feel alone. This is just like it was before."

Queen Constance was dressed in a flowing white dress and golden crown. She glowed radiantly. He smiled and felt the comforting, inward warmth when he held her hand.

"Every king, every emperor, and every leader is alone, no matter who surrounds them. This is the price you pay when God chooses you to take this responsibility."

"I wish you didn't die, Mother. I needed you so much . . . I need you still. Father died, and you died, Uncle Philip died, and Hector left. I'm to be crowned Holy Roman emperor, and I'm alone."

"I, too, wish I had more time with you, Frederick, but God chose a different path for both of us. God sent you another Constance."

"She is my wife, and the mother of my son. I love her, but she is not my mother."

"She is much more than a wife, Frederick. She has kept Sicily stable all these years while you fought in Germany. God sent her to you to be all the things you need to succeed and be happy. Cherish her for all the days you have with her, Frederick."

Her words lingered in his mind and soothed his soul. His perspective changed from looking up at her to looking directly into her eyes.

They walked to the lawn of the palace until they came upon the small herd of impala that had roamed the palace grounds when Frederick was a child. The calf, the baby impala that was brave enough to walk inside and allow Frederick to hold it in his arms, was now the leader of the herd.

"It's a lot of responsibility, Mother. I'm not sure I'm equal to the task ahead of me."

"You are a king of two kingdoms, my son. You have fought in battles in defense of your lands and defeated every foe put in front of you. You must continue to be brave and face your demons—on the battlefield and those in your mind, in your past and the future. You are a great man now. You have proven yourself in every challenge presented you. You are not the child that Pope Innocent bullied at the Vatican. You are my son, and I am very proud of your accomplishments."

Frederick woke at the break of dawn to a new morning.

XLVII

The Final Showdown

Frederick took five hundred knights with him to Rome but rode into the Vatican accompanied with only two civilian riders. Out of respect for the holy grounds, he decided to forego knights in armor that would usually escort him. His respect was in spite of the man behind the robes, the man who brought a curse upon the grounds in his eyes; instead, he wanted to honor the office and respect the position. Francis had made his point on that matter.

Innocent and Cencio met him when he rode into Vatican Square. Both men congratulated him on his victories in Germany, Cencio hugging him when he dismounted.

Frederick paused to take in the view, peering across the grounds. There, he spotted the garden he used to sneak into as a child. He couldn't help but smile. Nearby, he knew where to look to find the stable and the Vatican Guard's small outpost.

"Is my horse still here, Cencio?"

"I believe it is, Frederick. Still in good shape after all these years."

"I'm surprised he's still alive after so long."

"Thoroughbreds sometimes have a survival instinct that amazes us all."

"Indeed," Frederick said, smiling at Cencio.

"Does it all look the same to you, Frederick?" Innocent asked.

"It does, Your Holiness. I wonder if anything has changed."

—‑ɯ‑—

Innocent, Cencio, and Frederick went into the pope's office. For a while, things went cordially. Cencio tried to broker a civil discussion, but it finally unraveled when the topic of the empire arose.

"In the ceremony, I will ride a white horse to the stage," Pope Innocent said. "You will assist me by holding the stirrup on my left as I dismount. We will walk together to the stage, where I will place the crown on your head. You were able to collect the relics?"

"Yes," said Cencio, sensing a discomfort in Frederick to Innocent's arrogance. "Otto was in compliance."

"Otto was a good German," Innocent said. "The Welf family would not resist my orders."

Frederick fought the urge to say that Otto and the Welfs attacked a Papal protectorate and ignored excommunication to fight a war against his chosen emperor; instead, he smiled and looked at Cencio.

"*Was* a good German?" Frederick said.

"Yes, he died," Cencio said. "Just a few days ago."

"I'm sincerely sorry to hear that. I hope to one day reconcile with the Welf family and restore them to a leadership role in Germany as they once were. How did Otto die?"

"He died of disease due to the complications from injuries he sustained in battle," Cencio said. "That is what the physicians say."

"He was mortally expiated in atonement for his sins," Innocent said.

"What does that mean?" Frederick asked. "Mortally expiated?"

"He was beaten to death by the Abbott of Harzburg and his priests in atonement for his many wrongdoings."

"Otto allowed them to beat him to death?"

"It was the only way his soul could be cleansed for his journey to heaven."

"So the punishment and terms were laid out by the Vatican, and he accepted them in order to go to heaven?"

"He blatantly defied the Vatican by attacking my protectorate . . . you Frederick. His atonement had to be severe. You of all people should understand this."

"Let's move on from this," Cencio said.

"I guess he would be better off fighting and dying in the Albigensian Crusade," Frederick said. "That way he could go to heaven with the honor of fighting against heretics, right Your Holiness?"

"Frederick!" Cencio said firmly. "Let's move on."

"Very well," Frederick replied. "I understand the process of the service and am in agreement with everything we have discussed. I will be wearing my grandfather's coronation silks in honor of his memory."

"Very well, Frederick," Innocent said. You have my permission to do so. Now, we must discuss the matter of Sicily."

"I will be returning there after the coronation. There is a lot of work to do to restore Sicily to its former greatness."

"You can't have Sicily, Frederick. If you are to be crowned emperor, then Sicily has to remain a protectorate of the Papacy. You may not be king of both."

"I am king of Germany and king of Sicily, Your Holiness. Neither of those titles is in dispute. You agreed to both of those outcomes long ago. In fact—"

"I will not have one person ruling both kingdoms," Innocent interrupted. "You will not have the resources to protect and improve them both."

"And at what point did the Papacy protect and develop Sicily, Your Holiness? My kingdom was invaded three times, and I was taken hostage as a child. Your protectorate was in financial shambles, and the roads, castles and docks crumbled beneath our feet. No, Your Holiness, I suspect it is not the fear that I won't develop and protect Sicily; it is the fear that the Papacy will lose revenue from Sicily and that my lands will then surround you."

"I'm sorry you feel that way, Frederick, but you will not be both king of Sicily and king of the Germans as long as I am pope," he said with condescension, the tone quickly bringing Frederick back to his childhood.

"I am already king of both, Pope Innocent. I fought a war to defend both, and you endorsed me in claiming those titles. The princes of

Germany nominated and elected me. The Sicilian crown was always mine when all others fled in fear. There is no dispute in either case. Do not forget you supported me in both instances."

"Don't play games, Frederick. You know I agreed to let you rule over Sicily simply to have a title for your war against Otto. The Germans wouldn't have chosen a boy from Sicily to be king unless he was already credentialed. It was never the plan for you to keep Sicily once you were emperor, and I hold you to that now. You knew I was not giving you Sicily, Frederick."

"You speak the truth, Pope Innocent. You did not give me Sicily; it was never yours to give. It was rightfully mine all along, and I claimed what was mine. There is no challenger to me in Sicily. There is no basis for my kingdom to stay in protectorate status. The lone claim to my kingdom lives in this room."

"Think what you wish, Frederick, but if you remain stubborn about Sicily, then you will not be emperor. You simply cannot have Sicily and the Holy Roman Empire. And when the princes of Germany hear I won't let you be emperor, they will strip you of your German crown."

"I fought a war to be king of the Germans, Your Holiness," Frederick said with contempt and anger in his voice. "You will call me King Frederick, or this discussion ends now. And I am king of Sicily as well. These crowns are not yours to select."

Pope Innocent began to object, but Frederick cut him off.

"However, I do accept your position as pope to choose who will be Holy Roman emperor. Your opinion is that the princes who fought alongside me at Bouvines will strip me of my title as king of the Germans because you refuse to coronate me as Holy Roman emperor. My impression is that they will take it as an insult by you against their king. My opinion is that they will travel to Rome and burn the Vatican to the ground as retribution against the offense. So if it is to be someone other than the king of the Germans as your Holy Roman emperor, you should inform the princes of Germany."

Innocent attempted to refute Frederick but was interrupted again.

"And the five hundred knights I have in Rome? Perhaps they won't see this decision of yours as an implied insult. Even though they are already outraged at the idea of not being pure of spirit enough to enter the hallowed Vatican grounds because they are warriors . . . even though they fought and died in defense of the very same church that sees them as unfit to walk the grounds. Perhaps they will not lay siege to the Vatican, but it's hard to predict what will set off that many unholy knights."

Frederick turned his back to Pope Innocent and headed to the door. Then he turned around and addressed Cencio.

"I will be at the ceremony tomorrow morning to help the pope off his horse. I will stay in Rome until then. If my presence is not needed, please send word."

Frederick walked out the door without waiting for a response. Pope Innocent looked at Cencio and smiled for a moment.

"All grown up," said Cencio.

"See that he attends the crusade sermons after the coronation," Pope Innocent said.

The next morning, Pope Innocent presided over the coronation ceremony and crowned King Frederick as Holy Roman emperor. Frederick wore the robes of a Saracen, carried the sword of a Byzantine king, and had his grandfather's tunic inscribed in Arabic. It was his symbolic way of communicating his intention to be open to all cultures and religions throughout his reign.

He stayed for the crusade sermons and was moved enough by them to vow himself to undertake a crusade in the near future, but for now, he was very focused on his return to Sicily, Constance, and Henry . . . save one brief delay.

XLVIII

Christmas with Francis of Assisi

After the coronation, Frederick had his knights turn north toward Assisi. He had gotten word that Francis was performing the Christmas Eve mass, and he wanted to be there.

It was quite a surprise to the knights, who had never seen Frederick show any interest in religion or the church. If anything, he showed a silent contempt for it. Now he was changing his plans in order to see an unknown priest in an unimportant town in the wrong direction from Sicily.

—⁂—

Francis was once again proving to be the most authentic and unique priest in all of Italy. He decorated the church as if it were a stable, both inside and out. Where the pulpit typically stood, a manger scene had taken its place. The horses, donkeys, and other animals of Assisi's farms were brought inside the chapel and seemed to settle around the perimeter of the pews. Hay lined the floors and the makeshift stall on the stage, where the crib was constructed. The stench of the stable was now beginning to resonate in the church, yet there was not a single seat available. Francis had filled Assisi's church, not that it was of any concern to him; he would preach to the birds in a tree if that were his audience.

"What is he doing to our church?" one elder asked another. "We shall never get rid of the smell. This church should be sacred."

"If Pope Innocent has enough faith in our own priest from Assisi to approve an Order in his name, then we should match his faith as well," replied the other elder. "Francis is one of us. We can always cleanse a temple."

Francis was making that very point. The temple was a building. Jesus was born in a stable, not a cathedral. He was recreating the manger scene to accurately illustrate the birth narrative of Jesus so the people of Assisi could experience it the same way it was experienced in Bethlehem.

Frederick rode into town with only a small guard of knights. His larger force camped just outside of Assisi. He was still relatively unknown to southern Italy and able to arrive at the Assisi cathedral with very little recognition. This evening was about Francis and his message. Frederick was happy to blend into the crowd.

They stood in the back of the church, quietly awaiting Francis's entrance. While other churches were celebrating with all possible pomp and circumstance—orchestras providing the regal music for the senior priests, bishops, and the pope to proceed to the pulpit—Francis chose a different way.

He rode to the stage on a donkey.

"Hard to imagine this man was given an order by Pope Innocent," remarked one knights.

"It was probably his best decision," Frederick said.

Francis dismounted the donkey and immediately began speaking, even as the audience continued to chatter.

"Brothers and sisters of Assisi, it is indeed an honor to spend this evening with you, the night of our savior's birth. Imagine that perfect night in Bethlehem—a poor family is unable to find better lodging than a stable. And in a manger, Mary gives birth to Jesus before the stars outside, for the whole world to see. Jesus came from very humble beginnings and remained in that state His entire life. Despite His many gifts, talents, and blessings from God, He never aspired to do anything more than bring man closer to His father. He never wore expensive silks, royal clothing, or the uniform of a knight. He never possessed or even aspired to great wealth or property."

In Frederick's mind, the words were aimed straight at him. Many there thought the same thing. It was the effect a great preacher had on his flock.

"And now the church and royalty want to lift Him up from His poor and simple background because they struggle to accept their savior in such a manner. But remember, brothers and sisters: Jesus came to Earth a helpless baby from a poor family, and He departed Earth a poor man," he said in a booming voice. "He expects us to do the same."

The church was silent while they pondered his exact meaning. Was he being literal, or metaphoric? In his case, there could be no doubt. Francis would not even touch coinage and did not allow his followers to either. But was he preaching that all of society should follow suit?

While most of the church began to buzz about his meaning (just as Francis had intended), Francis glanced back at Frederick. The idea that we should draw closer to and search for God and leave the world penniless resonated with him.

"For some of you, leaving the world without possessions will be easier than for others," he joked with the poor section of the crowd to lift the tension and quiet the chatter he'd created.

"But for all of us brothers and sisters we must be in relationship with our savior and creator Jesus Christ. Our life's mission must be to share with others the joy we have found in Him. It doesn't have to be in a cathedral on a specific day, my brothers. Be an example to others every day in life and in spirit, no matter your station in life or name of your family. All of you are royalty in God's eyes."

"Amen, brother Francis," people echoed.

The mass ended with Francis riding away on the donkey that had brought him in, only this time, the crowd was on its feet, cheering his words, and feeling closer to their savior and more spiritual than ever before. It would be a difficult message for the priests of Assisi to follow in the future. Even the skeptical church elders stood and cheered; the rebellious son of Assisi was now their favorite.

—⁓—

Frederick hugged Francis after the mass. It had been some time since they had seen one another.

"So you are the leader of the Franciscan Order," Frederick said. "I would have given anything to have heard the discussion between you and Pope Innocent."

"It was either lead an order or be charged with heresy," joked Francis. "And there are already enough heretics in Europe that he needs me to convince otherwise."

"I would prefer your persuasive sermons to a crusade against European towns."

"In all sincerity, some of the Cathars beliefs are similar to mine," said Francis. "Their thoughts on poverty are almost exactly my own. But I respect the pope on larger matters like these. My mission will always be what God sends me to do. I pray for the Cathars. I pray they will meet God in heaven."

"I'm not so sure the pope's mission is as holy in spirit as yours is, Francis. His politics are often at the forefront of his decisions. He is a disgrace to the title."

"No, Frederick. We must always respect the pope," Francis said in a stern voice. "No matter what you think of the man, respect his relationship with God . . . but let me show respect for your accomplishments, Emperor Frederick. You are king of the Germans and Holy Roman emperor; a very impressive run, my friend."

"And king of Sicily," he said, smiling at his correction. "It's been so long. It's great to see you again."

"It's good to see you, too. We have certainly come a long way since our first meeting in the forest."

XLIX

A Return to Sicily

Frederick and his knights crossed the Straits of Messina and arrived in Palermo to a crowd that seemed to include every person living in Sicily. He rode in the lead position until he arrived at the end of the procession, where Constance and his son Henry awaited.

He feared the years away would make his love for her diminish, but the moment he looked in her eyes he knew it was if he had never left.

"I have missed you with the intensity of a thousand suns, Constance. Of all the accomplishments I have achieved since I left, returning to you was my greatest."

Constance smiled, and tears of joy filled her eyes. She hugged Frederick for what felt like an eternity.

"It is beyond words with which to describe my joy at your return, my king," she said. "Here is your son Henry."

He held his child for the very first time and smiled at Constance, then waved at the adoring crowd. It was in stark contrast to his departure from Sicily a few years ago. The boy who left for the wars was now very much a man, a father, a husband, a king, and an emperor. His title as king of Sicily was now very much earned.

He thought about his mother and father as he sat down on his throne. He wished they could be here for this, but wondered if it would have happened this way if they were. He wished Hector were here, too, but understood and agreed with his staying in France.

Constance, Henry, and Sicily would be Frederick's focus now. He was no longer the student, the protégé, or the boy king. He had fought in wars and stabilized Germany and the Holy Roman Empire. He had successfully negotiated with the pope.

Frederick arose from his throne and walked into the palace with his family, pausing to wave again to the Sicilians who had come to celebrate his return. This was to be his newest proving ground, to restore Sicily to its prosperous days, and take care of its people.

All along this had been his mother's dream. Now it was his.

About the Author

After reading a short biography on Frederick II, Reggie Connell became fascinated with this little-known historical figure from medieval times and felt his story had to be told. He has been working on Falconland and its accompanying second volume ever since.

Reggie is the Vice President of Peak Publications and the Board Chairman of his church – **Inspire** in Apopka, Florida. He is the former owner and publisher of *City Magazine*, but first and foremost he is a storyteller.

He lives in Altamonte Springs, Florida, with his wife Christina, three cats and a dog.

Falconland: Volume Two
Coming Soon!

For a sneak peek at *Falconland's* sequel, go to **reggieconnell.com**. *Falconland: Volume Two* is scheduled to publish in the summer of 2015.